a few kinds of wrong

a few kinds of wrong

a novel

TINA CHAULK

BREAKWATER

LIBRARY AND ARCHIVES CANADA CATALOGUING IN PUBLICATION

Chaulk, Tina, 1966-
A few kinds of wrong / Tina Chaulk.
ISBN 978-1-55081-268-8
I. Title.
PS8605.H394F48 2009   C813'.6   C2009-902810-7

©2009 Tina Chaulk
Cover photo: Pete Leonard/CORBIS

ALL RIGHTS RESERVED. No part of this publication may be reproduced, stored in a retrieval system or transmitted, in any form or by any means, without the prior written consent of the publisher or a licence from The Canadian Copyright Licensing Agency (Access Copyright). For an Access Copyright licence, visit www.accesscopyright.ca or call toll free to 1-800-893-5777.

Canada Council   Conseil des Arts
for the Arts   du Canada

Newfoundland and Labrador
Arts Council

BREAKWATER BOOKS LTD. acknowledges the support of the Canada Council for the Arts which last year invested $20.1 million in writing and publishing throughout Canada. We acknowledge the financial support of the Government of Canada through the Book Publishing Industry Development Program for our publishing activities. We acknowledge the financial support of the Government of Newfoundland and Labrador through the department of Tourism, Culture and Recreation for our publishing activities.

Printed in Canada

FOR BEN

1

MAYBE EVERYONE SHOULD have a time machine, a way to go back to where the bad memories haven't happened yet. Mine was created five years ago, slowly becoming exactly what I needed just when I needed it. At first I feared it, avoided it, but now I look forward to the time machine. I know that her small, beige room is the only place I have almost been happy in months. I know that when I'm with her, sometimes I can curve my mouth into a shape resembling a smile and she, if I'm lucky, will believe there is cheerfulness behind the move.

The hall leading to my time machine, in the Hoyles-Escasoni Senior Citizens' Complex, smells like medical disinfectant, urine, bleach, mothballs, and pine trees. Walking along there, I wave at Mrs. Turnbull, who lives in the room next to my grandmother's. She waves back.

"Who's that?" she shouts to her roommate.

"Don't know," replies Mrs. Crane, even though I often drop by to say hello to them on the way to visit Nan. "She's a pretty little thing though."

I stop outside Nan's room and take a deep breath. Some days she doesn't know who I am. I have to prepare for that possibility every time I see her now, even as I hope she doesn't remember too much more than my name.

I peek in without a word and see her sitting in a wooden glider chair in the corner. Her eyes, finding my face, light up.

"Hi, Nan."

"Hello, Jennifer, my lover, how are you?" Her sweatshirt, part of a navy two-piece sweat suit, is on backwards. The left half of her white hair looks groomed and I wonder if she forgot to do the other half or just gave up, her arthritic joints unable to do any more.

Her face is etched deeply with years of worry, pain, and pleasure. I find myself, from time to time, thinking of tracing the lines to make a map of her life: her brother drowning at eight years old; the January morning she lost a child during birth, his body perfect except for the blue tinge that turned her joy to grief; the creases from years of laughter, of being the life of the party, the deep ones made from over sixty years of smoking, only stopped when she forgot she did it.

I bend down to kiss her cheek. She turns and I get her lips instead. They are wet and turn into a smile when I stand up to take off my coat. I feel the moistness on my mouth, want to wipe it off, but can't.

"How was school, my dear?" she asks and I know the time machine has brought us back at least fifteen years to when I was still in high school.

"It was okay," I play along. "I did good in my math test."

"Yes, I dare say you did. You was always good in math."

I smile, reflecting her proud grin.

"Did you get your hair cut?" she asks and makes me wonder when my dirty-blond hair was longer than it is now. A little longer than shoulder length and in its usual ponytail, it's been like this as long as I can remember.

"No."

"Where's your mom and dad?" she asks, at once making my heart beat a little faster and my stomach tighten, making the trip to our past worthwhile.

"Mom's home. Dad's at work," I say. "It's busy at the garage."

"You're not at it, though, are you? You're not a real lady if you goes at that old dirt." Her face puckers up.

"Not lately, Nan. Too busy at school."

"You should get a man, have some youngsters, and keep a nice house. Never mind doing that man's work. Your father can fix them cars. He don't need you to help."

I nod. It's just as well for Nan to tell me not to breathe. Fixing cars is my passion. I have worked at my dad's garage since I was six. When other fathers were calling their little girls "princess," mine called me his little grease monkey. I'd be sixteen before getting my first paycheque, but I could change a spark plug at eight and change the oil at ten.

It was in my blood, my mom always said. I'd toss my Barbie aside to play with her pink, plastic car, and soon my parents started buying me dinkies instead of dolls. My Princess Magic Wand was a pretend screwdriver when I'd flip the dinkies over to fix them, so plastic tools soon followed. I begged Dad until I nearly drove him cracked and he had little choice but to take me to the garage.

"Did you know Brady was pregnant?" Nan asks me. "And with her brother's baby. The like of it. My God, I'll never understand it all." My mind goes through everyone I know and I reach back into the family history to try to remember a Brady. I realize she is referring to a character on a soap opera. I'm not sure if today she thinks the people on the soap are real or if she is just sharing the details of the show with me. Not much different from most people that way.

"That's going to cause a big problem with Deirdre," I say.

Nan tuts.

"Want me to brush your hair?" I ask.

"No, my lover, I can do that myself." She touches her hair and says, "There," as if the task is now complete with the gesture.

Nan turns on the tiny TV in her small bookcase and sits back to watch the story. On the screen, a woman stands between two men, waving her arms and crying. I sit on Nan's bed. We watch for a few minutes. I'm wrapped up in some lover's triangle on the screen when a knock wakes me out of this pleasant illusion.

"Hello," I hear and instantly recognize the voice as my aunt, Henrietta.

"Oh Mom, good, you already got a visitor," Henrietta says. She stops and looks at me, her face turning sad. "Hello, Jennifer. You okay? My dear God, I can't believe it. Can you?"

I shrug an answer. Henrietta shakes her head. She peels the coat off her broad body, revealing a tight, lime-green t-shirt that accentuates rolls around her stomach and cuts into her sausage arms.

"Dear heavenly father. You're like a bear," Nan says.

Henrietta rolls her eyes. "Where and when are you today, Mom? Sure, do you even know it's 2008? I've been big as a bear since I had Sarah."

Confusion fills Nan's face. Her eyes look from me to Henrietta to the TV, at pictures on the wall. She seems to be searching for some compass to guide her in time.

"I knows," she says with a slight nod. "We was just talking." She points to me. "Me and her there."

"Jennifer." Henrietta raises her voice, as if Nan's disappearing memory is affecting her ears.

"I knows. Jack's girl. He's busy at the garage or he'd be here too. We was just talking about him."

"Mom," Henrietta says, shaking her head. She looks to me and frowns.

"How is Sarah doing in school?" I ask, sure that Henrietta will change the subject if I bring up her precious daughter.

"Oh, she's good. She loves French Immersion. I knew she'd do good at it. She got that knock for language."

I open my mouth to correct her but stop. Nan's eyes have changed from confused to terrified, and I suddenly don't have the energy to argue with Aunt Henrietta about "knock" versus "knack."

"She's a smart girl," I say.

Nan is picking at the back of her hand, studying it like an infant stares at her fingers when she first finds them. I want to reassure her, to help her understand, but I'm not ready.

"Does she use French at home much?"

"Oh, yes," Henrietta says before she follows my gaze and turns to Nan.

"Mom, what's wrong with your hand?"

Nan shakes her head. "It's not my hand. I don't have that big spot there and—"

"Mom, that's your hand." She grunts as she crouches down before Nan. "You knows that." Henrietta takes Nan's hand in hers. "You knows that hand and Jennifer and me. And you knows Jack's not at the garage working. You remembers, don't you?"

Henrietta stares at Nan's face, and I know she is looking for recognition, searching for a sign that her mother hasn't forgotten.

More than anything, I want what Henrietta fears.

"You knows Jack's dead, Mom. Don't you? He's dead a year today." Henrietta looks down and whispers, "Poor Jack."

Nan turns to me. She looks confused, struggling to find some way to understand. I watch her shatter as a realization enters the room, and she lets out a tiny gasp. I'm not sure if she remembers or if the pain in my face lets her know the truth, but Nan and I are back in the present.

Tears are streaming down Nan's face, running the path of deep lines down to her chin. I sit still in my chair, afraid that if I move or speak, the tears I'm managing to keep back will betray me and escape.

Henrietta looks at me and shows me a smile filled with sadness. "See, she's not that bad. She remembers."

As angry as I feel toward Henrietta, as much as I despise her for making Nan see the truth, I hate myself as much for assisting in the deceit of the disease.

Maybe everyone should have a time machine. But she shouldn't be able to cry.

☞

On a cool fall day when I was eleven years old, my mother curled my hair with a thin curling iron covered in dried hairspray. I squirmed in my chair, complaining that I didn't need curly hair to go to Linda Mouland's birthday party.

"You're such a pretty girl," Mom said.

She leaned over and whispered in my ear, "One day you will meet a wonderful man. I hope you'll feel safer with him than anywhere else and you'll love him with all your heart. But most of all, I hope he'll love you back. You deserve that, my darling."

I laughed. "I already have that, Mom."

Mom sighed and went back to curling my hair.

At that pre-teen age, I was positive I couldn't love anyone as much as the man who lived down the hall from me. I knew the man I adored smelled like gasoline and orange-scented hand-cleaner. My dream man had calloused hands, full of cuts, with dirt engraved in his pores and staining his nails. He was patient and kind, taking time to show me new things over and over until I understood. No one could ever be as important to me as my father.

That was, until thirteen years later, at a bar on George Street, when Jamie Flynn sauntered into my life. When he walked up to me and asked me to dance, tingles travelled my spine at the sound of his voice. He wore a faded blue-jean jacket, black t-shirt, skin-tight jeans, and cowboy boots. His dirty-blond hair came down to just above his shoulders, and he peered at me through bangs so long only the sparkle in his eyes could be seen. No discernible colour peeked out from the tangle of hair. Waiting for me to answer, he reached his hand out while he used his other hand to pull back his hair and expose eyes the colour of the sky after a rainstorm, a kind of grey-blue that Crayola has never managed to reproduce.

His smooth hand grasped mine and held it there as he stared at my face and grinned.

Soon, there was another man who tucked me in at night.

So, I have loved two men in my life. The first was lost to me with a thud to the garage floor, seconds after he grabbed his left arm and gasped loud enough to get someone's attention. The second is supposed to be out of my life. But Jamie decided differently.

෴

There's a sweet spot in St. John's, a time in the morning when it's not too early to go to work and just before everyone seems to descend on the coffee shops and road-ways. Five minutes too late can mean long line-ups at lights, drive-thrus and coffee counters. If I leave my house at 7:35, I can hit that sweet spot, but this morning I lose a button on my one remaining clean uniform shirt and can't justify taking a dirty one from the laundry. There's no such thing as a little dirty once you've worn a shirt to the garage.

The time it takes to find a safety pin puts me behind. Maybe I could do without the button, but without it, I feel like I'd be verging on looking like I'm on one of the calendars the guys insist on putting up in the bathroom at work.

Drive-thru at Tim Hortons is too long and people are lined up back to the doorway for counter service, so I decide I'll settle for instant in the garage, at least until the coffee run during break time.

I try to be the first at the garage, Collins Motors, every morning but rarely succeed. I usually end up parking next to Bryce McNamara's car in the parking lot, and this morning there's a couple of other employee cars ahead of me too.

There are two huge garage doors in the side of the building and they're both already open. When I walk in, Alan Pittman is leaning against a Ford Explorer, talking to Rick Sutton, both of them with extra-large coffees in their hands.

"Got an extra coffee?" I ask.

"Nope. I'll run up and get you one if you want," Rick says.

"Nah, that's okay. I'll get one later on."

"Take some of Rick's," Alan volunteers with a grin.

"Ha, six sugars," I say, walking on to the office. "I like my teeth too much."

The garage office is at the back of the six-bay garage, far away from the front desk in the corner where Gerry Saunders deals with the customers and parts. Most of one office wall is a large window that overlooks the garage, but it works both ways and there's no privacy in the 10 x 15 office.

Bryce is already in the office, sipping a cup of tea from his big mug with Santa Claus on the side, a birthday gift from me a few years ago. A private joke that made us laugh at the time.

Bryce is my right-hand man, just like he was my father's. He is as much a part of Collins Motors as any Collins.

"Another sucky day today," I say.

"Good morning to you."

"Sorry. Morning."

"How'd you get on after, yesterday?" Bryce asks.

I had left early to pick up Mom and go to Dad's grave with her.

"I didn't pick up Mom. I went to see Nan," I say.

"Oh. How is she?"

"The same. Maybe a little worse. According to the nurses. How about you? It was a hard day for you too."

He nods. He doesn't look at me with those blue, steely eyes I almost never see. Tall and muscular, with an almost bald head, Bryce would be imposing if he had the voice to back it up or could look someone in the eyes. He was my father's best friend since before I was born. I've seen him laugh and cry, was there when his wife died of ovarian cancer eight years ago, and learned as much about cars from him as from Dad. I even learned how to drive from him. Dad wouldn't even try, saying Bryce would have ten times the patience he ever could. I adore him, and losing Dad has been a little easier because I know Bryce is still around. But, he also reminds me of my father — in the way they cared for each other, depended on each other, but mostly in the pain I see whenever I do get a glance at Bryce's eyes. I know I remind him of Dad too, and the memory sears him as it does me.

He reaches over and touches my hand. His skin is rough. An ache rises in me so profound I want to tear my hand away.

"I'm sorry," he says and I try to keep back the tears my mother's side of the family has cursed me with.

"I know."

Bryce takes my jacket off the chair where I laid it and hangs it on a hook on the back of the door. A crease runs down the sleeve of his shirt, exactly like the one on his black pants. I've never known why he made sure the uniforms we picked for the garage — dark-grey button-down shirts with Collins Motors embroidered in red on the front left and a light grey nametag on the right, along with black pants — were made of wrinkle-free material.

He frowns at the safety pin in my shirt. "Couldn't find a sewing needle?"

"Because I don't have one." I look down at the shirt. "It's not that bad. I was going to staple it."

Bryce shakes his head. He is the only person I know who polishes his workboots, even if they never seem clean enough for him. A weird line of work for a neat freak, but Bryce is one of the best mechanics I know. He's just slower than everyone else.

"So, he starts today?" Bryce asks, talking about my soon-to-be ex-husband, Jamie. He picks up a couple of work orders and shuffles through them.

"Yup. I can't believe I have to put up with him working here."

"Not for long, I can bet." His mouth moves a little, making what passes for a smile from him. "But I can't believe you have to put up with it either."

"If I knew that investing in the company would mean I'd have to work with him—"

"Jack would have lost the business. You know damn well he wouldn't take the money from me."

Three and a half years ago, Dad had decided it was a good time to expand, but he moved too much too fast, and when the cost of labour and materials skyrocketed, Dad had two choices: take my money or go under. So Jamie and I combined the $20,000 I had and the $5000 Jamie's parents gave him to become part owners of Collins Motors.

"But why did I have to let Jamie in on the investment? Now I'm stuck with his terms or he's going to go after fifty percent."

"I don't understand why he wants a job here anyway. Not like he likes cars or knows anything about them." Bryce doesn't look up from the work order he's writing on.

"No. Maybe he just wants to torture me. Doesn't matter why, I suppose. Twenty percent and a full-time job is what he wants and that's what I'm stuck with."

"He won't be around long," Bryce says. "You wait and see."

I want to believe him but think back to a year before, when Bryce said the words, "He'll be okay."

"Maybe," I say and head off to the lunchroom to boil the kettle.

☞

The rest of the morning flies and by eleven, I'm dismantling the dashboard of a Ford Windstar in order to replace the bulb in the speedometer. The job is frustrating and to make matters worse, the minivan I'm working in smells like something has long since died inside it. The stench hit me when I opened the door, making my eyes water. I hold my breath as long as I can before leaning out of the car to take another deep breath of fresh air. I won't dare get too close to the fast food bags strewn over the back seat and piled up on the floor.

Something touches my leg and I exhale a blast of air with a start and a squeal.

"Hi, partner," Jamie says as I look out of the van.

"I'm busy."

"I see." He leans down and looks in the van. "Can I help?"

"No. Go see Bryce. He'll tell you what to do. Maybe you can try something easy, like change a tire or something."

"Yeah, I'd like to learn how to do that." Jamie smiles and I want him away from me. I hate him too much to like that smile.

I try to return to the dashboard but I want to know where Jamie is and what he's doing. I lean out of the van and see Jamie talking to Bryce. Jamie is grinning and Bryce's face can best be described as a scowl.

Looking at Jamie studying a work order Bryce is pointing at, I realize that both the men I loved will now be in the garage — one in the flesh and the other in memories represented by a horrible place on the floor next to the toolbox I won't let anyone close.

☙

I manage to avoid Jamie most of the day and leave the long-empty garage at 8:20. I make a stop at the liquor store on Kelsey Drive to buy a bottle of Bacardi Dark Rum. Driving up Kenmount Road, I put on my sunglasses and even then it's hard to see with the late May sun so low in the sky, filling my windshield with brightness. I turn left into the Anglican cemetery, the only place I can visit Dad. He is between Alfred Taylor, who lived to be eight years old in 1967, and a couple by the name of Sherren, who have a heart-shaped headstone and died within two years of each other.

Pulling my nylon coat tight around me, I still feel the cool wind cut through, making me shiver. I'm the only one here in the cemetery. I suddenly feel lonely. At least until I reach Dad.

Dad's headstone is a plain one. "Beloved father and husband" is etched on the face, along with a verse from a bible Dad never looked at or believed in. I hadn't wanted the verse on the stone. Mom said it wouldn't hurt to hedge his bets since he'd only ever been in a church five or six times in his life, including his own funeral. I told Mom that he didn't need to go to church and God would know what a good man he was. Didn't matter. She insisted on a line from Psalm 30: *Weeping may endure for a night, but joy cometh in the morning.* And there it is, right there under *March 16, 1948 - May 29, 2007.* The verse almost feels as wrong as the date somehow, like anything joyful could ever come out of this painful place.

"Hey, Dad." Somehow I hoped it would be easier after a year, that I'd be able to breathe again and stand here without hurting.

I kneel down and straighten up the flowers I brought

yesterday. I always bring marigolds. They smell a little bad but are pretty and they remind me of him in a way. All that sweetness with a little bit of stink, just from being yourself and doing what you do.

"I wish I had something good to tell you, but nothing's changed since I was here yesterday. He showed up at work today, all smiley like he always is. I always loved his smile and now I want to slap it off his face. Bryce is not happy about it either, but he says we have to deal with it. He's the sensible one now. Now that you're gone."

My hand runs over his name on the headstone without even meaning to. I realize my hand is touching it only when I feel the roughness under my fingers.

"Dr. Carson was in this afternoon. He's been in Germany on sabbatical for two years, so when he came in he asked for you. He said it so easily: 'Where's Jack?' and I couldn't say anything. I just stared at him with my mouth open, trying to find something to say. I must have opened and closed my mouth a half dozen times. I was like a guppy. But Bryce must have known what was going on. He came over and walked away with Dr. Carson. I wish I could have told him you were at the dentist or something, maybe lied so we could both pretend for a few minutes that you were still there. He came over again and apologized. He felt so bad. I said it was okay. I didn't cry."

I shake my head. "Haven't cried at all today. I decided that I wouldn't cry anymore and so far today, it's worked."

I feel silly for saying it, for pointing out something we never really talked about. I cry at coffee commercials and insurance ads. Just like Mom. Just like Nan Philpott. Handed down to me just like my upturned, little nose and my small frame. Dad would always turn away and pretend he didn't see when I started to cry or when I tried to resist my tears.

I stand up and rub my knees. Our talks are usually not long and sometimes I just sit here, but being with him, touching base with him makes me feel a little better.

"Bye, Dad. I'll see you tomorrow. Maybe you could put in a word to God about Jamie. Maybe arrange some smiting or something. Or at least ask God to have Jamie not want to work at the garage anymore." I pat the headstone before I turn to leave.

ॐ

I drive to my duplex off Thorburn Road. This was the house I shared with Jamie, and I probably should have moved, but everything was already there and I just never got around to it. Even though the house next door has two Rottweilers in the backyard that scare the bejeesus out of me, it's home. I like to be here during the few hours a day I'm not in the garage.

My answering machine isn't blinking and I wonder once again why I bother to look. My friends know not to call. I see them on weekends. My mom also never phones. She knows I'll see her on Sunday for our usual weekly visit. We sometimes watch a movie, talk about the week, have supper, and try to ignore the empty place at the head of the table.

I walk to the answering machine and press play anyway, knowing there is one message there. It waits every night for me.

"I finished the Tobin job, so no need to come in tomorrow. Mom is cooking dinner anyway so we'll see you then." Dad's voice echoes through death and to my ears. His strong, deep voice speaks offhandedly, unaware how many times I will listen to his message.

Twenty-two words preserved on my answering machine's cassette and duplicated on two other tapes in case I might lose one. They were not Dad's last words, but they are the only ones I have left.

I pour Bacardi into a tumbler Jamie bought when he moved into the house. He decorated everything, always having a better eye for things like that. If not for Jamie, I'd still have the old green couch Mom and Dad gave me from their rec room and milk crates with a sheet over them as a coffee table. Instead, I have a maple cocktail table and a plush, navy living room set of sofa, loveseat, and chair.

Jamie insisted I go with him to pick out the furniture, so I went along and nodded my agreement with whatever he suggested. At least until he wanted the beige couch. Looking at the fabric, I recalled years of my mother's frustration with trying to keep everything clean from dirty hands. I remembered the sound of plastic squeaking when I sat on Mom's light-grey sofa because Dad said a man should not have to change his clothes before he sat on his own sofa. I looked around the furniture store and told Jamie to find something darker or none of my money would be used to pay for it. Since I was the only one with any money, Jamie relented. My one and only decorating choice in the whole house.

I turn on the TV and flick through the channels, stopping on a biography of Jane Fonda for a moment before moving on and finding an old black-and-white movie on AMC. Katherine Hepburn is in a boat with a greasy-looking Humphrey Bogart.

The rum tastes good and before I know it, half the bottle is gone. My eyelids are heavier than I can manage to keep up. Just before I pass out on my usual place on the couch, I think maybe Bogey looks a little like Dad and don't even bother to fight the tears I have struggled against all day.

2

AT SIX THE next morning, I clear off a small space on my dining room table, pushing aside piles of bills and junk mail. I put my coffee on top of a coupon for Subway and open up a small notepad I dug out from a kitchen drawer. I write my name on a page then write it again, continuing for two 4" x 5" pages of my name. More than five years of writing Jennifer Flynn and initialling everything JF, means I have to relearn my old signature. You would think that writing Jennifer Collins again would be like riding a bike, but more often than not, the C in Collins, despite my best efforts, looks like it started as an F.

Although I haven't legally changed my name back, I decided I don't want to use Flynn anymore. I really haven't been Jennifer Flynn in a while. I stopped being married to Jamie more than three months ago.

That morning had been warm for February. The fog was so thick I couldn't see the cars in the parking lot outside the garage. I was working, when I heard a song on the radio. "Happy" by Bruce Springsteen. Our song. The song we had played for our first dance at our wedding reception. The song Jamie so often sang to me after we made love. I finished the job I was working on, showered in the garage, and decided to see Jamie before going out with the girls for our usual Saturday afternoon brunch. I just wanted to see him and to talk, maybe even something more if time and mood permitted. I used my key and walked in. I knew Jamie would be surprised.

I heard a sound coming from the back of the apartment and didn't realize right away what it was. It was a moment later, when I got closer to the sound and saw a stiletto shoe in the hall, then a bra in the bedroom doorway, that it all made sense. I had heard the same sound many times before. Despite not wanting to, in spite of knowing it would change everything if I walked through that door, I did. I saw Jamie's naked body bent over someone who was on all fours on the bed, banging on her, each movement accentuated with his groan. The back of this nameless woman's head snapped back with each forceful thrust from Jamie, her long hair flicking around like a whip slapping Jamie's face. His back glistened with sweat. I knew if I could see his face, his eyes would have that hungry look I thought was mine, and I thanked God his back was to me.

They had no idea I was in the room. I was quiet, unable to speak because they had stolen all of the air from my lungs. I just stood there for two or three minutes, staring, hurting, dying, suppressing a scream until something seemed to snap and rage took over where the pain had been. I went straight from denial to anger in seconds, a new record for Kübler-Ross's stages of grief.

I could tell from his pace of movement and panting that he was about to finish. I thought about screaming to stop him before he could, but then my eye caught the other shoe, the twin from the one in the hall. I looked from the shoe to Jamie, back to the shoe, back to Jamie.

The scream Jamie let out a few seconds later was not one I had heard before, and it was not the natural culmination of the act he'd been consumed by. It was the sound of footwear hitting the back of his head, and I left before he could turn around. I could still hear his swearing and crying when I walked out the front door with a smirk on my face and tears in my eyes.

I return to the notepad. If only getting back to who I used to be was as easy as learning to sign my name again.

℘

A couple of weeks after Jamie started work, I walk into the garage and see Aunt Henrietta waiting in my office. This is the third time she has been here in the past month. Bryce calls her a hypocardiac and she isn't alone in her obsession with her car. A few of our customers have the same problem and, although they make us a lot of money by coming in so often, dealing with them is rarely worth the income.

"Morning," I say. Bryce nods. Henrietta doesn't bother with the formality of hello.

"That back tire is making an awful racket and Bryce is going to have a look at it. He says it's probably the hubscrew." She nods and furrows her brow, reflecting the seriousness of announcing that she has cancer or that the sky is falling.

"You want my car so you can go shopping or something while you wait?" I ask.

"Will it take a while to fix the hubscrew?" She glances at Bryce but her questioning stare lands on me.

"Umm." I look to Bryce. He returns a small grin.

"Nah," Bryce says. "Loose hubscrew shouldn't take more than ten minutes."

I nod.

Aunt Henrietta doesn't pay for any of the work we do on her car. She never has. Bryce was the first one to come up with our fake repairs on her car. He spent several hours looking for a strange sound Henrietta had heard in her car, including removing the centre console between the seats, and the lower dash. Then he finally figured out that Henrietta had been hearing the movement of a Coke can with the pull tab inside, which would roll forward and backward under the seat, rattling as it did. He swore that he would never waste that kind of time again.

The next time Henrietta came in with a vibration, Bryce checked to make sure all was okay. When he could find nothing wrong, according to the story that has been told over and over, Bryce told her she had a broken stilt assembly. Dad, who had been there, looked at Bryce with question marks all over his face. Dad didn't crack a smile but he and Bryce laughed for a straight half hour after Aunt Henrietta left with her car exactly the same as it was when it came in.

Over the years Aunt Henrietta has had hundreds of repairs done to her car, many of them real but the majority fictitious. The hubscrew has been used before, but it's a good one and it makes Henrietta happy.

Jamie walks in fifteen minutes later, when Henrietta is showing Bryce and me the latest pictures of her five-year-old Sarah. Henrietta refers to Sarah as her miracle child. She was conceived when Henrietta was forty-six years old, after doctors had assured her, years before, that she could never have a baby. No child has ever been as smart or kind or beautiful as my cousin Sarah, at least that's what Henrietta thinks. I think she always has a runny nose and spends way too much time styling her dolls' hair.

When Jamie sees Henrietta through the office window, he turns around and is walking away from the office when Henrietta spots him.

"Jamie," she shouts, her voice jolting me. "Did you take my Tupperware container on Sunday?"

I feel like I've fallen through a rip in the universe and landed somewhere else, maybe in another time. Is Aunt Henrietta having a stroke or something? Why is she talking to Jamie about Tupperware?

"What?" I ask.

Aunt Henrietta turns to me. "I think Jamie took my green cookie container. You know, the one that used to be Mom's."

No, I don't know. I don't know the colour of anyone's Tupperware. Ever. I turn and catch Jamie making some kind of signals to Aunt Henrietta.

"Where would he have been to take your cookie container?"

"Mom's." Henrietta shrugs.

I turn to Jamie who has come up next to me. "You were at Nan's? Why?"

Before Jamie can even open his mouth, Aunt Henrietta

pipes up. "He goes there every week. Every Sunday at two like clockwork." She looks around and must notice the faces on Bryce and Jamie. They look like someone has just blurted out the non-existence of Santa Claus, the tooth fairy and the Easter bunny to a four-year-old.

"What?" Henrietta says, looking to Jamie and Bryce. "She's not a youngster. I don't see what the big deal is."

"How long have you been visiting Nan?" I ask Jamie, close enough to his face that I can smell the coffee on his breath.

"Since you split up," Henrietta answers.

"Are you a ventriloquist, Jamie? Because whenever I ask you a question, this one answers and it's getting confusing."

"Excuse me?" Aunt Henrietta says, her voice up an octave on "me." "I will not be spoken to like that. I'm just telling you the truth. That's more than anyone else. Big deal. Jamie visits Mom. Who cares?"

"Then why didn't you tell me?" I ask her.

"Because everyone figured you'd be angry if you knew about it."

"Well, I am now. Because you kept it from me. Like I'm too fragile to hear something as simple as that. Wonderful. Glad to know my family thinks so much of me." I start to walk away, to get out of the office before I smack something when the question hits me.

"Did Mom know this?" I turn around and three faces have the wordless answer written on them.

In my bay, I pick up a cloth and start to clean a wrench. I don't have a work order and I don't want to go back in the office. I think about the Sundays I suggested to Mom that we visit Nan and how she always talked me out of it.

I can't believe they wouldn't tell me something as simple as this. Like it's a big deal or something. Like I'd be upset. Just because I told Jamie never to show his face around me or my family again. Just because I may have told Nan that Jamie died, made her cry before she forgot my stupid lie.

I suddenly feel gripped by a panic, wondering what else has been going on. There's been a concerted effort to keep something from me. A minor thing. Something that shouldn't really matter. What if there are other big things? Maybe Mom has cancer or they all helped Jamie get part of the garage. They obviously still kept in some form of contact with him since we split. Maybe he's over at Mom's house for dinner regularly and Bryce goes to hockey games with him.

Bryce comes out to my bay and I jump on him with questions. "What else are you not telling me? Is there a whole load of stuff I don't know?"

"No."

"Swear on Dad's grave."

"I don't swear on anything, let alone a dead man."

"Then why should I believe you?"

"Because I said it."

"Yes," I say. His words, the sparseness of them brings me back to reality. Sometimes the truth doesn't need a lot of frills.

I turn away and pick up my air gun, ready to turn it on and drown him out if he pisses me off.

"What's the part that's bothering you?" Bryce asks after a couple of minutes.

"Nothing."

My hand is on the trigger. Bryce reaches around me and lays his hand on the air gun. He gently pulls it out of my hand.

"That even you didn't tell me," I say, turning to him. "You kept it from me."

Bryce stares at me, face unchanging. If he blinks, I don't see it.

"And I wish Jamie wasn't so nice. I wish he could be a bastard everyone hates. We could all hate him together."

"Yeah, I know what you mean." Bryce lays down the air gun.

"Why'd he have to be so nice. To visit my nan in an Alzheimer's unit. And everyone likes him. Even you. I saw the way you put your hand on his shoulder the other day. You like him, don't you?"

Bryce knew Ray for three years before he got a shoulder clap. Some of the guys still haven't gotten one.

"He tries hard. He don't have a goddamned clue about cars, but he tries with everything he got. And he'll do whatever you ask. No matter what. I'm after giving him the dirtiest, greasiest, stinkiest jobs I could find and even made some up, but he does every one of them with a smile."

I think back to Jamie's second day when he showed up looking too good for an ex to look. Bryce had told him I'd be showing him paperwork so he should dress appropriately, but when he got to work, things had changed.

"Got a Mercedes for you to work on first," Bryce said. "Very important customer."

"Oh. Should I change?"

"Nope. No time. Need this done ASAP." Bryce knew

the customer was out of town for the weekend and wouldn't need the car until Monday. "Seems Mrs. Dwyer's keyless entry is not working."

"Keyless entry?"

Bryce stared at him and I watched his right hand curl into a fist at his side.

"On a remote. Press the button and you can unlock the doors or pop the trunk."

"Oh, I thought that was just called a remote starter." Jamie chuckled. "So we just have to check the starter, or the keyless entry thing or whatever and that's it. Sounds pretty simple."

"There's nothing simple about a keyless entry problem," Bryce said, straightening up. "That's a complicated system. Could be one of a dozen things."

"Really?" The question surprised me. I didn't think he knew enough even to question Bryce on the keyless entry.

Bryce looked Jamie up and down, from the tip of his shiny leather loafers to the white collar on his perfectly pressed shirt. "We'll start with the oil. We'll change that then see where we go from there. That's always your first check with a keyless entry problem."

As I watched Bryce talk to Jamie, I noticed three guys come up behind them, standing there with grins on their faces. Jamie was nodding to Bryce while Ray, Alan, and Rick were all looking at the same spark plug Alan was holding while looking at Bryce from the corners of their eyes. I walked over to see the same spark plug. Jamie turned to watch me.

"How's the gap there?" I asked Alan and smiled. Stupid question no one ever asks a mechanic. That's why we have feeler gauges to measure the gaps in spark plugs, but I was sure Jamie didn't know that. I'd have been shocked if Jamie even knew the thing Alan was holding was called a spark plug.

"Looking good," Alan said and winked.

We all stared at the spark plug but I watched Jamie too. He was still looking at me, at least until Bryce smacked him on the arm.

"You want to do this or not?" Bryce asked, making Jamie turn back to him.

"Oh, yeah. Sorry."

"I'd check the gear oil too," Rick said. "Goddamned dirty old thing to do, but I've seen that fuck up a keyless entry system before."

Three and a half hours later, Jamie's perfect outfit was blotched with oil and sweat and he smelled like he'd taken a bath in gasoline and gear oil. Bryce had told him there were no extra coveralls for him to wear.

"Now, I think we should replace the battery in the remote transmitter," Bryce said.

"What?" Jamie asked.

"Most likely the battery in the transmitter needs to be replaced."

Jamie turned when he heard us laughing. For a second he looked hurt, but only for a second, before his big, Jamie grin came back on his face.

"Sure." He nodded. "The battery. Of course." His smile broadened. He turned so he addressed Bryce and the rest of us too. "You know I could have just replaced the battery, but I learned how to change the oil, and checked the gear oil, and bled the brakes. Thanks, Bryce. I'm learning a lot."

In my bay I wipe my hand on my coveralls then pick up a wrench. "It's all that good stuff that pisses me off. It makes it hard to hate him. And Nan loves him so much. I bet he made her happy with his visits." I look straight at Bryce. "Why can't he change into someone awful?"

"He's not going to change. Maybe you'll have to." And Bryce is gone, walking back to the office before I can reply. My voice of reason and of few words.

I decide to let this one go, not even to mention Jamie's visits to Nan when I see Mom again. They all expect me to be upset and I won't give them the satisfaction. I don't have to feel angry about every little thing he does. I realize my hand hurts and look down to see that my hand is clasped around the wrench so tightly it's digging into my fingers.

℘

If variety is the spice of life then I must lead a bland existence. A creature of habit, Dad called me. Set in my ways, Jamie's always said of me. No matter what you label it, I work all day during the week from eight to whenever I finish up, except for my standing date with Nan on Tuesday afternoons. Saturday mornings I work until noon then have brunch with the girls at Bernie's Pub and Restaurant. Sunday afternoons I visit Mom, at least since Dad passed away.

The only difference in my schedule now is that I go out with the girls on Saturday nights now too instead of renting a movie and staying home with Jamie or going downtown with him to watch him in the latest band he's in. And Sunday afternoons now, Mom and I don't always eat at her house. Sometimes we go out to a movie or a play or for supper at a restaurant.

With the exception of a couple of illnesses, a few weddings — mine included — and one funeral, the girls and I have managed to keep the standing date for several years now. Bernie's is small, with an even smaller deck outside for those rare occasions when one can eat on a deck in St. John's. If it's actually sunny and warm, there are usually flies or the dreaded wasps of summer. At Bernie's, we know we'll have our full meals of soggy bacon, runny eggs, toast, and warmed-up frozen hash browns before us — and the best Bloody Caesars in St. John's. Some things are more important than food.

After two full weeks with Jamie at the garage, I look forward to the usual Saturday. A sunny day in June makes us feel brave and we decide to eat outside on the deck. A bank of fog sits just outside the harbour, threatening to make our day darker.

"I think we should go inside," Michelle says, wrapping her jacket around her shoulders. "You said it would only get up to twelve degrees. That's not exactly outside weather."

"Shut up complaining," BJ says, rolling her eyes. "It's already fifteen, according to the thermometer in my car."

"Well, that means you were wrong about how warm it would be. Anyway it feels colder than that with the wind."

BJ puts her hand on her chest. "Oh my God. The weather person was wrong. Stop the presses. Call all media. This is a first in history."

"Did you put extra sarcasm on your corn flakes this morning?" I ask BJ.

"You know I snort it straight up. No diluting it with milk

for me."

BJ smiles and Michelle sticks her arms into the sleeves of her jacket then zips it up to the neck. With hands laden down with one or two rings on each finger, she flicks her mousy brown hair out of her green eyes.

"Come on then, let's go inside," BJ says, touching Michelle's arm.

Michelle Connors is broad in the shoulders and the jacket makes her look like a linebacker. Her face has a distinctive orange tint, thanks to her foundation, which today is matched with red lipstick and pink blush. Mom kindly said once of Michelle that she liked to "lay the make-up on thick" and added, "Strange for someone who works in a lab all the time. She must get mascara all over her microscopes."

A waitress I haven't seen before comes over to take our orders. She stares at BJ and smiles. Michelle orders our food and drinks, but the waitress doesn't write anything down, doesn't even seem to notice that Michelle is talking.

"I'm a big fan," she finally says to BJ.

"Thank you." BJ smiles the fake smile she reserves for people who annoy her with their adoration when she's trying to eat or go to the bathroom or buy tampons.

BJ Brown is the kind of friend you could easily hate if you didn't love her so much. Brown hair, blue eyes, dark skin that seems to tan even when it's cloudy, buxom chest, tiny waist, white teeth, perfect everything.

"Uh, excuse me," Michelle says to the waitress, waving her hand, making the six gold bangles on her arm jangle. "Did you hear anything I said?"

"Oh, no, sorry. What would you like, Miss Brown?" The waitress turns from glancing at Michelle to focus on BJ.

"I'd like you to listen to my friend while she orders, please." Again a smile but less so.

Once Michelle has placed our order, the waitress smiles at BJ again before walking away.

"It always pisses me off when people ignore us because you're there, but she was particularly bad." Michelle doesn't look at BJ as she speaks.

"No," I say. "The time that guy pushed me out of the way and onto the ground so he could talk to BJ was particularly bad. She was just mildly rude."

"Sorry, guys. I can't help it."

"Maybe you should wear a disguise," I say.

"My God, I just read the weather on the news. I'm not a movie star."

"You might as well be. You're a big fish in a goldfish bowl," Michelle tells her.

We both stare at Michelle. I don't know what's going through BJ's mind, but I'm pretty sure she's wondering, like I am, if Michelle meant the statement to reflect how small Newfoundland is and how big a minor celebrity can be here, or if she just mixed up her clichés. The first choice would be a surprise. The second would be expected.

"What?" Michelle asks, her green eyes opening wide.

"Nothing." BJ giggles and shakes her head.

I shiver a little and pull my coat on as subtly as I can, pulling my ponytail outside once I have the coat on. Underneath, I'm wearing my usual casual-wear t-shirt and low-rise jeans. My collection of t-shirts with funny sayings or comics or something Newfoundland-related means I'm an easy person to buy for. Today I'm wearing the t-shirt BJ gave me for my birthday. This one says *Department of Redundancy Department,* and people either read it and don't get it or they read it, take a moment, and laugh.

The three of us grew up on Shea Street and have been best friends since elementary school. An odd combination of the beauty, the scientist, and the mechanic. Michelle went to university to study biology and followed it up with a job working in a lab at the Health Sciences Centre, while BJ lucked out after she won Miss Teen Newfoundland and was offered a summer job travelling around the island promoting an FM radio station. From there she caught the eye of a TV station manager who let her replace the regular weather guy when he went on vacation. After the weather guy "retired" following charges of marijuana possession, BJ became the regular weather person and occasional anchor-person on holidays and vacation fill-in.

The waitress is back with our Caesars in what seems like an impossibly fast time, if I didn't know that Kelly Parsons, the muscular Irish bartender, had started making them when he saw us coming in. Being regulars at this place means Kelly never makes us wait too long.

"Okay, dish out all the dirt," BJ says, flicking her napkin open with a snap and laying it on her lap. She is looking straight at me.

"Huh? What dirt?"

"Yeah, Jennifer has so much dirt at her work, what kind do you want? Brake fluid? Grease? Oil?" Michelle laughs as she speaks.

"I don't mean actual dirt," BJ says in her talking to a two-year-old tone. She turns to me. "I mean the dirt on Jamie."

"What?"

"You said in your email when he started at the garage that you didn't want to talk about him, and I went along with that for a couple of weeks, but you can't expect Jamie to be a non-subject for too long."

"Yes, I can. There's nothing to discuss. He's working there. I hate it. End of discussion."

"Does he still look good?" Michelle asks as the waitress brings us three more Caesars.

"From the man at the bar," the waitress says. A balding man, with his shirt open way too far, nods and waves. Winks at BJ. I'm pretty sure Michelle and I could be extra chairs at the table for all he knows.

We all nod back at him. Michelle and BJ smile.

"Did you hear that Jane Simon's mom has cancer?" I ask.

"Nice try," BJ says. "Topic is Jamie. No new topics until this one is finished."

"Are you the conversation police?"

BJ just stares and I know there is no point in trying to get out of this.

"Bertha Jean, leave me alone."

"Shhh," BJ says.

BJ's only weakness, if you can call it that — more of a sore spot — is her name. Bertha was her grandmother's name and since her grandmother died a week before Bertha was born, her parents gave their baby girl the name as a sign of love and remembrance. The name haunted her until grade six when Michelle found out Bertha's middle name and started to call her friend BJ. I started using the nickname too, and by junior high no one remembered BJ as anything but BJ. Not that she wasn't teased about that name a time or a hundred. But we still had "Bertha" as a little word we could poke her with every now and then.

BJ narrows her eyes at me. "Let me guess how it went with Jamie. He started out shaky. Not a favourite of anyone in the garage and clueless about all things mechanical. We know that. The guy can barely pump his own gas. But he's starting to grow on them. People like him and he's doing pretty good at the garage. He's catching on fast and trying really hard, just like he always does." BJ finishes her spiel, sits back and crosses her arms.

"Yeah, right."

I wish I could laugh and tell her she's wrong. Jamie's charm and passion for life are as predictable as BJ thinks they are.

If anything could prove that Jamie is a special kind of person, it's my father's acceptance of him, first as my boyfriend and then as my husband.

"What does he do?" Dad asked after he overheard the guys in the garage talking about my new boyfriend, gossip they rarely got to share.

"Well, he's a jack-of-all-trades. Right now he's playing bass guitar in a band called—"

"A band?" Dad's voice went down an octave and he crossed his arms.

"Right now. He does roofing sometimes. And he worked on a supply boat for a couple of months last year." I could see by my father's face that every word was digging a bigger hole for Jamie.

"Where does he live?"

"In an apartment." Something told me not to include the part that he shared the two-bedroom with four other guys.

"And who pays when you go to dinner?"

"We take turns." It was one of the few lies I ever told my father.

"I think it's time we meet this fellow. Bring him over to dinner on Sunday. And don't expect me to be nice to him. I don't tolerate slackers."

And Dad hadn't at first. He practically told Jamie that he didn't think he was right for his daughter. But Jamie kept coming back to the house, undeterred by anything or anyone, and a little over a year later, after Dad walked me up the aisle, Dad shook Jamie's hand and smiled. Such is the power of Jamie.

As the waitress comes with our food, BJ smiles.

"I know I'm right," she says, opening a bottle of ketchup. "That's exactly what Jamie would do."

"Change of subject," Michelle pipes up. "How's your nan?"

I shrug. "Same."

"When I went to see Pop at the home, Mrs. Talbot said your nan started to take off her clothes in the common room. But the aides stopped her and brought her back to her room."

"Jesus," BJ says, "why did you tell her that?"

"Why not?"

"Because there's some things you just don't need to know."

42

a few kinds of wrong

"Like what?" Michelle leans back in her chair.

"Like what you just told Jennifer."

"What else?"

"I don't know. Lots of stuff."

"Ha. Good rebating skills, BJ. 'Lots of stuff' really straightens that up for me."

"Like that the word is 'debating,' not 'rebating.' Like you get lots of words wrong." BJ starts to wave her hands as she speaks. "It's not cancer of the Eucharist that Mrs. Simon has, it's cancer of the uterus; like an octopus has eight tentacles, not eight testicles; like—"

"That's not the same as what Michelle told me," I join in. "Michelle can do something about those things. She can stop using the wrong words. I can't do anything about what Nan did in the home."

BJ stares at me, blinking her eyes in an exaggerated way and I know she's debating, not rebating, whether or not to say something. "You could buy her body suits that snap up in the crotch to make it harder to get her clothes off." She blinks again. "And you know we've pointed out stuff Michelle says all the time but she never learns. So it's exactly the same as what she said about your nan."

"I don't say that much wrong," Michelle says. "You make it sound like I'm an idiot. I'm a biologist."

"Yeah, you are, and a brilliant one at that. Book smart doesn't mean everything though."

After a minute of silence at the table, Michelle turns to me and says, "My friend Sarah, at work, says BJ looks like she's gaining weight."

"What? I'm not."

Michelle shrugs. "That's what she said."

"Well, Sarah is one to talk, I know. She's not exactly easy on the scales."

They continue to argue as I sip my Caesar. There's comfort in their back and forth, in the loving bickering the three of us share. Like I imagine I'd have with sisters if I had them. Sometimes BJ, with her cutting remarks, crosses the line, but Michelle often doesn't get it, and I usually give back as good or better than what BJ gives me. For a few minutes I don't join in the fray. I just drink and watch, like an outsider, a voyeur with full access to listen to these people without having to participate.

"Hello," BJ says, snapping her fingers in front of my face. "What do you think?"

"About what?"

"You're thinking about Jamie, aren't you? You're lusting after him." BJ smiles the way she always does when she's said something she's not sure she can get away with.

"No. I hate him. I can barely stand to be in the same room as him. I'm not lusting after him. And I won't. Ever."

"Okay, okay. No lusting after the sexiest man anywhere near your garage. Of course you don't want to feel those strong arms around you," BJ says.

"No," I say and slam down my napkin. Everyone looks at us and then the whispers and pointing start. Everyone who hadn't already noticed now sees that BJ Brown is sitting with us. I try to ignore it and whisper to them, "Why do you think I'd want anything to do with him? Don't you think he hurt me enough?"

"Well," BJ says while Michelle says nothing.

a few kinds of wrong

"Damn it. You always think it's my own fault, don't you? Some friends you are." I stand up to leave before I hit something or cry, my two responses to this kind of frustration. Michelle grabs my arm.

"I have some really big news. Subject changed. Okay?"

I hesitate. BJ mouths "I'm sorry," and I sit down. The Caesar is just too good to leave it.

"Well, what's the news?" BJ asks.

"I met someone," she says with a smirk on her face.

"I thought you said this was news," I say.

"Yeah. He's new."

"Yes, but you met someone last week, and the week before, and the week before," BJ says.

"And the week before the week before, and the week before that, then two days before that," I add.

Michelle's face is grim. "Well, I tried to change the subject for you. We can go back to Jamie if you'd like. Or I can tell you about the new guy."

"Tell us about him," I say before BJ can open her mouth.

And as Michelle starts to tell us about her new love, I once again find relief in the same old, same old.

꙳

The next morning, I whisper out loud, asking God to create some kind of head-removal device so I can function a little without the gnawing pain in my skull. I normally don't have hangovers if I just stick to one thing, usually rum, but yesterday started with Caesars and ended at nearly three in the morning with Jello shots. The time in between was filled with a wide assortment of shooters, fruity cocktails and beer. I think it was the beer that got me.

Getting home is fuzzy. I try to remember anything past standing outside Shooter's bar, shouting "BJ Brown is named for what she does best, baby. Step right up and try her out." Poor BJ had to practically beat them off with a stick and that's where I lost the timeline.

I look around. No guy here. That's good. Still in my clothes. Good, since that probably means I didn't get sick on them on the way home. I have to call BJ and make sure she's okay. And I need a bucket of water to drink. Everyone knows the cure for headaches is water.

Sitting up in bed turns out to be a bad decision as I'm compelled by the sensation in the back of my throat to find something to get sick in. The bathroom is too far away, I know. This is happening. Now.

There is nothing around. Nothing except the jeans lying on the floor next to my bed, and I grab them without thinking. With the legs balled up, it turns out to be a good container. In about five minutes my stomach feels better, my throat and mouth much worse. My jeans are a multicoloured, sour-smelling design. I run to the bathroom and lay them on the tile floor before I go out to the kitchen to get a garbage bag. No garbage bags.

"Shit," I say out loud. I turn to open the garbage can in the kitchen, but seeing the banana peel and potato chip bag hanging out over the side, I remember that I've needed garbage bags for a while now. I open the cabinet under the sink and find a nice sturdy, large shopping bag. Thank God for the Newfoundland Liquor Corporation and their thick plastic bags.

Back in the bathroom I fill the bag with jeans and yuck while trying not to look. This doesn't work and some stuff I'd rather not see spills out.

"Shit. Shit. Shit."

I try to clean it up, also while not looking at it, and use almost a whole roll of toilet paper to do it. When I flush, the toilet starts to overflow with way too much toilet paper and puke. I sit on the floor and cry, at least until I hear the sound of water pouring onto the floor. Clogged toilets can be wept over; overflowing toilets must be dealt with. I grab the plunger, and in a few minutes, I've unclogged the drain and cleaned up the remaining mess with a bath towel, which joins my jeans in the liquor store bag. I have to get garbage bags. And a mop.

I grab a shower after brushing my teeth for five minutes. Still tastes like crap inside there. I wipe enough steam away from the mirror to look at my face. My mom would tell me I look sick.

I throw my towel in the hamper and go to my room to dry my hair.

"You're still a pleasure to wake up with, babe." A voice stops me in my tracks.

I don't have to look. I'd know it anywhere. Still, I need to know why and how he is here, even where he is in the house. But I'm also naked so I run to my room, saying "no" with every step.

"What are you doing here?" I yell, looking around for something clean to wear. Those were my last clean pair of jeans. I search in the laundry hamper and find a pair that looks reasonably clean.

"You don't remember?" Jamie shouts.

I grab a t-shirt that says *I couldn't repair your brakes so I made your horn louder* from my drawer and try again to remember anything. Nothing comes. Picking up the telephone on my bedside table, I dial BJ's number.

"Why is Jamie here?" I ask before she can finish her hello.

"What? Jamie's there?"

"You don't know either? I don't remember anything."

"Not even the bouncer from Greensleeves who had to rescue me from the assholes you encouraged to ask me for blow-jobs?"

"I'm really sorry, Beej. I'm such an idiot."

"Yes, you are but don't be sorry. That bouncer has muscles in places I didn't even know had muscles. Now, I'd like to get back to him, please."

"He's there?"

"Duh. How do you think I know about his muscles? Hey, maybe I wasn't the only one who got lucky last night. Is Jamie dressed?"

"Don't know. Haven't seen him. Only heard his voice. Anyway, get back to the bouncer."

"Okay, but I want an email later with details about this Jamie thing. Or I'll call you and bug the shit out of you."

"Yeah, okay."

I call Michelle but get her machine and hang up without leaving a message. Best she doesn't know about this anyway.

I don't want to tell Jamie I don't remember anything. I shut the bedroom door and hope he'll go away. The sound of the blow dryer will drown out anything he might say, and even when my hair is dry I sit on the bed with the dryer pointing at the mirror. No need to rush out there to see Jamie.

My makeup is in the bathroom so I need a way to get there. I don't usually use much makeup, only on the weekends with the girls, but I must be the only mechanic who makes sure there is eyeliner and lipstick in her toolbox at all times. Those were always my staples. For the past few months I haven't been wearing them much, but right now my face is so pale it could use a little outlining just to reinforce that it's a face.

I figure the best way to get my makeup is to make a dash for the bathroom — head down, straight ahead. Jamie will just think I'm getting sick again. Oh, God, Jamie heard me getting sick. He saw me walking around with a vomit-filled pair of jeans. And I'm worrying that he doesn't see me without eyeliner.

Ripping open the door to start my dash to the bathroom, I run face and eyes into Jamie with a thud. He topples backwards and only stops himself from hitting the floor by grabbing my shoulders. Now I'm face to face with Jamie, my eyes so close to his I can see the flecks of gold. Jamie steps back and pushes me away.

"Sorry," he says. "I was just going to check and make sure you were okay."

"I have to go to the bathroom."

Two seconds in front of the mirror in the bathroom tells

me eyeliner and lipstick are not going to help much, but I try anyway.

"I have to go somewhere, Jamie," I say through the door as I try to line my lips with a shaky hand. "So you'll have to leave."

"You're welcome." He is right outside the door.

"What?"

"I come over when you call me at almost four in the morning, I let you cry on my shoulder, and I fight you off when you come onto me, and this is all the thanks I get. Great."

I don't know how to begin processing this, let alone to decide which part of Jamie's story to refute. I open the door.

"Fought me off? I don't think you remember that right."

"And *you* do? Do you remember anything? What did you say when you called me?"

"That doesn't matter now. What matters is that you didn't fight me off and I have somewhere to go. Right now."

"You took off your shirt and almost had your bra off before I stopped you."

I don't want him to be right, but he is here, and I must have let him in. He has no key. I let him stay here. I must have wanted him here, wanted to talk to him.

"We had a good talk, Jen," Jamie says. He reaches his hand out like he is going to touch my face but I step back. He puts his hand back down by his side. "I thought we straightened some things out."

"I have to go. I need to go into work for a bit. Tough

job and I need to get it done before I go see Mom."

He opens his mouth, as if to say something, but closes it again. "Okay."

He puts his shoes on and I stand there. He straightens up. "But it changed last night. You kissed me again and I won't let you forget it. You'll forgive me one day."

"Forgive you for what? You've always said you didn't do anything wrong."

"Not for that. For what you really hate me for."

"Goodbye, Jamie."

"Yeah, I'll see you soon." And he is gone, leaving me and the truth alone in the house again.

3

THE AFTERNOON IS the usual. I pick up a large double, double for me and a medium with two cream for Mom at Tim Hortons and drive to the home I was literally born in.

"Eager to get in the world," Nan still says of me when she remembers who I am. Two weeks early and twenty minutes of labour.

The house would look worn down if it wasn't for Bryce, who helps out with the leaky faucets, paints the eaves and windowsills, and fixes the creaky step. Mom doesn't even have to call him. He just shows up from time to time, tools in hand, and starts to fix some exterior problem he's noticed as he drives by, then asks Mom if there's anything else to be done inside. Mom once commented that the house looks better now than when Dad was alive.

"That man will do anything for a home-cooked meal," Mom says all the time, but I know she's happy Bryce helps out. Even knowing he lives just down the street seems to comfort her. Any strange noises in the night and Bryce can be there in two minutes, one if he runs. I'd say there would have to be a burglar beating down her door in order for her to call him, but just the knowing is sometimes all we need to make us feel at ease.

Getting out of my car, I wave to Mom's next-door neighbour, Ray Chafe. The sky is threatening rain. You can smell the dampness in the air, but he's mowing his lawn again even though he probably did it yesterday. He mows no matter what the weather, waters the lawn at the first sign of it not being saturated, fertilizes, limes, spreads manure on his lawn, even tried kelp once. They say fences make good neighbours, but I can guarantee that kelp and manure make for bad ones. Since his wife died, he's gone onto mowing other people's lawns and Mom's is always manicured.

The bungalow is yellow and white with a veranda and four steps in front. Purple and pink flowers hang in baskets along the front of the veranda. I'm pretty sure they're real because Mom never puts them out until at least the second week of June. She swears that summer in Newfoundland doesn't begin until that last frost in June and she's usually right.

I put Mom's coffee on top of mine, freeing one hand to open the front door, trying not to knock off the flowery wreath hanging in the centre.

"Hello," I shout as I walk in the porch. The smell of apples and cinnamon comes out to meet me.

Mom walks around the corner and gives me a peck on the cheek, then wipes off the lipstick she inevitably leaves there. Mom believes everyone needs lipstick. Over the years, she has started to rely more heavily on other makeup like concealers and wrinkle-hiding foundations. I rarely see her now without her face on.

Most people refer to Mom as "small" or "tiny" but she calls herself petite. Short and thin, she could still manage to buy clothes in the girls' section except she swears there's nothing there suitable for a woman of her age so she gets everything tailored to fit her right. Her short hair is kept trim and chestnut brown with a monthly cut and colour.

"Hello," Mom says, taking her coffee. She takes a big sip then pulls a sliver of hair behind her ear.

"I see Mr. Chafe is mowing again."

Mom nods.

"And your lawn looks good too."

"He did that yesterday."

"I'm telling you, he wants to mow more than your lawn. You should watch out for him."

"Oh, Jennifer," Mom says. She smiles and there is something in it that makes my heart hurt.

"You baking a pie?"

"No." She bends to pick something up but straightens up again and turns to me. "Do you want me to make you a pie?"

"No, just smells like apples and cinnamon."

"Oh." She chuckles. "Plug-in air freshener. It's nice, isn't it?"

"Yeah."

"You want it? I can get another one."

"No, no, that's okay." My mind goes to the overflowing garbage and bag of jeans and vomit back at my place and I'm tempted.

a few kinds of wrong

"You sure?"

"Yes, I'm sure. I don't want an air freshener. Honest."

My words are meant to curtail a long back and forth of *please take it* and *no, that's okay,* but I think I miscalculated my tone and Mom's smile leaves.

"Thanks, though."

Mom nods. "You coming in?"

"Nah, I thought you said you'd like to go to a movie."

"I was thinking we could go to that new movie with that guy in it. You know, the one you like," Mom says as she puts on a pair of shoes then straightens up the remaining pairs on the shoe rack.

"No, Mom, I don't know. Which one? I like most of them."

"That cute one."

I roll my eyes. "Doesn't narrow down the Hollywood acting scene much."

She snaps her fingers. "He used to be in that show, the one with Sarah in it."

"Sarah who?"

"You know, Sarah from *The Young and the Restless.*"

I connect my TV and movie dots, trying to remember what Sarah looks like, what other show she was in, who starred with her in it, and then come up with the answer. "Benjamin Ritchie."

Mom smiles. "Yes, him. Just like I said. Anyway, want to see that movie?"

A film about a guy who holds a prostitute hostage, tortures her, then ends up falling in love with her over sexual toys. Not exactly a great afternoon with Mom.

"Not really. How about that new one with Kevin Costner?"

"Don't like him," Mom says, shaking her head. "There's a book launch down at the Anglican Crypt. We could go to that."

Yes, and I could poke sticks in my eyes.

"Our book club is going to read it so I wouldn't mind seeing the author."

"How's that going? The book club. You like it?"

Mom smiles. "Yes, I do. It's fun and I like getting out and talking to people."

"That's good. The book launch sounds great," I say.

Two hours later, I, and the four other people in attendance at the crypt, have listened to the most boring reading in the history of the world and Mom and I are sitting in a Thai restaurant. Mom decided she wouldn't cook today and was dying to try this restaurant.

"When did you even know there was such a thing as Thai food around here?" I asked Mom when she first suggested the restaurant.

"Someone at the book club told me," she explained.

I almost collide with a knee-high elephant statue just inside the entryway. The thin lanterns hanging from the ceiling don't throw much light, and since it's raining outside now, there's not much light coming from the windows. We forego the cushions and low tables and pick a booth on the side of the restaurant. We are barely seated when two brightly coloured drinks come to our table.

"Compliments of the manager," the pimply-faced waiter says as he spills some of my drink while setting it down. "Oops,

I'll get you another one."

"That's okay," Mom says. "It was just an accident. And please tell the manager we said thank you." She looks so proud that someone gave her a drink. I don't want to tell her it's just a promotional thing new restaurants do for new customers to keep them coming back. No different than the complete car wash we give a first-time customer at the garage.

"I'm not sure what to order," Mom says.

I have to admit I'm not much help. The dishes all sound so unfamiliar: *Goong Hom Pa, Pla Lad Prig, Peek Gai Yad Sai, Tom Yum Koong.* I can't even guess what they are. I have no reference to guide me. High school French won't help here. I can't even place the rich smells permeating the restaurant. Strong spices, peppers, a hint of lemon maybe, fish, and some other mysterious scents make my mouth water.

"Excuse me," my mother says while waving at the waiter. "Could you help us with this menu?"

"Allow me," a gentle voice comes out of nowhere from behind Mom.

"Oh, Petch," Mom says. "Thank you so much for the drinks. You didn't have to."

Petch? How does Mom know anyone named Petch? Her most exotic adventure in life was going to a luau party at the Skinners' house.

"My pleasure," this man says, taking my mother's hand and bending to kiss it.

Mom smiles, not just with her mouth but with her whole face, lines I haven't seen in a while forming at the corners of her eyes. I clear my throat and she looks to me, pulling her hand away.

"Petch, this is my daughter, Jennifer. Darling, this is Petch. He's in my book club."

"Hi," I say as he kisses my hand too.

"Charmed," he says.

He is short and dark-skinned. His cheekbones are high and gorgeous. Dark eyes twinkle with a smile, but his eyes are no longer on mine. They are focussed on my mother and I don't like the way they look.

"Excuse us, Petch, but we're having our supper," I say.

"Jennifer," Mom says. "Petch is only saying hello. He owns this place and he can help us with the menu." She turns to him and says, "Would you, Petch?"

He sits down, takes the menu, leans into Mom and starts to explain all the food. Watching her talking with him, laughing at his lame jokes, touching his arm as he speaks, I feel a distinct hatred for Petch rise up in me, and an increasing dislike for Mom. She's flirting. Say what you want about her but she is flirting. I want to reach out, grab her and run out the door before this can go where I think it might be going. I'll also need to lock her in the house, just to make sure she doesn't attend this book club anymore.

"Well, that sounds great, doesn't it, Jennifer?" Mom says.

"Yeah, sure."

"We'll have that."

"I shall make it with my own two hands." Petch kisses Mom's hand again.

"Yes, you seem pretty active with your hands there," I say. I grunt as Mom's foot makes contact with my calf.

Petch says goodbye and Mom sits quietly for a minute,

lining up her fork with the top of her napkin. I'm just about to break the silence when she beats me to it.

"You were very rude, Jennifer. Petch was just being nice."

"And you. You seemed pretty nice too. I could go home if you two want to get a room or something."

"How dare you?" Mom says, slamming her hand down on the table. Glasses shake. Forks and knives clink. People at other tables turn to stare.

"I think it's pretty obvious what was going on. I don't think acting all coy and innocent is going change how pathetic you looked."

"Pathetic? Is that what I am?" Her eyes look sad and I remember seeing that look so many times over the years.

No, not pathetic, I want to say. I want to tell her I didn't mean it, to make that hurt look go away.

"Yes."

She takes a deep breath in and I watch her struggle with the tears threatening to come out. Such a crappy thing to be a weeper, your emotions always betraying you — voice breaking, eyes filling — all when you don't want them to.

"I think we should go," Mom says.

"No, you stay and talk with Petch there. Have dinner with him. I'll go."

"I came here to be with my daughter, not Petch."

"Oh, it just so happens that the first time we go somewhere other than the Bagel Cafe in months and it's the very restaurant your new boyfriend owns." I lean in closer and whisper, "How could you, Mom? Dad's not cold yet."

Mom moves her drink around a little and looks past me

59

tina chaulk

when she speaks. "I think you're right. Perhaps you should leave."

"Fine." I stand up and bang my knee on the edge of the table. "With pleasure," I say through clenched teeth.

"And I think he's well past cold," she says. "He would be so ashamed of you now."

This isn't where I wanted the day to go, and as I walk out the door of the restaurant, I wish I could have said something different, had any control over my idiotic mouth, but it seems like she is betraying my father, our family. I can't feel comfortable with this new Mom. For a brief moment I envy her and how she can smile so easily, seeming to feel it and not just go through the motions of showing teeth and turning up her mouth. I wonder if I will ever feel a smile again.

4

THE DAY WHEN Nan kept turning the dials on her stove while trying to change the radio station, the damage to her house was mostly just from the smoke. The call that afternoon from Nan's neighbour changed things, and we all knew right away that Nan would never live alone again. Mom was the perfect daughter-in-law and told Dad that Nan could stay with them for as long as was needed.

Dad, who still believed Nan was just a bit forgetful, looked wary of it all. I didn't doubt Dad's opinion, but the smoky house meant Nan couldn't stay there for a while anyway, so I thought, Why not let her go to Mom and Dad's house? I promised I'd come by and help out when I could. Dad reluctantly agreed while Nan held firm that she was not leaving her house. That was until Dad got stern with her, and Nan, as everyone did when Dad got stern, relented.

"Won't be so bad," Dad said to Nan and Mom at once. The irony of his words would become evident much sooner than we could imagine.

The first night Nan stayed at my parents' house, I decided to go home with Dad and see that Nan was settled. Dad and I arrived home a little after eight and Mom's tear-stained face met us at the door.

"I don't know what to do," Mom said, looking past me and searching Dad for something, her eyes roaming his face. "I'm sorry," she said.

"What?" Dad said.

"Your mom." Mom started to cry but continued to talk, sobs making her words incomprehensible as she shook her head.

"What's wrong with her?" Dad asked, running through the kitchen without taking off his boots.

Mom buried her face in her hands. I reached out to touch her, comfort her, but decided to go with Dad and see if I could help him.

Walking into the living room, I saw Dad crouching over Nan, who was on the floor, curled in the fetal position, rocking back and forth. A mournful, muted wail came from somewhere around her.

"Mom?" Dad said in a feeble voice I'd never heard from him. I just stood there, staring at him. I didn't look at Nan, tried to pretend that sound wasn't coming from her.

"Dad," I said. "What's happening?"

I waited for the inevitable reassurances, for him to tell me it would be fine, to explain what was going on, to touch Nan and make everything okay. He just shook his head.

Mom came in and I suddenly felt like I had left myself, as if I could see all of this happening outside my body. I watched me standing helplessly, Mom behind me crying while

a few kinds of wrong

Dad kneeled next to his moaning mother, his trembling hand stretched out to touch her, hovering just inches above her. I wondered what stopped him, why his hand remained so close to her without making contact.

"Jack, what should I do?" Mom spoke through sobs.

He didn't answer. His hand slowly moved closer to Nan. He exhaled, seeming to deflate before me, then closed his eyes. Waiting for half a breath, he put his hand on Nan's arm.

The room exploded. My seventy-six-year-old grandmother, weighing all of 110 pounds, hurled herself at her son with the fury of flames surging through a dry forest, hitting him over and over, all while she screamed obscenities at him. Words not meant to come from her mouth came out and slapped us all. The house filled with violence as Mom and I ran to help Dad, to try to get her off him. Her rage turned on Mom for a second but soon went to me.

"Don't touch me, you bitch," she shouted at me, her words punctuated with spittle that ran down her chin and flew at me.

Dad was on her in a flash, grabbing her hands and clasping them together as he yelled at Mom to get Nan's medicine and at me to get Maisie, the nurse who lived four doors down.

"What will I tell her?" I asked as I heard Mom running up the hall.

"Go get her," he roared at me. It was the first time in my life he had raised his voice to me. The loudness startled me and I ran out of the house, as much to get away from the awfulness there as to get help to fix it.

On the way to Maisie's house, I tried to figure out what to say. Everything in my life with Mom and Dad had been about keeping up appearances to the outside world. When the business was struggling a few years earlier, Dad put a new coat of paint on the house. The time Mom told me she was leaving Dad and moved in with Nan Philpott, Dad got a station wagon just like Mom's and parked it in the driveway. No one knew that she was gone, at least not until she showed up again one day in the passenger side of Dad's car. Mom cooked supper that night, her absence never brought up, my questions going to sleep with me but never finding a way to be asked.

So I wondered how to put a good spin on telling Maisie that my dad currently had Nan pinned on his living room floor after she spit at us and cursed on me.

I knocked on Maisie's door, trying different sentences: "Nan is having a spell." "Dad wants you to come because Nan is sick." Before I decided on something, Maisie's husband Bill answered the door.

"Is Maisie here?" I asked, panting from the sprint to their house. "It's Nan."

"Maisie," Bill called out and I heard a thudding as she walked toward us. "It's her grandmother."

Tall and broad, Maisie took up most of the doorway. No words passed my lips as Maisie slipped on beach sandals over her white socks and walked onto the steps.

"What is it?" Maisie asked as she marched up the street while I tried to keep up with her.

"It's Nan. She was all curled up and then she went wild. She hit Dad and called me a name." My voice trembled as I spoke.

Tears threatened to escape my eyes and I thought I had

them under control until Maisie touched my arm and said, "Oh, sweetie, she didn't mean it."

I nodded because I knew if I opened my mouth, the pain would come out.

An hour later Mom, Dad, Maisie, and I were sitting at the table drinking tea and Nan was asleep in her room.

"After supper she was up in her room and I heard her screaming," Mom explained once she'd calmed down enough. "When I went up there she kept saying, 'Get out.' She was pointing at her bureau. I didn't know what she was talking about first, but then I realized she must be talking to herself, her reflection in the mirror. And when I tried to explain she got so mad." Mom turned to Dad. "Oh, Jack, I didn't know she was this bad. I don't know how she stayed on her own this long."

Dad stared into his tea. He hadn't looked up from it since Mom placed it in front of him.

Maisie reached over and laid her hand on Mom's. "Nighttime is the worst," Maisie said. "Sundown Syndrome, it's called. Moving somewhere new might have set it off so it might not always be as bad as this. First night might be the worst. But other nights could be hard." She turned to Dad. "Maybe you could consider getting home care."

Dad shook his head, still not moving his eyes from his cup. "We can do it. Like you said, it's just the first night. She'll be all right."

Maisie stared at Dad. She opened her mouth twice to say something but didn't.

"I can't do this," Mom said, before Maisie could decide on whatever she wanted to say. "I didn't know what I was

65

tina chaulk

getting into. I'll try with some help from home care but I don't think I can do this."

"Maybe you can't, my love," Maisie said. Her prophetic words would linger in the house, and I thought of them often when I helped Mom with Nan, especially at night.

༄

After I leave Mom at the restaurant, I go straight to the seniors' home to visit Nan. I don't even make it to Nan's door, when a nurse, Carrie, runs up to me.

"Bad night," she says, "and not a much better day."

"Oh." I don't want to ask. The details always seem worse than the summary. "So, best not to go in?"

She shakes her head.

But I want to see her. Just let me look at her.

"Maybe I could try."

"Up to you. But she's not remembering much now. She might remember you. She thinks she got a baby in there with her today. It's the pillow, mind you, but she's after putting a towel around its bottom twice now, cleaning it with a facecloth first and asking us for baby powder.

"Then she's not aggressive?"

"No, no, not at all so far today. Now, last night. Well, last night was bad but today she's all about the baby." Carrie lowers her voice, as if she's telling me some secret only she and I must know. "Says it's her boy, Jack."

I decide to go in there. Most of the time I listen to the nurses. I don't go in when they tell me it's best not to. I know they're trying to protect me as well as her. They understand that I'll remember what happens with each visit, while her cruel, yet kind memory will let her lose it once I'm gone. But some days I don't listen. Some days I think I know better.

"Hello," I say, knocking on Nan's door. "Mrs. Collins?"

"Yes?" She looks at me without a trace of recognition.

"I'm a volunteer here. Would you like a visit?" I know the routine.

"Oh my God, my dear. I needs a nap. That youngster won't let me sleep for two minutes. He's after soaking through six cloths today. I can't hardly keep up."

"Well, I can help. I can watch him while you have a nap if you like."

"You sure?"

I nod.

Nan touches my face as her eyes roam over it. "You're a pretty little thing. Do you have any of your own?"

"No," I say softly.

"Best get going then, my love. You're getting up there, aren't you?"

I nod and touch her hand, keeping it on my face perhaps a bit longer than she would have. I tell her to go ahead and take the nap. She lies on the bed, pulling the duvet over her rail-thin body. Her wide blue eyes stare at me from just over the top of the blanket. I pick up a pillow with a towel tied around one end for a diaper.

"His name is Jack," she says, her eyes closing for a minute.

"Hi, Jack," I say to the pillow, smiling at the white cotton with the words *Central Laundry* stamped on it, my father's name almost sticking in my throat.

I sit down in Nan's chair and start to rock, imagining a baby there, sure I'm only doing it for Nan. Just until she goes to sleep. I start to hum. The glider underneath moves me effortlessly as I hum and rock, hum and rock, hum and rock. Now this is my kind of kid, I think. No crying, no real poopy diapers, just serene rocking and humming. I am peaceful. No guilt over the argument with Mom, no sadness, just this make-believe baby, a sleepy Nan, and me.

It doesn't last long. A light knock on the door is followed by a nurse's face peeking in.

"God love her," the nurse says, looking at Nan. "You calmed her down." She smiles at me. "Your mom's here looking for you."

"Tell her I can't let go of the baby. Nan will flip if she wakes up and the baby's not being looked after."

"I'll stay here until you get back."

I want to tell her that I don't want to talk to Mom. I think better of it and leave the room after handing the pillow gently to the nurse.

In the hallway, Mom is leaning against the wall opposite Nan's door, arms crossed and lips pursed.

"Why are you here?" I ask.

"I know this is where you come when you're upset."

"I'm not upset."

"Then why are you here?"

"To see Nan."

"Okay." Mom steps across to me. "I didn't like the way we left things."

"I know. I didn't either."

We look at each other for what seems like a long time,

the silence standing between us like a presence I can feel. Suddenly I hear screaming coming from Nan's room.

We run in, getting there before any of the nurses. Nan is trying to smack the nurse who is grappling with her. Mom and I join in and have Nan's arms before two other nurses come in and grab her, wrestling her down to her bed.

Carrie looks right at me. "You'd better leave," she says in a voice that seems soft despite the force behind it.

I turn to leave immediately. I know what they are going to do and I don't want to see it. It's bad enough that I hear Nan screaming "no" and "stop." I fight back the same tears I see Mom struggling against.

"Oh, Jennifer," Mom says out in the hall. She turns and looks me straight in the eyes. "You don't understand."

"She just had a rough night. She'll be okay," I say, trying to keep my voice stronger than my emotions are.

"I don't mean her. I know she'll be … fine. I'm talking about the restaurant."

"Mom—"

"I just want to be happy," she says and looks away. "Just for once in my life," she whispers.

"What?" I say. My voice echoes down the hall, the loudness of it startling me.

"I just want to be happy," she repeats, her eyes wide.

"For once in your life? What's that supposed to mean? Does that mean you've never been happy? Not once in your entire life? So you were never happy with Dad?"

Or me? The words sit on my tongue, burning it as I want to say them but can't. I remember the way she looked at me most of my life: with something other than love, something

I never understood. I always assumed it was disappointment. I never liked the girly clothes she bought me, didn't play with the dolls she gave me, refused to join her in the conversations about womanly issues she always wanted to share with me.

"Your period is the beginning of a new part of your life," she told me the day I got embarrassed by the red stain on my jeans. "Today you are a young woman. This is all about the blossoming of who you are." Her smile was so bright, so hopeful. "Every month your body releases an egg and your uterus—"

"Ewwwww. No! No uterus. No period talk of any kind," I screamed with my hands over my ears. "I don't want to be a young woman. No eggs. Ever."

The way she looked at me in that moment, that face I took as disappointment, had been there every time she looked at me ever since.

"I'm sorry," Mom says to me, as Nan's screaming gets louder when a nurse opens the door to her room. "I shouldn't have said that."

"Well, you can't unsay it."

"Of course, I was happy," Mom says. "We had money and a good house." She smiles as tears rim her eyes.

I can't find the words to ask what I want to. I can't even muster breathing very well. Nan is screaming in the background and I have a million questions and a thousand things I long to say, but none of it goes anywhere as I turn and walk away, hoping Mom won't follow me.

The elevator opens the instant I push the button. I rush inside, pressing the Close Door button repeatedly, but Mom is quick and gets in before the door shuts.

a few kinds of wrong

"I'm sorry," she repeats.

I stare at the closed elevator door, willing the contraption to move faster so I can get out.

Mom gently grabs my shoulder, then stands in front of me. "Say something," she says.

I shrug and look away. "I don't know what to say."

"I'm not dating Petch. He hasn't asked me out. There is nothing there. I just want you to know that I intend to be happy. I'm not sure how, but I want to be happy."

The door opens and I run out into the lobby, then outside, running to my car as Mom calls behind me. I'm inside the car when Mom catches up and knocks on my window.

"I'm sorry," her muffled voice says through glass. I drive away. I don't ever want to stop the car again.

☞

I arrive at the cemetery just before seven. The traffic on the way out Kenmount Road is slower than usual, people probably just going for a drive, trying to drag out the remnants of a wet Sunday. I sit in the car for a long time before I get out. There's a light drizzle now that makes everything look slick, but I'm pretty sure it would take a long time to make me feel wet.

I'm not sure what to say or do. Does Dad know about my fight with Mom, about her admitting to never being happy with him? Does he know about her unhappiness already? Was it all shown to him in one flashing moment after his death when all was revealed to him? And should I say anything or just ignore it, pretend it's not happening?

I decide that ignoring it is the best idea. No need to get into heart-to-hearts we didn't have while he was alive.

"Hi, Dad. I saw Nan today. She was having a rough day. She remembered you as a baby and was taking care of you. I wonder how it feels to hold a pillow and think it's really a baby. The brain is pretty cool to make that into something sweet for a bit."

A car stops in the parking lot and two people with flowers get out. A man and a woman. I've seen the man here before many times, but the woman doesn't come here very often. At least not when I'm here. Out of the corner of my eye I watch them walk to a headstone with a metal sculpture tricycle next to it. The man takes her flowers, bends down and places them on the grave. She remains standing, looking everywhere except at the grave.

The drizzle is heavier now and I put the hood up on my jacket. I pull it back a little so I can watch the woman without turning my head. I can't take my eyes off her.

"Me and Mom went to a book launch. Some book about someone around the bay a long time ago, fishing and stuff. I think the woman read about twenty minutes on a description of a boat and the lobster pots in it. And the lobsters they caught and about how they'd cook them. Made me feel envious of the lobsters. But Mom seemed into it. She said afterward that it was vivid imagery. More like all style, no substance to me. All icing, no cake, like Pop used to say."

The man over at the other gravesite is rubbing the woman's back now, but she's still not looked down at the grave once. She moves his arm away and turns around, walking slower than I've ever seen anyone walk.

"We're all booked up tomorrow. Wouldn't have time to put a new spark plug in if someone wanted. I suppose Jamie could do it. If someone drew pictures for him and wrote down specific instructions and stood over him telling him what he was doing wrong. He thinks he's a big help when we're busy but I keep telling him he's not, that it takes a man or woman away from the job to have to stand with him and teach him. Well, takes a man away because I'm definitely not going to show him anything. It's hard enough not to get him to bend right over into the car and slam the hood down on his head."

I think of Dad's obsession with safety in the garage, of making sure everyone followed all the rules, ever since John Carrigan lost his eye when he was chiselling a bearing race off a hub and a piece of metal went in his eye because he wasn't wearing his safety goggles.

"Not that I'd really do that, Dad." I think about it for a minute. "Wouldn't want our insurance to go up."

I leave the cemetery after my goodbye. No mention of Petch or fighting or anyone's unhappiness. I think, maybe like the woman who was at the other grave, that some things are better left alone.

5

FOR MY SIXTEENTH birthday, Mom threw a big party with a few good friends and lots of family. While BJ, Michelle, my friend Karen, and I sat in the corner, Mom passed around finger sandwiches, meatballs, and cookies, smiled and made small talk. Dad and Bryce smoked cigars downstairs in the rec room, where I made my way before long.

"Hey," Dad said. "I have a surprise for you."

"Really?" I said. "Can I have a cigar?"

"Ladies don't smoke cigars," Bryce said with a smile then puffed the cigar, a cloud of smoke forming around his head.

"I'm not a lady."

"A lady is the one who's going to get my surprise, so I guess you can't have it."

"Okay, I'm a lady. But it better not be a dress."

Dad grinned, stood up and told me to close my eyes and open my hand. When I did I felt something metal and something round. I opened my eyes and blinked twice. I stared at Dad, my mouth open, unable to find any words.

"Say something," Dad finally said after a too long silence.

"Ahh." I shook my head and fought back tears. "I can drive her?"

"She's yours."

"But, no one can even—"

"Yours," he said.

In my hand was a key and a crystal ball key chain. The key chain and the key were a legend in my house. It unlocked what Dad frequently referred to as his second favourite girl, winking at me when he said it. A powder-blue 1956 Chev Bel Air named Bessie sat in our house's attached garage, the only car allowed inside there. Dad and Bryce spent hours doing her up while I watched and bugged them with questions. They'd heard about the car from an old buddy of Pop Collins and drove to Coley's Point to pick it up then towed it on the back of a trailer truck Dad borrowed from Bryce's brother-in-law. The car wasn't much more than a rusty shell that had been left to rot in the garden of a saltbox house, but over many hours, days, months, and years they fixed up the car to make her something fantastic.

Mom hated the car and said so many times. Dad spent almost all his time at the garage as it was and whatever leftover time he had went to fixing up Bessie. I liked it because I got to watch and sometimes I got to help out too. But mostly I got to spend that time with Dad. I always toted tools to him and brought small parts over. All while Mom watched TV or stayed in the kitchen baking or did the dishes. Mom seemed to take hours in the evenings doing the dishes. On Tuesday nights Mom went to bingo with Mrs. Murphy. That was the night Dad and I ate fast food in the truck on the way home and went straight to work on the car.

Dad had never taken a vacation before he got Bessie. But in the six years it took to fix her up, he took three weeks each year. Every day of it was spent with Bessie, except one day in the second year when Dad wanted to take me fishing. Mom was invited to come but decided against it, sighing when she said, "It would be nice to do something as a family while you're on vacation."

"This is a family trip," Dad said, touching Mom's arm, an act as affectionate as I'd ever seen between them. "If you come with us."

"I don't like fishing," Mom said, pulling her arm away. "And you know it." She went to their bedroom, shutting the door with a firm bang. Not a slam so much as an aggressive close.

The next day Dad told me we weren't going fishing. We were going to drive to Butter Pot Park with Aunt Henrietta's fold-down camper trailer to camp for the whole weekend.

We didn't last one night. At about three in the morning we drove back to St. John's. A small tear in the mesh around the trailer had allowed entry to tiny visitors. I awoke to a nightmarish choir of hundreds of whining mosquitoes and the feeling of them biting into my flesh. I started to cry. A rain that could soak you in seconds had started so Dad took me out of the trailer and into the truck in a garbage bag with holes cut out for my head and arms.

Mom and Dad were dripping wet on the ride back, the silence in the car broken only by our incessant scratching and the monotonous sound of the windshield wipers that lulled me into a restless sleep full of insect nightmares. When I was settled into my bed at home, calamine lotion on my numerous fly bites, I heard them first talking, then yelling, the sounds of their anger muffled by the walls between us.

On that day of my sixteenth birthday, I squealed in the rec room. As we were leaving to go to the garage, Mom came in and asked if everything was okay.

"Mom, look what Dad gave me," I said, my voice trembling with excitement.

"Wow, he's going to let you drive it. He's never even let me drive it." She smiled at me then looked to Dad where her smile faded.

"No, no, Mom, he gave her to me. Bessie is mine."

She stared at the key in my hand until finally she reached over, kissed me on the cheek and whispered, in a dull and breaking voice, "That's wonderful. Happy birthday." She turned and walked out, not even looking at Dad before she left.

"You didn't tell Mom?" I asked, knowing that it didn't seem right to make such a large decision without her input. Bryce followed Mom outside and I heard them whispering in the hallway.

"Your mother don't bother with stuff like that. I'd say she'll be happy that the old car will belong to someone else. I think she might be a bit jealous of the old girl," he said with a wink.

Dad's words didn't change what I felt. As much as I wanted to get behind the wheel of that gorgeous old blue car, I saw something in Mom's face, a sadness I wanted to make better.

"Mom," I called out after her.

Mom poked her head back in and I saw the remnants of tears in her eyes.

"Want to drive her first?"

I didn't look at Dad, didn't want to see how he might feel about what I was doing with this very generous gift. I just looked at Mom and saw her face fill with a broad smile. I don't think I'd ever seen her look so happy and so sad all at once.

"You go ahead. Maybe another time," she said, her voice thick with uncried tears.

My father beamed at me as I pulled the gearshift on the side of the steering wheel down into reverse. As I backed out, I saw a figure out of the corner of my eye. It was Mom, standing inside the garage, arms at her sides, shoulders slouched. The look on her face stopped me for a moment, long enough to smile at her then watch her as we left the garage. I didn't recognize it then, still not sure I know what it is now, but I've seen it in the mirror from time to time in recent months before the Bacardi makes the look go blurry first, then fade completely.

As I drink my supper that night, feel its warmth make me feel something better than awful, I try to get the picture of Mom's face those years ago out of my mind, try to wash it away but it's too fresh and easy to find in my memory because it was the same look I saw today, as I drove away from the seniors' home, leaving her standing in the parking lot.

☙

On Wednesday morning, I go to work early. Sleeping hasn't been easy the past couple of nights since I fought with Mom. I've managed to avoid her since I don't normally see her. But for two evenings I've gone home to find messages from her on my answering machine. She wanted to talk. I didn't return the calls.

Wednesdays are no different than any other day to me but sometimes I hate them. Even more than Mondays. They sit there in the middle of my week, boring and usually not as busy as other days. Mondays are busy. Fridays can be too as people think they better get their cars fixed before the weekend. But somehow people seem to think they can put things off on Wednesdays.

The only job I've had this morning is done, returned, and paid for when the customer who owns the car asks for the mechanic who worked on it. I wash my hands, walk out to him and make my mouth smile, extending my hand the way Dad taught me to do.

"Hi, I worked on your car. Is there a problem?"

The man's eyes twinkle for a second before he laughs out loud, his jowls shaking. The bad toupee on his head shifts a little as he moves.

"What?" I ask, confused by his sudden outburst.

"That's a good one, little lady. Now, go find the mechanic that worked on my car, will you?"

I've been fighting the assumption that I can't do this job my whole life, starting with Nan.

"Jack, why in the world did you take that child to the garage?" Nan said to Dad the weekend after my first visit to Dad's work. "Just because you wanted a boy, you can't make

79

tina chaulk

her into one." She said this at the dinner table when we had our bi-weekly Jiggs dinner at Nan's house.

"Because she wanted to." Dad shrugged. "She kept on and on. I figured she'd hate it, to tell the truth, but she didn't. She seems to like it." He didn't look at me as he spoke, just at Nan.

"Well, still, I hope you won't take her again."

"I want to go to the garage. I love being with Daddy."

"My lover, you can be with Daddy somewhere other than the garage, I suppose," Nan said. Mom looked at Nan with a tired question on her face.

"But that's where he lives," I said. Mom's mouth held the trace of a smile. "So that's where I want to be."

"He don't live there. He don't sleep there so he don't live there," Nan continued to argue. "It don't matter anyway. A garage is no place for a lady and it never will be."

"Well, I'll never be a lady." I folded my arms and put on a practiced pout while Nan ended the conversation with a tsk.

No matter what Nan, or anyone else, said, I didn't doubt I belonged in the garage. Even the fact that I never saw another woman work in Dad's, or in any other garage, wouldn't make me doubt that I could do it. That would change when I was twelve years old and Dad hired a mechanic named Jed Cleary.

Jed Cleary was in his early twenties and seemed old to me at the time. He had dark hair, a dark moustache and brown eyes. He was Tom Selleck, right there in Dad's garage, and my young hormones, just finding their way to places I had yet to fully discover, told me I liked him. A lot.

His first day at work was in the summer, when I worked

pretty much full-time in the garage. He saw me in the office, work order in hand, and asked me to give it to him.

"What?" I asked.

"The work order."

"It's mine. I'm working on it." I smiled. I remember the pride I felt at that moment.

"Enough playing around, little girl," he said, raising his voice.

"It's mine," I said, sensing an emotion creeping toward me but not yet sure what it was. "I'm going to change the spark plugs on this car. I wrote the work order."

He grabbed the work order from my hand, tore it, so I was left with the torn corner in my hand. I looked down and stared at that small piece of ripped paper, mouth open.

"I don't have enough time to play around with little girls. This is a man's job. Go play with your dolls or something."

I looked up to tell him that I didn't play with dolls, but the man standing behind him, the four men, with arms crossed, stopped my voice.

"Take your toolbox and go home," Dad said to Tom Selleck.

"She's just a little kid," he answered back.

"She's more mechanic than you'll ever hope to be," Bryce said. "Now, Mr. Collins asked you to leave, and I and my friends here suggest you do as he says."

As he left, his toolbox not yet unpacked, I was shaken. It was just one of the many times that Dad or Bryce picked up for me. One of the numerous times someone told me I couldn't, or shouldn't, be who I was, but it was the first time I doubted myself. It was the first time I was dismissed and understood it as that. Jed Cleary ripped more than the paper from my hand. The torn piece of me he left behind grew into an adamant feminist. I believed in nothing less than equality because I could do anything a man could do and could often do it better, but I also believed in it because good men stood behind me and they knew I could do it too.

In front of the bad wig man, I put my hand on my hip, lean on one leg and look him in the eyes. "I fixed your car. I, this little lady, as you call me. I took your transmission out and replaced your clutch disk, release bearing, pressure plate, and slave cylinder. Me. And you paid eighty-five bucks an hour for me to do it. So, if you want to talk to the person who fixed your car, go ahead."

He laughs again, less loud now. Like he still doesn't quite believe me yet but just might be starting to.

"Well, I think I should have that bill reduced. I mean, you're a woman so you don't get paid as much as a man."

"Actually, I get paid more than anyone else here because I'm the Collins in Collins Motors. And so I can tell you to get out of my garage and never come back again. I know a couple of garages with some very crooked male mechanics. Maybe next time they can fix your car. But expect to pay through the nose and remember," I say, pointing to him, "there's no such thing as a hubscrew."

I turn and walk away.

"Miss," he calls after me.

I turn around.

"You can expect a call from my lawyer about this."

"Sure." I can't resist a smile, the first in such a long time. "But I bet mine's better than yours. *She's* a real firecracker."

As I walk away again, I can't help wondering what it was he wanted to speak to me about in the first place. My curiosity doesn't stop me from going in the office and watching him as he leaves.

༄

The next morning, it takes a while to figure out the noise that wakes me. A knocking that intensifies to a pounding. My clock radio tells me it's 6:30. Who is at my door at 6:30? I'd think Mom, but she hates people dropping in as much as I do and would never show up without calling me first. The only other alternative is someone who would want to annoy me and wake me on a Thursday morning. Jamie.

"Go away," I say, too low for anyone more than a few inches away from me to hear.

The pounding continues a couple more minutes before it stops. Seconds later I hear the door open. One person has the key to my house.

"Beej?" I call out.

Six feet of legs, breasts and hair fill my doorway.

"What are you doing here?" I ask and put my hands over my eyes. Maybe if I don't see this, it's not real and I can just go back to sleep.

"Breakfast," BJ says, holding up a bag with golden arches on it. My favourite. If my stomach will agree, maybe in an hour or two, I'll enjoy it.

"What are you doing here?" I repeat.

"Break-fast," she says slowly.

"At 6:30?" I shake my head. "Were you by chance

83

tina chaulk

talking to my mother?"

She shrugs.

BJ talks to Mom several times a month and they see each other almost as much as I see either of them. BJ needs a surrogate mom since hers ran away with a Baptist minister from Wisconsin when BJ was fifteen so I understand that. But why does it have to be *my* mom?

This new relationship started shortly after my father's death. BJ ran into Mom at a local store and they started to chat. A few minutes in, BJ asked her if she wanted to grab a coffee at the donut shop next door. Two hours later, BJ and Mom were chummy-chummy and I lost out on someone to bitch about my mom with. Not that I bitch much about Mom, but every now and then you need to vent about the woman who irons her sheets.

"What did she say?" I ask.

"I'm not talking to you while I'm standing and you're lying in bed."

"I'm not getting up yet," I say. "I'm tired."

"There's two empty flasks on your coffee table. You're more than tired."

I pull myself up to half sitting and lean back on my elbows. "There was almost nothing left in one of them when I started."

"I'm not here to measure what you drink. I'm here to give you breakfast and to tell you that your mom is sorry and wants to talk to you." BJ lays the cup of coffee on my bedside table and the bag on my bed.

I sit up and take a good gulp of coffee before I speak. "She said she was never happy with Dad."

"I can't win if I say anything, but she's sorry."

"What does that mean?"

"You heard me." BJ walks to the door and turns, her long brown hair flicking around. Even at 6:30 in the morning she looks like a supermodel on the catwalk. I should hate her. If I could muster the energy, I might find a way.

"Have a good day and call your mom," BJ says.

"BJ, what do you mean, you can't win if you say anything else? Did Mom tell you anything about why she was never happy?"

"No, she doesn't talk to me about stuff like that. But …"

"But what?" I want to know almost as much as I'm scared to know.

"Just think about her life, that's all. Just think of her life as anyone else's, not your mom's. How many times did they go to dinner together? To a movie? How many evenings was he even home an hour before he went to bed? How many days did he spend more time with her than at work? Than with you?"

"What?"

"Just ask yourself," BJ says with another shrug. "And while you're at it, ask yourself when you ever talked to him about something other than work."

After she leaves, her words hang in the house and pick at my fuzzy head. I wish I'd saved something in one of the bottles on the coffee table. My coffee needs something extra this morning.

6

AN HOUR AND a half later I show up at work for a day of busy. A day to keep my mind off where my mind wants to go. Face and eyes into an engine job or a complicated electrical problem and I'll forget everything BJ said. I just have to go to the office and find the hardest job in the stack of work orders.

As I walk in the garage, I see that Bryce and Jamie are talking to someone in the office. Even before I see who it is, a sick feeling in my stomach tells me it's Mom. I turn to leave. Good day to call in sick.

"Jennifer," Rick shouts out, and when I turn, I see the three faces in the office staring at me. Mom's smile looks like more of a plea. She waves.

With a big grin on his face, Jamie sticks his head out and calls me into the office. I know he knows I don't want to go in there. My upper lip twitches.

"I have a lot of work to do," I call out to him.

"You haven't got a work order yet," he shouts. "And we're not even fully booked." His smile broadens and my eyes go searching for something heavy I can hit him over the head with, even if it just has to be in my imagination. A rubber mallet fits the bill and, as I go to the office, I stop to pick it up. At least I'll have the option if the urge overtakes me.

"Hi," I say. Everyone looks uncomfortable, except Jamie, who is still giving the Cheshire Cat a run for his money.

"Let's go to work, boy," Bryce says, grabbing Jamie by the arm. Jamie opens his mouth but the look from Bryce shuts it. "I got a nice greasy job for you."

"How are you?" Mom asks. She leans against the desk then stands up, moves slightly then leans against the desk again.

"Tired. Your messenger woke me at 6:30."

Mom puts her hand to her throat, a move I once told Jamie was her effort to try to find something to say, to encourage her throat to utter the right words. Every time she doesn't know what to say, Mom's hand flies to her throat.

"I just asked her to talk to you, not to wake you."

"And when did you decide to come here and speak for yourself?" I don't care that my tone is angrier than I thought it would be.

"Please," she says in a whisper.

Please what? I think about asking, but I know there are a number of requests behind that one pleading syllable. Please forgive me. Please understand. Please let me be happy. Please love me. Please don't speak to me harshly. Please make everything right. Please don't drag this unpleasantness out.

BJ's questions from this morning play in my head, as they have every second since she uttered them. Something in them makes me feel guilty. I give Mom a huge hug.

"I'm sorry," I whisper.

The resulting smile on her face looks out of place with

the tears in her eyes. I can't help wondering if she is happy or if, like me, she's just relieved that we've avoided all the things we don't want to say.

Mom says she has a hair appointment to get to and walks out with Bryce. I watch them walk until they stop to talk. Right in front of Dad's toolbox. She is almost touching it, unaware it was Dad's, that no one is allowed to touch it, that I won't let anyone use the bay so I won't have to clean out the toolbox. Won't have to remove the probably long-melted candy bars he kept in the small middle drawer. Won't have to touch the chain with the little gold wrench I gave him after I got my first paycheque, the necklace he took off every morning and placed in the toolbox to keep from getting broken or caught in machinery, then put back on his neck each evening before he closed his box. Won't have to touch the pliers full of concrete paint I spilled on them or the digital calliper I gave him that he refused to use, believing it could never be as accurate as the old dial one he'd had for twenty years. Won't have to find a place to put every tool with every story behind it, the metal and grime reminding me of everything I miss and love about the man who used them to make machinery hum.

I can't stop looking at Mom standing there, oblivious to all that she's close to. Bryce seems to be moving away from the box, trying to draw her away. A voice behind me makes me jump.

"Everything okay?" Jamie asks.

I nod, not turning around.

"Bryce seemed really surprised to see her. Said she never comes by."

"Nah, it's no big deal. She's been here before."

Not strictly a lie. She had been here once, that I remember, the time she forgot her wallet when she went to the mall.

"Are you happy for her?"

I turn around. "What?"

"Happy for her?"

I just look at him.

"Didn't she tell you?"

"Tell me what?"

"Guess not. I'll let her tell you."

"No, you don't get to do that. You brought it up, now what are you talking about? Why should I be happy for her?"

In the back of my mind, I'm thinking that if the word "Petch" is used in this conversation, this place is going to erupt into something ugly.

"I won't tell her that you told me," I say, and suddenly I'm conspiring with Jamie, as if we are old friends, willing to plot secrets together, willing to hold something dishonest between us. Jamie won't go along with it, I realize. His downfall was always that he's honest to a fault.

"It's not that big a deal to keep secret. She's taking a couple of courses at MUN," he says, referring to Memorial University of Newfoundland. "One in English Literature and one in Theatre. Did you know she almost had her degree thirty-odd years ago?"

"Sure," I say, voice thick with the lie I give it to tell. "I didn't realize you were talking about that. I think it's pretty sad, really, her trying to recapture the past like that. You can't go back in time."

He stares at me and starts to shuffle from one foot to

the other. The Jamie shuffle, all his friends and family call it. When he debates doing or saying something, he rocks back and forth, bouncing as if his body is playing the same back and forth as his mind.

"I think it's more like she's moving forward. I'm happy for her. I think she's brave. She's getting on with her life and doing things she wants to do. She's not trying to go back in time. She's trying to go ahead. She could stand still, I suppose. Could go to the cemetery every day, or maybe every night, and tell a headstone about her day. She could listen to an old message on her answering machine over and over and drink and cry herself to sleep at night. But really, don't you think *that* would be sad?"

I open my mouth to ask him how he knows that, but some foggy memory from the other morning answers my question before I can ask it. I turn away and don't look up again until I hear the office door close.

ᏋᎧ

It's after 10:00 pm when I hear the door to the office open and turn to find Jamie standing there, grin wider than usual.

"Fancy you being here," he says. "Later than normal, aren't you?"

I nod.

"Not doing anything this evening but paperwork?"

"I was thinking of ..." I hesitate, not wanting to talk to him but wanting so badly to tell him he's wrong. I can move on too and I'll prove it to him. "Of going to Mom's to surprise her, but I didn't realize it was this late."

"I'm sure she won't mind. You'd probably make her day, maybe even her week."

"Yeah, but she goes to bed pretty early. She's probably asleep now."

"You won't know if you don't try."

"Maybe."

"You go on. I'll lock up."

"What are you doing here anyway?"

"Was driving by and saw the light on." He smiles. "Thought maybe you were in here trying to cook the books."

I pass him the stack of papers and motion to the computer I've been plugging numbers into. "Here, check it out. And then lock up, will you? I have somewhere to go."

He nods and I'm glad he doesn't do or say anything more than that.

Leaving the parking lot, the car almost tries to turn left on its own, up Kenmount Road to the cemetery. I sit there in the car as the traffic light a few metres up the street changes from red to green and back again several times. No signal light on, debating which way to go.

The world is silent as falling snow. There is nothing but the sound of an unblinking signal light, waiting to see which way this car, this day, this life, will turn.

It decides to turn right and drive down Kenmount Road, onto Freshwater Road to stop at Stockwoods Bakery and pick up some of the chocolate éclairs and macaroons Mom loves. It will be a nice surprise for her.

As I drive, I feel something lift from my chest and I take a deep breath, deeper than I've breathed in months. A whole breath, unencumbered by the hunch of my shoulders or the desire not to cry. I know I'll never let Jamie know it, but I'm pleased with myself. I'm not sure if I'm moving forward, but at least I'm not standing still.

A variety of goodies from Stockwoods sits next to me in the car as I pull into Mom's driveway. The lights in the house are all off. I debate waking her up, but decide against it. I can leave the treats for her anyway. Finding a piece of paper in the glove box, I grab the pen in my shirt pocket and jot a quick note:

> *Came for a visit but saw you were gone to bed.*
> *Enjoy these for breakfast.*
> *Love*
> *J*

The click of the lock is barely audible as I gently turn the key and open the door. I lean into the porch to place the Stockwoods bag on the deacon's bench by the door. I'm back outside and pulling the door shut when I see it, out of the corner of my eye. It's just in my peripheral vision for what must be half a second, and I almost have the door locked again when it registers. I push open the door again and there it is, plain as the white hair on Nan's head. A jacket with a perfectly pressed seam running down the arm, hanging on a hanger on the coat rack like it's always been there. It looks as at home as anything I've ever seen on that rack.

Slowly, my eyes make their way down to the boot mat next to the rack and what I see confirms something that makes no sense. Polished workboots sit perfectly lined up against the wall.

But all the lights are out, I tell myself. He can't be here. A nauseating, stabbing pain running from the pit of my stomach to the compressed feeling in my chest, opens the door and drags me inside. I hold my breath as I tiptoe into the house, feeling as if someone else's feet are making the journey. I creep through the kitchen, into the hallway, past the room that was mine for so long, past the room where Nan's body stayed as her mind left her, past the spare room where Dad would so often sleep rather than wake Mom when he'd go to bed late, moving forward until I'm in the doorway of the master bedroom.

I stand motionless until my eyes adjust to the darkness. I'm conscious of my breathing, trying to ensure that I continue it, despite the involuntary way I seem to be holding my breath. While at the same time I'm afraid my breath will be too loud and will be heard in the room. I make out the image of two forms asleep in the bed. Close enough to almost touch, the contented sounds of comfort coming from them.

On each side of the bed an alarm clock sits on an oak table. The clock on Mom's side says 10:24. From the red glow of the one on Dad's side of the bed, I can see a book and reading glasses. A bookmark is tucked inside, about three quarters of the way through the book. The reading glasses sit on Dad's box, the one Mom called a jewellery box but Dad called his change box, where he would dump a pocketful of change every night and empty it back into a clean pocket the next morning.

A water glass sits full on the table, on a wooden coaster. The red lights of the clock make its contents look like

Kool-Aid or Purity Syrup. Purity Syrup like Dad loved. With a bit of light rum. Purity Syrup like I'd leave for Santa, who visited me after supper every Christmas Eve, telling me to go to bed early as Mom and Dad looked on with smiles. Until I was nine and learned who Santa really was.

For minutes I focus on their chests. The way they rise and fall in such peaceful slumber. I can't stop thinking about chests. The way Dad's stopped moving that day, the way it was compressed by Rick as Alan breathed into Dad's mouth. Nan's chest and the way she touches it when she can't remember something, as if she can find it in there somewhere, hiding inside her heart. Mom's chest and the sigh I heard and felt when she exhaled in our hug this morning.

I'm hoping my body will soon regain some of its feeling so I can move. The only thing I can feel is a sickening ache in my chest. Chests. I try to avoid Mom's and focus on her face. The contented look I see there worsens the pain, and I crouch down, praying that I won't get sick, not quite able to stand up and not willing to sit down.

The thoughts come: Where do we go from here? How can I move on now? It's followed quickly by another thought that's been my companion for months now: maybe I won't have to.

Some nights the drinks don't seem enough to help me sleep, and sleep doesn't even seem up to numbing the ache inside me. So occasionally I've mixed some of the Atasol 30s left over from my shoulder injury with some tranquilizers the doctors prescribed for me after Dad died, and added lots of alcohol. I have been purposely careless. I'd never try to kill myself. I'm just frequently disappointed when I wake up in the morning.

When the feeling starts to return to my body, my muscles ache. I slowly stand up, tingly legs quivering with the effort. Mom's clock says 10:48 and I have lost twenty-four minutes. Twenty-four minutes of being in the presence of this truth and it still does not register.

For the first time since I got here, I turn away. I look down the hall and see Dad there, staggering with sleep to the bathroom in the middle of the night, his grey boxers on, tufts of hair stuck off everywhere as he scratches his head and walks with half-closed eyes, not seeing me there. How can his ghost walk down the hall? How can it not be standing here beside me, sharing the burden of this moment?

I look back to the bed and nothing has changed. Everything has changed. Eventually they will wake up, I tell myself, and, less prepared to see their eyes open than to watch them closed, I tell myself I must move.

Just turn your head again then let your feet follow. You can do it. One step in front of the other, step by step, until the door, then open the door and quietly walk out. You can do this. You have to. Leave, or stay here and face them.

My head turns, and my feet, just as planned, go with it. Once moving, the momentum brings me through the house, and in seconds I have the front door open and am standing where I was half an hour ago.

The wind has picked up outside and it blows through the doorway, rustling the plastic bag from Stockwoods. I cringe, wanting to keep quiet. Stepping outside, before I can stop myself, some part of me slams the door as the sound reverberates outside. I can only imagine what it sounds like inside.

My feet carry me quickly to the car. I find my keys in the ignition where I left them when I had no idea how long dropping off Mom's surprise would take or how my idea of a surprise would change once I opened her door.

The cab light goes out a few seconds after I sit behind the wheel. In the dark of the driveway, I know I have to start the car but I'm trapped in my stillness.

I see lights go on inside the house — first in the hall, then the living room, and finally the porch. The front door opens and he fills the doorway, his eyes scanning the night until they stop on my car.

He stands. Unmoving. Staring.

Minutes pass before Mom appears behind him in the doorway, her robe carefully tied around her waist. I watch as she speaks but he continues to stare ahead. His lips don't move and hers stop once her gaze follows his and finds me.

I start the engine and back straight out of the driveway, not taking my eyes off them. Unsure again which way to turn the car, I choose left and drive.

7

THE THING I found most confusing about the morning my mother left us, was the lack of tears. I was used to seeing my mother crying or fighting back tears in any sad or touching situation, but that morning her eyes remained dry.

I was excited when Mom said she would drive me to school. It meant that I wouldn't have to go on the bus and could stay home a little longer and watch TV.

I ran to the TV and switched it on, only to have Mom follow me and turn it off. "I have to talk to you about something," she said, her right hand rubbing the material on her black polyester pants.

"I want to watch TV," I said, folding my arms and putting on a practiced pout.

"I know but this is very important. You see ..." Mom's eyes searched the room and finally landed on a spot above my head. "I am leaving your dad and going to live with Nanny Philpott. I am *not* leaving you." She looked right in my eyes. "I am leaving your father. You are the greatest thing in my life, the most wonderful thing I've ever done. And this is the hardest thing I'll ever do. But I have to do it." Both her fists were clenched at her sides.

"But why? Daddy is so great."

"Yes, he is," Mom said with a smile even my eight-year-old eyes could see was fake. "But ..." She paused for a long time and chewed on her lip.

She kneeled down and looked at me. "Sometimes even the best man in the word can't make you happy." Her eyes were different than the soft, caring ones I was used to.

"And I can't make you happy?" I looked down when my voice broke on the word "happy." One tear escaped down my cheek.

"You're the one that has made me happy, Jennifer Matilda. And you always will. But I'm starting to find happy a hard thing to feel."

"Are you feeling sad? I can tell you a joke Robbie Hynes told me in school. It's about a frog and the frog—"

Her hand gently touched my face and I stopped speaking.

"I'm not sad, sweetheart. Maybe one day you'll understand that there's a feeling other than happy or sad. But know that nothing, absolutely nothing, can make my love for you go away."

"When will I see you again?" I asked, wiping more tears away.

"I don't know. I need some time first. Then your father and I will talk about where you'll live."

"I want to live with Daddy," I said without a thought about how it would make her feel. "I have to live with Daddy

98

a few kinds of wrong

or he won't take me to the garage."

She closed her eyes. "Yes, I know. That's why this is the hardest thing I'll ever do." She stood up, turned away and went to her room, returning moments later with a sweater around her shoulders.

At school, when she dropped me off, she hugged me until I told her she was hurting me.

"I'll see you before you know it," she said. "I love you so much." She touched the side of my face. "And I'm going to call you tonight and every single night after that. So don't be sad, okay?"

"Okay," I said. And when I closed the door on the station wagon, I didn't feel any sadness. I felt a certainty that it would be fine. It would have to be. For the first time in my life, my mother had watched me cry, had hugged me tight, and had told me she loved me, all without a tear in her eyes. If my mother, of all people, couldn't find a tear for this occasion, then her leaving couldn't be so sad at all. And yet something in my chest ached as I watched her drive away.

 infinity

After leaving Mom's house and driving to Conception Bay South, Paradise, through St. Phillips, and up to Portugal Cove, I find myself back at the garage. It's like the car drove me on its own. I don't remember the decision to make my way here, to not go to my house. But I'm not surprised. I know my house contains only empty bottles, while at the garage I have a not-so-secret stash. It sits in a place of honour, next to "the cure."

"The cure" — Dad's nickname for the contents of the third drawer in a battered four-drawer file cabinet in his office — a forty-ouncer of Canadian Club Whiskey and four lead crystal glasses. I never saw him pour out more than two glasses at a time but Dad was a better-safe-than-sorry kind of guy.

"Cure for all that ails you," Dad would say while he raised his glass whenever he drank the cure in my presence. The first time he gave me a drink, I was seventeen years old.

I'd had an awful experience that day. Lying under a fish truck in the heat of August, trying to remove the starter, I heard something drop on the floor next to my head. I didn't think much of it until I heard another thing land on the floor, then another and another. I felt something cold land on my hand and saw something white fall on my cheek. Its coldness didn't startle me, or its colour. It was its movement that caused me to flick it off, turn sideways and see what it was. I pushed my creeper out from under that truck so fast, I heard whizzing as I passed the back tires. I'm not squeamish, but when I looked down and saw what peppered my body, my hair and the floor below the truck, I screamed.

My movements in the garage that day have been forever referred to as the Maggot Dance and never a Christmas party passes without at least one performance of the hopping and squealing I did that day. Every time a new mechanic comes to work, he is warned to check for dead cats under the hood before he gets under any vehicle.

After I showered off the remnants of the little creatures, Bryce told me Dad was waiting for me in the office. I went in there with some hesitation, fearing that he might be angry, that I may have embarrassed him. Instead, his smiling face and two stiff drinks of whiskey greeted me.

"A day like this calls for the cure," he said as he handed me a drink.

"For the love of Jesus, don't tell your mother," Dad said as I sat down.

I winced with that first taste of whiskey. I drank the full glass, cringing with every sip, while Dad laughed.

"You might be a rum girl," Dad said.

And he was right. Next to "the cure" I keep a bottle of Bacardi Dark Rum so I can have a drink if I need one. No one is allowed to touch the other bottle in the drawer, the one that's two-thirds full and smeared with greasy fingerprints.

I don't even bother with a glass before I chug down a good hard slug. The office is dark and I decide it's best to keep it that way. I consider that I should do something worthwhile as long as I'm here. I don't like wasting time at work and it seems insane to sit here at midnight, drinking in the dark.

This is it. I have to change things and it has to start now. I have to work out how to go forward. Maybe it's as simple as making one step — turning on the light. I just have to turn on the light and I can start again and figure things out and everything will be okay. Flick the switch to on and step into the world of fine.

But the light stays off and I continue to drink, trying to will myself to make a move, to do something other than feel angry and hurt. Finally I move my hand to the radio and turn on the classic rock station. Music I listened to in my late teens blares at me. How is that classic rock?

The song changes to Bruce Springsteen's "Born to Run," perfect for anything — drinking, dancing, driving, anything but crying and that sits well with me.

I turn it up and start to move, start to sing along with Bruce and the band, begin wailing about Wendy and tramps like us. I'm singing and dancing, playing air drums with the hand that's not clutching the bottle. Bruce is the man and we are getting to the good part, to the big, roaring, drumming, climax when someone turns on the light. I scream, turn around and raise my fist.

"Whoa!" Jamie yells, his hands out to fend me off.

"You nearly gave me a heart attack," I say, smacking his arm. "What are you doing here?"

"I just dropped by to check on the garage." He shrugs. "I do that all the time."

"Oh, for Christ's sake. They called you, didn't they?"

He closes his eyes. Even Jamie doesn't know what to say or do with this revelation I've been punched with tonight. Unflappable Jamie. Lucky Jamie. Jamie with the horseshoe up his ass, as his friends call him. Jamie who always lands on his feet. Jamie who never has anything bad happen to him. Jamie who saunters through life without being touched by anything bad. The only thing he ever lost was me and even then he got a partnership in a thriving business. Jamie just doesn't have wrongs. They're all mine.

"Are you okay?" Jamie asks. He crosses one arm over his chest in a pose he must have patented. I've never seen anyone else cross only one arm. It's like he's wearing an invisible sling.

"I'm fine." I take another drink. "No big deal. I can't believe they called you. My real friends not available?"

"I don't know. I just know they're worried about you. Both of them are. You know you should be happy for—"

I cover his lips in a fierce kiss. I lay the bottle down on the desk as my tongue slips in his mouth. His hands explore familiar, foreign areas. I press my jeans against his, feeling how ready he is for what I want. He pulls me even closer to him so my back arches and I lean back, a moan escaping my lips. His hand goes around the back of my neck, pulling me back to him. He pushes his hungry mouth on mine. I reach down to his button-up jeans, stretched tight across his hardness, and frantically try to get the top button undone, claw at it, would rip the buttons off if I could just get my fingers to work right, and then he pulls away.

"No," he says, hands on my shoulders, pushing me away.

"No?" There's a no?

"You've been drinking and you've had a big shock. I don't want to take advantage." He touches the side of my face. His eyes are the colour of pity. "I know you're hurting. I can't make that go away."

It starts at my toes — a wave of something inescapable I can't name, an intense urge for something, anything. It moves up my legs, through my torso, out my arms, up my neck and lingers at the edges of my eyes in the form of tears that hover, waiting for me to do something, wanting me to break. It will only take a word to make it happen and it comes out in a desperate whisper.

"Please."

The sobs come the same time I do, the same time Jamie does, and he holds me, lying naked on his jacket on the office floor as I weep onto his chest until I'm gasping for breath.

Half an hour must pass before I realize I'm shivering and that Jamie's arm, resting under my head, is covered in goose bumps. I lift my head to look at him. His tear-stained face brings me back to now, brings me back to then, and rips the moment away.

"I'm so sorry, babe." His voice is barely audible and I wonder if he spoke the words out loud or just moved his mouth to form them. I know this isn't about Bryce or Mom or the divorce. It's about us and the parking lot. Just when I think I can't cry any more, a memory proves me wrong.

8

IT WAS THE sound that turned my head, a person falling to the floor, a thump as flesh met concrete. How I even heard it above the noise in the garage, I don't know. Shouts and words bounced off walls and came into the office where I was talking on the phone, receiver against ear, in the last seconds of the life I'd loved. Just a quiet thud and it was gone. In a heartbeat. In the loss of one.

I ran to the sound, ran in cold tar, legs moving quickly with little forward momentum. How is it possible that so many steps, in such rapid succession, could keep me in almost the same spot until what seemed like long eons later I was standing over Dad? His ashen face seemed devoid of Dad, like the absence of him was lying on the floor. His cheeks looked sunken even though they puffed out every time Alan breathed into Dad's mouth.

Everything seemed distant, like I'd been sucked away and was suddenly watching it, smelling it, from far away. There was just a faint whiff of garage — grease and sweat. It was all lessened in the moment. Except the sounds, as if all of my other senses had diminished and joined together to make footsteps echo like cannons and the puffs of air into Dad's mouth sound like Wreckhouse winds. My heart thudded in my chest, in my ears, in my eyes, in the tips of my fingers and the bottoms of my feet. The piercing siren of the ambulance made me cringe with pain in my ears, like music in earphones on bust, undulating back and forth from ear to ear with each revolution of the siren.

But when Bryce spoke to me — held my arm and guided me away, telling me he was taking me to the Health Sciences Centre where the ambulance would take Dad — his voice was almost drowned out, coming from some remote place, muted by the electric sound of the defibrillator as it jerked Dad into the air, arched his body in some kind of sick ballet. I nodded at Bryce and followed him to the car.

As we drove, Bryce spoke, said words I couldn't comprehend. Just muffled mutterings that filled the car but stayed outside of me. Except three words that stood out, seemed louder and clearer than the rest: "He'll be okay."

At the hospital, a nurse ushered us into a family room. In the centre of a ring of chairs was a chipped laminate coffee table with the name *Carla G* carved in it. A phone sat on the table. Seeing it, I spoke for the first time since the sounds started.

"Mom."

"Let me," Bryce said. It seemed like only a second later that his lips moved into the phone receiver.

The family room door opened time and time again. Mom, Aunt Henrietta and Uncle Charlie, the guys from the garage. Mom held onto me like I was a life preserver and she was about to go down for the third time. But nothing came into focus until Jamie walked into the room. The world resumed. Touch, sights, even scents were back as I felt Jamie's arms around me and smelled him — coconut soap and Neutrogena shampoo.

I withered in Jamie's arms. I felt a hand, Mom's, I think, rub my back as I sobbed into his chest.

"He'll be okay," Jamie said, sliding his palm over my hair and down my back in one fluid motion.

"I don't know," I said between sobs. "You promise?"

"I promise," he whispered.

I paced, cried, hugged, and most of all, prayed. Prayer comes in three forms: ritual, desperate and grateful. My petitions were of the second variety. "Please let him live, please let him live, please let him live," repeated almost every second until the door opened again and I heard the shuffling of chairs, felt Jamie stand up, felt myself standing with him, pulled by his embrace.

A man in a white coat, his hair in a crewcut, spoke to Mom through echoed words, asked if she was Mrs. Collins.

"Yes," she said and grabbed my arm. "And this is my daughter Jennifer." Her fingers dug into my flesh, hurting so much I wanted to cry out, but somehow feeling anything except scared felt good, a strange relief.

The doctor stood before Mom, closed his eyes, and shook his head in what looked like a practiced move. In the months since, I have seen that move many times in the moments before sleep and just as I wake. I can almost picture the doctor looking in a mirror or standing before a wife and asking, "Is this sombre enough? Should I keep the sigh or just shake my head?"

In a sudden sludge of time when things moved at the speed of a broken clock, the doctor opened his mouth and I watched the words "I'm" and "sorry" come out of his mouth like they were enclosed in a cartoon bubble.

"No," my own bubble said in a long, slow, low sound, and I wrenched away from Jamie, holding onto me on one side, and Mom, on the other, walked past Bryce, leaning against the wall by the door, and out into the hall, where the sluggish world sped up again until I was running, running like Donovan Bailey, through the waiting room, trying to catch a breath while hyperventilating.

The hospital doors opened to rain that battered my face. No idea where I was running to, but sure of what I was running from, I kept going, almost across the parking lot, past the doctors' parking spaces, the police parking, the cancer patient parking — hair soaked, clothes soaked, skin soaked — when a hand grabbed my arm and pulled me back.

Jamie held onto my arm, his other arm spread out to embrace me. I yanked away from him and stepped back then moved in next to him again. I grabbed his arm, tearing at it, panting but unable to get a breath. I moved next to his ear.

"Don't say it," I whispered. "Please don't say it. For God's sake, Jamie, don't say it."

I pulled back and looked at his face. He stared at me long seconds, the rain drenching both of us, rain falling down his long bangs and off his nose. He just looked at me, obeying my order, my threat. Until I broke the spell and turned away. What was it in my eyes that held him still until I looked away?

I turned back to him again. He touched my face and before I could beg him again, he spoke in a whisper, "He's dead, babe. I'm so sorry but he's dead."

The roar inside of me came out in fists and screams and kicks until Bryce and Mom pulled me off him. Blood ran down his cheek from a cut somewhere and his top lip was swelling as they pulled me away. Bryce held me up off my feet, my legs flailing, wanting to make contact with Jamie again.

"Never again," I said to him as they brought me to Bryce's car. "I don't want to ever see you again," I shouted, stretching the limits of my vocal chords so I'd be hoarse for two days after.

And I didn't see him until the next day when I called his mother's house and cried into the phone for half an hour. He stayed on the phone, not saying a word the whole time. But I'm not sure I ever forgave him for not listening to me, even though he'd just told me the truth. A truth I had to hear. Still, sometimes when I look at him, I remember the rainy face that whispered sadness into my life.

෴

Jamie and I are in the office, locked in shivering silence, when I hear shouting across the garage.

"Jennifer," a voice I recognize as Michelle's yells. "The door was unlocked."

"Idiot," I say, slapping Jamie's chest. I hop up, grabbing my shirt as I do. If I can just get the shirt on, it's long enough to cover everything important. "You left the door unlocked."

"I didn't know how long I'd be here." He pulls on his pants as he speaks.

"Oh," Michelle says, eyes and mouth wide. "Oh." She raises her voice then. "Oh my God. Oh my God. This is so great. I knew you'd get back together."

"Stop talking now." I pull on my jeans and Jamie slips into his white button-up shirt, covering the tattoo I'd almost forgotten about: J^2, the same one I used to have on my shoulder blade where scarred, lasered skin is now. "Why are you here, Michelle?"

"Your mom left a message on my machine, saying she was worried about you and could I try to find you?"

"When?"

"I don't know. A while ago."

Looking her over, I realize she's wearing a short, black dress, fancy updo, and extra makeup. Rather like adding icing to an already iced cake.

"Where were you until then?"

"The mayor had a thing and Steve was invited," she says of her closeted gay politician friend who often takes Michelle to public functions.

"Well, everything is fine here. Mom doesn't have to worry. And we're not back together." I search for a missing sock.

"We're not?" Jamie raises his eyebrows. "I thought we were."

"I needed something to make it go away. There was only so much Bacardi left so you had to do."

He stares at me for a few seconds then looks down at the floor. "Goodbye, Michelle," he says before he walks out of the office.

I give Michelle the stay sign and run after him. After a few steps I slow down, my feet not as coordinated as I thought they'd be. I remember all the rum I drank before Jamie came.

"Jamie."

He stops and turns around, eyes heavy with hurt.

"You didn't think it was anything more than that, did you? It was the office floor, for God's sake."

"You cried on me for the past half hour. Do you honestly think any guy would do that for you? Would you open up that much to anyone but me?"

I have no answer. At least not one I care to express.

"You're so selfish, you don't care how you make anyone else feel, do you? You used to care."

"About you, yeah, but you decided to change that."

He laughs. "Man, you don't know anything, do you? You don't see anything. You shut all of us out — me, your mom, BJ, Michelle. You shut us all out in one way or another. And as long as you're miserable and angry, you want us to be too." He raises his hands. "Well, if it makes you happy, I have been miserable. I miss you. I miss the way you laugh, and your awful scrambled eggs, and how you rob all the sheets from my side of the bed, and those ugly green track pants you wear on Sundays, and the small of your back, and the way you kissed me and ..." He looks around the garage and pulls his hand through his tousled hair. "And the—"

"I get it, Jamie, I get it."

"No, no you don't or you wouldn't have said that to me. No Bacardi so it was me. Fuck."

Jamie shakes his head and shuffles. A minute passes before he speaks, locking onto my eyes. "She was the only one since you, and I never saw her again after that day. Everyone tells me to get past you, I should let it go. But I don't. I don't want someone new because ... not one of them knows how ticklish my shoulders are or how I faint at the sight of blood or where that little scar over my left eyebrow came from. And I don't want to have to tell anyone new those things. I don't need to because everything I ever wanted is right here in front of me. And nothing will change that. Not even how rotten you've been all this time."

I dig my fingernails into my palm to focus my energy on the pain there instead of the threat of tears in his eyes.

"So, you might think we're not back together but I don't. I'll wait for you. For Jennifer. The one I married. I'll wait forever for her. But I won't wait long for this girl who fucks a guy on the floor just to get a little relief from life."

My hand nearly makes contact with his face when he catches my arm. "Don't bother to pretend you're insulted. You know the truth better than me. That's why you're either working or drunk all the time. It's not that you can't face your father being gone. It's that you can't face yourself."

He turns and I scream at him as he walks away.

I don't move for a long time. I just stare at the doorway Jamie left through.

"Jennifer?" I hear Michelle say after a few minutes. "Everything okay?"

I wipe my eyes before I turn around and answer her. "Can I get a ride home?"

She jiggles the keys in an affirmative. "You okay?"

"Perfect."

"Good."

She smiles and I can't help thinking how happy I am that it was Michelle and not BJ who found us.

☞

The next morning starts with a pain in my neck. I'm face down on what feels like a small hill. I open my eyes and see that it's the highest and hardest pillow I've ever seen. I lift my head, wiggle my neck around, turn over to see where I am, and scream.

Clowns surround me. They line shelves on the wall, are piled into bookcases, and hang from the ceiling on strings. I know where I am now.

Michelle runs into the room, and asks if I'm okay. Her hair is wild, her makeup from last night faded but not removed. She's wearing a short nightshirt that reveals more than I want to see despite how she keeps pulling it down.

"I'm in clown hell. No, I'm not okay." I rub my neck. "What kind of weird pillow is that? I can hardly move my neck."

"Oh, that's a massaging pillow and if you plug it in it also puts out different smells like roses or lavender. Want to try it?" She walks toward the pillow and bends to pick up the AC adapter, flashing me way too much information about her personal area.

"No, no, no. I don't want any rose or lavender smell." I rub my neck again. "How are you even my friend?"

"You're welcome."

tina chaulk

"For what?"

"Keeping you safe. You passed out in my car. I was afraid to leave you alone at your house so I brought you here."

Her huge, silly grin reminds me of what she saw last night.

The time between lying with Jamie in the office and getting to Michelle's comes back to me little by little. The whole night comes back to me and I curse my memory for working so well.

"Yeah, thank you. I appreciate it." I remember Jamie's shot last night, about how I treat everyone. "I really do."

"Oh, you're welcome." Michelle sighs in the doorway and says, "Jamie loves you so much."

I want to throw up. "I have to get to work," I say, trying not to move my neck too much as the rest of me stands up.

I follow Michelle out to the living room and look at my watch: 7:45. Jamie's probably not at work yet, so little chance he's fired Bryce. I called Jamie just before I left the garage last night and left a message on his voicemail: "I'll be in at one, and I don't want Bryce there when I get in. Fire him." And then I hung up.

"So, you and Jamie, hey?" Michelle's smile keeps getting wider and I know for sure where I don't want to be.

I pick up the phone, dial, and give the cab company Michelle's address.

"I'll get a cab to the house and get cleaned up," I say, pulling my sneakers on and then getting my coat on. "Thanks for putting me up."

"Just wait a few minutes for me to shower and get ready

and I'll drive you."

"No, I really have to go. Thanks a million. I'll see you at brunch."

I shut the door and realize it's raining. I'm standing outside for ten minutes and am drenched by the time the taxi gets there.

☙

I'm soaking wet and sitting in a cab as the taxi drives along Water Street when I see the intersection for Patrick Street.

"Stop."

The taxi driver slams on his brakes, causing the driver behind us to veer his car around us and honk his horn.

"What?" the taxi driver says.

"Can you go up Patrick Street? I want to go there."

"I thought you wanted to go to Thorburn Road."

"I changed my mind."

I hadn't really. A question popped into my mind when I saw the intersection and now nothing matters but the answer.

BJ's house is a two-bedroom, fully attached house on Patrick Street. She bought it for $70,000 seven years ago, has renovated a lot — hardwood floors, claw bathtub, chrome faucets, handmade antique washstand — thousands of dollars to make the old house look old again. Her flair for style, renovations, and a real estate market full of buyers drooling for an older style home downtown means that BJ's recent appraisal by a real estate agent brought the house in at over $200,000.

No doubt, the fact that the house is owned by BJ Brown, weatherwoman on the nightly news, helps. BJ is the queen of visiting community events for live shots. Whether it's a potluck fundraiser supper, a doggie fashion show at the SPCA or a ribbon-cutting at the latest Fill-In-Your Disease/ Disorder-Here Centre, BJ is there, holding a microphone and wearing a warm, caring smile.

The taxi stops outside BJ's house. I step out of the car and make two steps to her front steps. I knock for five minutes. No answer. I know light-sleeper BJ sometimes sleeps late in a sensory deprived state, blindfold over her eyes and earplugs in her ears. I give up and walk around to the back of the house.

I throw small rocks at her window, then when they don't work, I go bigger. When the rocks get big enough that I'm afraid I might break the glass, I finally see the princess in the window, silk blindfold pushed up to her forehead. She furrows her brow.

"What's wrong?" she yells, her voice muffled through the glass. She pulls the earplugs out of her ears. I motion for her to go to the door and let me in. I'm not about to shout at her, figuring the neighbours have already called the police about a potential crazed stalker in BJ's back-yard.

Before I get through the door BJ is talking. "You can't be that big of a sook."

"What?"

"Waking me up early just to get me back for waking you yesterday morning. Come off it. Even you're more mature than that, for Jesus' sake."

a few kinds of wrong

Was that yesterday morning? It feels like I've lived a lifetime in the space between then and now.

"It's not that early. It's almost eight. Most normal people are up now." BJ and I step from her foyer into her living room through an archway on the left. BJ runs upstairs and comes back down with a towel which she passes to me. I take off my coat and shake most of the water off. BJ holds it with one finger and thumb and lays it across a radiator.

"Something happened last night," I say.

"Really? What?" BJ asks, her one eyebrow raised. "Is everything okay?"

We sit on her white leather couch and I notice the new decor. BJ changes around her living room like some people change their kitty litter. I'd been at her house three weeks before, with its blue walls, white trim, sheer curtains, and beige sofa. Now the walls are chocolate brown and the trim a baby blue, a new trend I don't understand.

"You didn't get a call from Mom last night?"

"No." Concern enters her voice. "I was on a date. Had my phone off. I didn't get in until almost two. Is everything okay?"

"I dropped by Mom's house last night after work. Late. To surprise her." I run my finger along the seam on the leg of my jeans. "It was me who got the surprise."

"Really?" BJ says, but I catch something in the second before her perfect camera face takes over.

"You knew," I say, sitting up straight. "You knew and you didn't tell me."

"Knew what?" BJ says, innocent face painted on perfectly.

"You know."

"No, I don't." She shakes her head.

"Then why did you look guilty for a second?"

"I didn't." She lets out an exasperated gasp.

We sit in silence for a minute or so until I decide to end it. "Why don't you guess what I saw?"

"Was she alone?"

"See, I knew you knew," I say, hopping to my feet. I start pacing. "I can't believe you didn't tell me."

"I don't know anything." She raises her voice. "I swear to God I don't."

"Yes, you do. I saw it in your face."

"What happened? Did you catch them in bed or something?"

I nod. "But not like you think. Mom was there asleep in bed with him. They seemed so at home in that bed together. I think it would have been easier to see them … well, I can't even think of that."

"I'm sorry."

"You didn't ask who it was," I say, my voice lowering to almost a whisper.

"I dropped by on her one night too," she says, picking at the red nail polish on her left index finger, "and he was there then. He was just sitting on the sofa. There wasn't anything for sure there. Just …"

"Just what?"

"Just something in the way she acted, the way she kept glancing at him. The way she shuffled her feet and didn't know what to do with her hands. Like she'd been caught."

"And you didn't tell me?" I look away. "I can't trust anyone."

"What was I supposed to say? Oh, guess what? I went by your mother's house and Bryce was there watching TV and your mom acted funny."

"Sure. Like you didn't ask her about it after. Like she didn't tell you what was going on."

"Jennifer, I'm not that kind of a friend with her. We went to cooking class a few times and now we go out for coffee and swap recipes. I don't tell her about my relationships and she sure as hell doesn't tell me about hers. The only time we ever talked about anything serious was the other night when she called me all upset and wanted me to talk to you about the fight you'd had."

I sit down and rub my forehead. "I wanted to be sick. I stood there just looking at them. It was like I couldn't not look but I didn't want to see it."

BJ reaches out and touches my hand. I pull away.

"I'm okay," I say, standing up to lean against the old cabinet hi-fi BJ had converted into the world's largest MP3 player.

"Then you should be happy for them. They both lost someone they loved and now they've found a new relationship with each other." BJ tilts her head at me. I'd find the look challenging from anyone else.

BJ continues to stare at me. "And what else? There's something else."

I glance at BJ then look away.

"My God, you got laid, didn't you?"

"How'd you get that?"

"You did." BJ smiles the way she always does. One grin can change her so she goes from gorgeous to breathtaking. Her smile, even when it's sarcastic and smarmy, softens everything around her. It has made me laugh while sad tears rolled down my face; it has made me remember something I didn't know I'd forgotten; and I looked for it in the days after Dad died. It didn't come for a long time, and when it did I wanted for it to make me better, to make things right again. But not even her smile filled the space left behind.

"BJ."

"I know these things. From the first time you did it with Craig Ferguson in Bessie's backseat, I can pick up on it. You always look a little guilty after you've done the deed. Well, a lot guilty after that time in Bessie." She giggles. "Man, we scrubbed that back seat so much I thought your dad would figure it out just by how clean it was. Never did that again, did you?"

I look at her and raise my eyebrows.

"Really?" she says.

"Jamie really liked that car."

"Yeah, me too. Anyway, I guess last night is the reason for … for this." Her index finger points its way up and down my body.

"What this?"

"This, this relaxed Jennifer thing. This, I don't know. It's like you let something go."

I roll my eyes. "I did the nasty with Jamie, BJ. I didn't have some kind of emotional awakening or anything."

BJ's eyes open almost as wide as her now gaping mouth. "Jamie? Well, you finally came to your senses, hey?" She smiles again. "I'm glad. It's about time."

"Came to my senses? How can you say that after what he did to me?"

"Come off it, Jennifer. We both know he bent over backwards for you and you locked him out."

"You always take his side. I caught him. With her."

"Doing something he had every right to do. You can't take away someone's food and then get mad when he lets someone else feed him."

"What? What kind of weird comparison is that?"

"It's called a metaphor."

"I'd call it stupid. And I'm sick of you always picking up for him. I don't understand. You always said he sponged off me and that he was lazy."

"But you were good together and you were happy with him. He can't be perfect."

I shake my head. "I just wonder whose side you're on."

Her tilted head makes me want to smack her.

"Yeah, just like I figured," I say. I pick up my coat and walk out the door.

"Jennifer. Don't leave. Come on. I was just saying."

"Yeah, I know what you're just saying." I slam the door behind me. On BJ's front step, I stare at the pouring rain. For once, I'm grateful for it. I can let my tears go and no one needs to know.

9

BEFORE DAD'S DEATH, the worst day of my life was one where I placed a piece of paper down on a desk.

I laid the cheque down in Dad's office. Jamie stood behind me and closed the door. Once the door closed, there was a strange silence that blocked out all the noise in the garage so that I heard Jamie's sneaker squeak on the floor when he moved.

"What's this?" Dad asked, looking up at me from the old orange desk chair. At least it used to be orange. It was more of a dark brown now with streaks of grease and dirt all over it. He suddenly looked small in that chair.

"It's a cheque."

"Yes, I can see that. But what's it for?" He picked up his Shoppers Drug Mart reading glasses and placed them on his nose, pulling the cheque back from his face then closer until it must have come into focus.

"This is for $25,000," he said, looking back up at me, over his glasses. "To Collins Motors."

"We want to invest in the business," I said.

He chuckled and shook his head, looking down. Without looking back up he tore the cheque in two, then four pieces. "It's not that bad."

"It is that bad, Dad. I see the books, remember? I know how much you owe the contractors and how much the lumber and supplies have gone up. I know you didn't bargain for that idiot not allowing for the ramps and the garage door when he put down the floor, and I know how much it cost to replace that floor. So, I know how bad it is."

He stood up. I couldn't read his face. Was it anger or hurt or pride or love? I didn't know. I never could read him, but in that moment I didn't know if there was any one thing he felt. Or was I just watching a struggle going on inside him?

"I can get more money from the bank. Now, go on out there and don't let me hear this from you ever again." His voice was stern, one reserved for slow-to-pay customers and errant mechanics. "It's just a shortfall."

I just stood there. I knew I couldn't leave the office, knew I had to accomplish this mission. But my mouth was so dry I knew I wouldn't be able to make a sound if I opened it.

"No, sir, you can't," Jamie's voice from behind me said. The exact reason he had come here with me.

We'd argued about it the night before.

"I don't need you to come with me, Jamie. You're nuts. He's my father," I'd said. I took my feet off the coffee table and stomped them on the floor.

Jamie was in the kitchen when he'd started the conversation. He walked out to the living room and stood over me.

"Yes, and that's exactly the problem. If he says 'no' or 'drop it' then you'll just give up. Damn it, why are you so stubborn with every single person except him? Oh, that's right, you *are* him." He motioned his hand toward me in a karate chop. "Stubborn, stubborn, stubborn. But if Daddy says 'boo,' you put your hands up and admit defeat."

"That's not true," I said, my voice even.

"See, just the fact that you're not screaming at me that you're right and I'm wrong means that I am so right." He knelt down in front of me and put his hands on my knees. "Where's my fighter? Where's my heels-dug-in, immovable object, battle-until-the-death fighter?"

"I'm here. I just don't want to fight Dad. You know he won't want to take it. Everyone knows that and still, here I am, committed to making sure he does. I'm all in on this. No going back now."

"*We're* all in on this."

"It's not the same for you and you know it," I said.

"Just because I didn't put in as much as you. If Mom and Dad could have loaned me more, I would have."

"I don't mean that. I know you gave everything you could."

"Nah, just another time I'm Jennifer's sponge."

"What?"

"You heard me. Jennifer's sponge. I know that's what BJ calls me. I heard her say it lots of times."

"It's just a joke, Jamie." I shook my head and smiled. "She doesn't mean it."

"She pretends it's a joke. She laughs and winks when she says it, but you know she means it. And I know you used to argue with her about it. I know you asked her not to say it."

"How …" But before I could form the question I realized the answer. "Michelle should shut up."

"It's not her. It's not even BJ." He touched the side of my face with his soft, gentle hand. "It's your opinion that matters." He took his hand away and turned his head. "And I overheard BJ call me that again the other night. At Billy Newman's party. And you didn't say a word to defend me. Just bent your elbow and tipped up your glass."

I didn't have anything honest to say to defend myself. "I didn't hear her say that."

"I just think that with both of us investing in this, I can feel like I'm contributing." He stood up, crossed one arm and his voice got soft. "I don't want to be the sponge. That's why I got the money from Mom and Dad."

I stared at him for a second or two, waiting to spot some sign that he could see the irony in what he just said. But I could tell he didn't.

"It doesn't matter either way, Jamie. He won't take it."

"Well, that's why I'll be there. I can stand up to him better than you." He looked down at the floor. "Even a sponge can stand up to him better than you."

In the office, Dad looked past me to Jamie. "What did you say to me?" Dad squinted his eyes and I knew it wasn't because he couldn't see Jamie.

"I said that you can't get money from the bank. Not against the debt you already have. With the garage already mortgaged and your house still not paid off, you can't get a loan for what you owe."

Those were my words I'd practiced the night before over

125

tina chaulk

and over. Jamie even used the same tone and intonation as I had in our kitchen, emphasis on both "can't's."

Jamie walked past me and put another cheque on the desk, the same as the one Dad had just torn up. I hated to think Dad was predictable, but Jamie had been exactly right in knowing what my father would do. Even though I argued with him and told him Dad would never tear up something I gave him.

"I can rip up this cheque too, you know," Dad said, standing up and staring Jamie in the face.

"Yes, I know you can. But we have a whole box of them and we can keep signing them as long as you keep tearing them." Jamie turned, put his hand around mine, and pulled me along with him, turning me around as he did. He opened the office door. I stopped and stood still until Jamie pulled a little harder. I took three steps toward the door before Dad spoke.

"Where'd you get the money?"

I took another step.

"Where'd you get the money?"

"I don't think that matters," Jamie said, standing outside the office door. I'd pulled my hand away but Jamie reached out to me, motioning to take his hand again.

"Jennifer. I know you don't make that much money to get another big loan. Not with the mortgage and the car … payment."

The pause after car. He knew and I didn't have to turn around to see it. I could feel it in the way the air in the office changed, in the way the hairs on the back of my neck stood up.

"Come on, Jennifer," Jamie said, stepping inside the doorway and touching my hand.

"Tell me that if I go out to Storage Mart, I'll still find her there in the container." Dad's voice was full of panic.

"She did what she had to do, Mr. Collins," Jamie said, squeezing my hand and looking past me as he spoke. "She said it was the hardest thing she's ever done but she did it. For you. And I got some money together too."

"Jennifer." Dad's voice sounded like someone was letting the air out of it. I heard the squeak of the orange chair as he sat down. "My dear, go buy it back." His voice was soft until his next word — loud, firm and angry. "Now!"

I shook my head, still not turning around. "Buddy'd never sell her back to me. He's been wanting one like her his whole life. He loves that car."

"Like me. Like you. Like you did."

I finally turned around. His face was full of anger and pain but mine was full of tears, and when he saw them he looked away.

"I did what I had to do, Dad. I, we, could lose her or you could lose everything. My car. My choice. I wish there was some other way but ..." I looked down. "My car. My choice."

This time, when I turned around, I managed to keep walking, out the office door, past Jamie, out to the bathroom where I stared at the grey concrete floor and cried.

Dad never said another word to me about it. His lawyer came in the garage the next day and Jamie and I signed partnership papers with lots of heretofores and aforementioneds and not withstandings and the party ofs. When it was done

Dad didn't hug me, which I didn't expect anyway, or didn't even shake Jamie's hand. He just got up and walked out of the garage. He didn't come back until the next morning when he greeted me as he always did, with a gruff "good morning" and a "probably going to be a slow day today," a phrase he used superstitiously to avoid such slow days.

Mom whispered to me, the following Sunday when we went for dinner at her house, "Thank you. He won't ever say it, but I know he appreciates it too." She shook her head. "And I'm sorry. I know how much that car meant to you."

"Do you really think he appreciates it? That he's not mad at me?" The words, the desperate tone behind them, were out before I could think not to say them.

"Yes." She touched my hand and nodded. "I know he appreciates it and I know he's not mad at you."

And just like that last year I still believed in Santa Claus but began to have my doubts — started noticing that Santa's gift wrapping and tags were always the same as the ones Mom bought and the wrapped presents under the tree always had a faint scent of Mom's perfume on them — I told myself she would not lie to me about something important like that.

ఞ

When I leave BJ's, it's too early to visit Nan. Mornings at the home are a time of bathing and breakfast and nursing reports. I need to kill a couple of hours before Bryce gets fired, so after I run home for a quick shower, I get dressed in workpants and a *Newfoundland Liberation Army* t-shirt from Living Planet, my favourite t-shirt store. I go outside town to Conception Bay South, where I don't expect to run into anyone I need to avoid.

I pick up a few groceries at Sobeys and a couple of bottles at the liquor store. When I come out of the store, the rain is gone and the sun is shining. The temperature gauge in my car tells me it's twenty-two degrees already. I wonder if it's this nice in town. I've seen it raining in St. John's and sunny and ten degrees hotter in CBS. Seen it the other way around a couple of times too but not many.

I'm on the way out the main road in Chamberlains, with a view of beautiful Conception Bay to the left of me. The water is dead calm, flat as the glass in the antique mirror Jamie gave me on our last anniversary, the one with the card that said *so you can see how beautiful you are.*

I take a detour to Topsail Beach, down the narrow, weaving road to the parking lot where I just sit and stare. There are sailboats in the bay, dogs chasing sticks thrown in the ocean; a toddler places his sneakered foot in the water in the second before his mother gets to him.

Nan would love to be here. How her face would light up whenever she'd see the salt water. A memory jabs me, places soft pain in the pleasure of this moment. A trip out here, not long before she went in the home.

"You got a new car, my lover," Nan had said as I held her arm and eased her into the seat of my convertible Mustang. "She's some nice."

"Thank you," I answered, despite the fact that I'd had the car for five years and she'd been it in many times.

We drove out to Conception Bay South, making our way to Holyrood first then back to Manuels. Nan remembered some things right, some things wrong and some things not at all, but throughout our drive she'd blended all of those memories into a collage of Nan. She spun yarns about Kenmount Road when it was just a remote place where people had cabins they would visit on the weekends, not the bustling commercial mainstay of car dealerships, hotels, taverns and restaurants it is now. She told me about cleaning house for the Crosbies when she was a young girl and remembered the day I was born.

"I never saw your father cry, not as a man, you know," she said, a slight smile on her wistful face. "But when he called me, he said, 'Grace had a girl.' I heard his voice break and he couldn't finish his words. Got all filled up, he did, and when he tried again, he still couldn't get it out. I told him, 'That's all right, my love. I knows what you're saying.'" She turned to me. "He was some proud."

I wanted to tell her she never told me that before, but I couldn't finish my words either.

We kept driving. Nan told me three more times that she liked my new car and must have ignored the layer of dust on the dash to even imagine it was new.

We stopped at Bergs and I went inside for an ice cream cone for each of us, idly telling her I'd be back in a moment. When I walked out of the store, hurrying to get the ice cream to Nan before it started to melt, I stopped at the sight of the empty car. I was so mad at myself for leaving her alone, as if my memory had failed me and somehow I'd forgotten who Nan had become. I scanned the area and saw her, sitting at a picnic table, smiling and waving at me. I stared at her, the arrested portrait of my Nan as she once was: a happy Nan, smiling and enjoying fresh air and waiting for ice cream. I stood looking at her until melted ice cream dripped down my hand and pulled me out of my spell. I ran to the picnic table, where we frantically ate our ice cream, running a race to finish it before the sun changed it to something else.

She'd told me she wanted to go to Topsail Beach after we left Bergs, but before I could get there she started to cry, to scream really, scared of something I didn't understand. I raced to get her back to somewhere familiar, but even Mom and Dad's house didn't do, and it took a long time to settle her down after I brought her back there.

The beach doesn't hold my interest anymore. I'm thinking of Nan and when my mind does wander to something else, thinking about Nan seems the better alternative, no matter how sad it is. At least I can't blame her for anything she does. More than I can say about most of the people in my life.

☞

At the home, the nurses are nowhere to be seen before I get to Nan's room. All busy, I suppose. Nan's door is open and I know this is a good sign. I poke my head in and look around.

"Jennifer, how good to see you," Nan says with a smile. Her hair is combed and she's wearing a pretty blue dress she used to wear to church. I realize how much weight she's lost as the dress hangs off her the same way Dad's shirt and pants hung off a scarecrow we made one Halloween.

"Nan, you look beautiful."

"Thank you. A lady has to keep herself up." She stands

up and twirls around. "Julie helped me with my hair," she says of her roommate, who's probably at her usual place in front of the piano in the common room.

She smiles for a bit before her face changes to a frown. "Why aren't you at work? Now, don't stay away just because Jamie's there." She tilts her head. "He's some sweet, Jennifer. You should get back together."

Oh, Nan, I need you to forget for today. Wrong time for one of your good days.

I wonder about these moments of semi-lucidity when things become clear. Does she recognize that she is in a home or that she forgets most of the time? She must, I think, because she's here in her room and has spoken of Julie. She remembers my name and the details of what's happening with me and Jamie. But she isn't crying as she sometimes does when she wishes she was in her old house, the one she shared with Pop for forty-six years. Perhaps there is some blessed part of her disease that lets her remember just enough and blacks out everything else.

"What's happening on your stories? Did Deirdre—"

"How's your mom?" Nan interrupts.

"Good."

"That's nice. She told me she's going back to school."

"More than she told me," I say before I can stop myself.

"What?"

"Nothing. Nan, I was out to Topsail Beach this morning—"

"Jennifer, your father's gone now. Your mother's all you got, my lover. So be nice to her."

Suddenly I'm nine years old and am getting told off for taking strawberries from Nan's garden.

"Did you hear me?"

"Yes, Nan, I heard you."

"Don't snap at me."

"I'm sorry. I didn't mean to snap." I don't know where to look so she won't find me, won't see me, won't judge me.

"All right. Now, tell me about Topsail Beach. I remembers when that seemed so far away. Sure, Kenmount Road was out in the country and the only thing out there was cabins."

"Did you have a cabin out there?" I ask. I can hear the story for the hundredth time. I don't mind a bit.

10

I LISTEN TO Nan tell me the history of St. John's until she has to eat dinner, then I go to Lucky's Chinese Restaurant for my own lunch. I walk into the garage a little after two, sure that, by now, Bryce would be applying for Employment Insurance in Pleasantville. One turn around the corner tells me I'm wrong. Bryce is sitting in the office. Jamie is nowhere to be seen.

The heat in the garage is stifling. It's twenty-five outside and maybe five or ten degrees hotter inside, even more if you're working on an engine. I'm never sure which time of year is worse in a garage — the heat of summer days when you can't seem to quench your thirst or breathe anything but a roasting heat, or the frozen days of winter when snow and ice melt off vehicles, water dripping down your neck and back while you work under the cars, a slow water torture all day, every day.

"Hey," I call out to Ray. "Is Jamie around?"

He points to a Toyota Camry and I see Jamie's black steel-toed boots sticking out from the car's interior.

"Flynn," I yell, walking toward the Toyota and causing several heads to turn my way. I don't look toward the office.

Jamie bumps his head on the edge of the car door as he tries to get out.

"Why is that man in my office?" I point at the office but still don't turn toward it.

"Our office. And I tried. He wouldn't leave."

"What do you mean, he wouldn't leave? I'm going out for an hour and if you have to call the cops to do it, he had better be gone when I get back."

"You'll need to do it yourself," Bryce says behind me.

"Fine. You're fired," I say, spinning around to face him. "Now get the hell out of my garage."

"What? What's going on?" Rick asks over the sound of an air gun across the garage.

"Do you want to do this here? Or in the office?" Bryce crosses his arms as he speaks.

"I've done it." I walk toward the office. I go so fast I almost break into a run, hoping Bryce isn't following me but with every certainty that he's doing just that.

I try to close the office door once I'm inside, but Bryce pushes back on it, keeping it open. He's inside the office and has the door closed in seconds, moving faster than I expect.

I look out the big office window and see Jamie standing in the middle of the garage, a couple of guys talking to him as he stares at me, mouth open. I don't feel hate for him in this moment. My anger is altered and the target of it stands next to me. From the corner of my eye I can see that his arms are still crossed and he leans against the door.

"Get out. Get out or I call the cops."

"No."

"Fine." I pick up the phone and realize I can't call 911. This isn't an emergency in any book but mine. I need the regular police phone number and so I look for the phone book amongst the rubble on the desk.

"What bothers you the most?" he asks.

"You're bothering me."

"No, what's bothering you the most? Is it me or her? Is it that she's happy?"

"I don't know that she's happy. Just that you found your way into her bed. Maybe she's just a—"

"Watch what you say about her," he interrupts, and I realize I'm not sure how I'd have finished the sentence. All the words that race through my mind make me feel like I'm less of a person for thinking them. I feel my face turning red.

"I'll say what I want. You're not my father. You just play him here. And now in his house too. You're not half the man he is."

"Was. The man he was. That's what you need to realize."

"Get out." A trickle of sweat runs down my face but I won't wipe it away.

"You're certainly his daughter though. Your way or the highway, isn't it? You don't care who it hurts as long as things go the way you want them to. You're just like your father. Selfish."

I feel his face on my hand before it registers what I'm doing. The red mark on his cheek stings my palm. I bite my lip until it hurts more than my hand does, and get the metallic taste of blood.

Bryce opens the door and turns away, standing in the doorway, his back to me. "Your problem is the truth. You can't accept it. It's not always pretty but the truth is the truth, and whether you like it or not, at some point you have to face it." He turns his head enough that he can look at me from the corner of his eye. "He's dead. She's not."

He closes the door behind him and I watch him walk out. He's shaking people's hands, patting them on the back. The guys are standing there with open mouths and wide eyes, shaking their heads. Every now and then one of them glances at the office then looks away.

It starts with Rick. He turns his look from Bryce to me, walks to his toolbox, puts the wrench he's been holding into a drawer, turns to me again and slams the box shut. Alan follows, then Ray. They all close their toolboxes. Rick walks over to Gerry, who leaves the counter and walks out of the garage with the rest of the guys.

Jamie stands in the middle of a quiet, empty garage and shrugs. I stare at him until he storms into the office.

"Do something," he shouts. I don't think I've ever seen him quite this panicked. "They're leaving. They're all quitting."

"I didn't ask them to leave. I can't work with Bryce." I shake my head. "There's nothing else I can do."

"Bullshit. You can ask them to come back. Let Bryce come back. I get a say in this, you know."

"How can I forget?"

The anger is draining out of me and I'm being filled with nothing else. I'm empty and I don't care anymore.

"If you can't work with Bryce and the guys won't work

without him, then maybe you should leave." He stands taller and pulls back his shoulders, thrusting out his chest. "Maybe you need to take one for the team."

I know that if I wasn't so devoid of feeling, I'd roll my eyes. Jamie and his crazy sense of drama. Take one for the team. Well, I'll match your drama.

"Yeah, you're probably right." Words I never thought would come out of my mouth. And I stand up, walk through the doorway, out the garage door, past the group of mechanics gathered in the parking lot who are telling me it's no good for me to try and change their minds, to the gravel parking lot behind the garage where all the staff park. All the stress lifts away from me as I get in the car and drive out onto Kenmount Road, to the liquor store, and then on to home.

 ෆ

In my dream, I'm in Dad's old 1986 Ford F150 truck with a black ghost. We're driving along and I'm trying to pretend that I'm okay with the ghost, when my back gets itchy. I ask Dad to scratch my back, but the ghost, who suddenly has eight-inch long fingernails, starts scratching. First it feels good and it's such a relief to get rid of that itch, but then it starts to hurt and the ghost is gouging my back and I'm still trying to act cool and not show any weakness. Then the engine starts knocking loudly and my dad starts shouting at me. "Jennifer, Jennifer, open the door. Open the door, Jennifer."

I wake up, unsure what's going on. Someone is banging on my front door and calling my name. It takes me a minute to even realize where I am. My mouth is dry and the room seems to move with every thud against my door. The clock on the VCR says 7:13, and with the blinds drawn, I can't tell if it's a.m. or p.m. There's only a quarter of a 26-ounce bottle of Bacardi on my coffee table.

I try to stand up and fall down, hitting my shoulder on the corner of the coffee table. I'm rolling around the floor, pain everywhere, and there's still the knocking on the door. I finally recognize the voice as Jamie's and decide to stay on the floor.

Until the knocking turns louder and I'm pretty sure it's Jamie's foot, not his hand that's banging against my door.

"I'm going to kick the door in," Jamie shouts as he continues kicking.

"I'm going to kick your ass," I say, as I stumble toward the door.

When I open the door, Jamie must be just about to make contact with it, but since I've moved the door out of the way, his foot lands between my chest and stomach and I fall back with a grunt, smacking my head on the hardwood floor.

"Oh my God," Jamie shouts, kneeling over me. "Are you okay?"

I can't manage any words, only a gasping for breath. The over-indulgent headache that had battered me seconds before is a memory now. The searing pain in the back of my head is dwarfed by the pain in my chest and the awful sensation of having the wind knocked out of me.

"Why?" I pant.

"Are you okay? I'm so sorry." Jamie is touching my head then my chest. "I thought maybe, I don't know, that you'd done something stupid to yourself. I saw the car outside and I was afraid you might have … done something."

I hadn't done anything. I'd gone home. I pulled down the blinds. I locked the door. I sat in front of the TV with my bottle on the coffee table, a glass in one hand and the remote in the other. I watched Nan's soap opera and found out the baby Brady was having for her brother isn't his at all but belongs to her boss, the cosmetic company magnate. I wondered what Nan thought of that revelation. I took a couple of tranquilizers, along with the drinks, because I figured they would help, and if bad things happened as a result, they weren't my fault. I finished most of my bottle in the hour it took to watch the soap and the next thing I knew steel-toed boots were hitting my door, preparing to knock me over. As pleasant an afternoon as I could hope for before the door-pounding.

"Idiot," I try to say but my breath has not returned yet and it comes out as a gasp.

"I just thought. Things have been changing so much lately and … I was afraid you'd, you know, do something. Bad. To yourself."

"I'm really hurting," I find the air to say.

"I know you are and I want to be there for you, to help you with everything. I think last night means we should be together. I know we're still right for each other and we've finally gotten through all the—"

"No, I'm really hurting," I interrupt with a whisper. "I can't breathe right. I think I might have broken something." I try to move and cringe.

"Oh shit, I better get you to the hospital."

Jamie tries to pull me up and I holler. "I'll do it myself," I whisper. I try to raise myself up on my elbows but it hurts too much to move.

"Just pull me. Count to three and pull me up." I lift my arms and Jamie takes my hands.

"One, two …" He pulls me up to my feet as I scream.

"I said on three." I punctuate every word with a smack to his arm.

"You'd tense up and it would hurt more."

"I can't even trust you to pull me up when you say you will."

Jamie puts his shoulder in my armpit and my hand grabs his other shoulder. We move at a pace of about ten steps per hour, but we finally make it to Jamie's old GMC Sierra truck.

"I can't climb up there. That's Mount Everest. We'll take my car."

"You sure?"

A grimaced look answers him.

I take the keys out of my jacket pocket. Passing the keys to him seems as easy and practiced as buttering toast. He hesitates for a second and I know dozens of times we handed off keys must be going through his head too. The day we had to put his dog Max down and he passed me the keys because he couldn't see through tear-blurred eyes. The time he collided with a cement post in drive-thru at McDonald's and I nagged him and teased him until he stopped the car in the middle of four-lane traffic on Prince Philip Drive, shut off the engine, and passed me the keys. The night of every last day of work before Christmas at the garage, when the boys and I would have a few drinks and I'd swear I'd be okay to drive myself home and he'd end up picking me up after a night of too much. Jamie, sober as the judge and grinning at me every second. The day I laughed and told Jamie he could take Bessie for a spin around the block as long as I went with him, handing over the crystal ball chain as I said it. It surprises me that moving a set of keys from my hand to his can cause such a flood of memories and a new, deeper ache in my chest.

On the drive to the Health Sciences Centre every pothole feels like a knife stabbing in my side. In St. John's this means my sides feel like they're stabbed every metre of the way. A muted grunt escapes my lips with every bump, and by the time Jamie turns onto Clinch Crescent my hands are wet from tears I keep trying to wipe away, turning my head toward the window and hoping he doesn't see. I look over and he averts his eyes.

The ride to the hospital seems like a leisurely stroll when it comes time for Jamie to help me out of the car. Nothing seems to work as we try a number of different ways to get me out, and the grunts are no longer muted as he tries to pull me. The smokers gathered around the ER entrance, standing under a cloud of nicotine fog, look at me with pity. A couple of them move forward tentatively, like they want to help but aren't sure if they should. Jamie says, "I'm sorry" after every second attempt to move me.

"If you say 'I'm sorry' one more time, I'm going to punch you in the face. I could do it. My arms aren't hurt."

"I know." And Jamie hauls me right out of the car and onto the sidewalk. No counting, no warning, just rips me out.

My feet are on the sidewalk and I'm bent at the waist.

"I'll help you straighten up now."

"No," I shout. "I'm good this way. I need to stay this way. And preferably not move. Ever."

"I think you have to move. And you'll look like you're searching for change if you walk like that."

"I don't care what I look like."

Walking, slow excruciating step by slow excruciating step, bent over and wincing, still fairly drunk and hungover all at once, I'm pretty sure I look about as pathetic as one can. This does not deter the ER nurse who makes me wait in line then asks me inane questions, takes my blood pressure, temperature, and pulse, then suggests I take a seat in the waiting room.

"I can't sit. I need to stay bent."

"Okay, then lean against a wall in the waiting room," she suggests.

I open my mouth but Jamie stands in front of me and tries to lead me away. "Don't piss off the nurses," he whispers.

"I didn't say anything." I walk, my body a right angle, to the waiting room.

"You were going to."

"She told me to lean against the wall. Not overly helpful, was she? And she didn't look too pleased with you when I told her you kicked me."

"You didn't need to say that. You could have said you fell against something."

Jamie sits in a chair and I remain standing, bent. He looks at me then stands up. Looking up at him hurts my neck.

"Sit down. And the nurses will have to know what happened. They'll figure it out. Telling the truth will never cause any problems."

Jamie raises an eyebrow. Can you rip off an eyebrow?

"Shut up," I say.

As I wait, I memorize the patch of floor over which my head hangs. CSI forensics could not know more about what's on the floor: a brown, faded shoeprint I hope is mud; a gum wrapper; a piece of old, petrified gum; two deep scratches, one below the gum and one next to the footprint; a soggy band-aid; and a cotton thread I'd guess is from some gauze. It doesn't help that I've been standing close to the garbage can. Aim, it seems, is not the forte of those in the hospital ER.

When my name is called, Jamie helps me get back to the triage area but is intercepted by the nurse before he can step inside.

"Patients only," says a tall, broad woman with a round face and porcelain skin. Her nametag says *Amy*. She helps me stand next to a seat and then notices Jamie hovering nearby. She stands up and marches over to him, with a firmness that makes her soft, white shoes thud on the floor. "Please wait in the waiting room," she says loud enough to make a couple of heads turn.

"But I want to help her if she needs to get back to the waiting room. Or if she goes inside to another room."

"What's your name?" she asks, picking up a pen and a piece of paper from the nearby desk.

"Jamie Flynn."

"I'll call you if she needs you. Now please sit down."

I don't see him once he moves beyond the counter and my much lower than usual line of sight.

The nurse touches my arm, bends down to face me and whispers, "You're safe now."

"What?"

"You're safe now. You can get help. You don't have to stay with him."

"With who? Can't you fix my ribs? I think they're broken."

"Your husband. We've called the police. It's best if you talk to them and tell them exactly what happened."

She is staring at me so intently that I don't quite know what's going on until it suddenly registers.

"Oh my God, no. He didn't abuse me or anything. We're not even together anymore. I mean we slept together last night but I was drunk and … I'll shut up now."

"There's a shelter where you can stay. There's lots of help out there. You can't stay in that situation."

"No. He's my ex-husband. Well, not yet. But soon. And he just kicked me because I opened the door when he was trying to kick it down. He was worried about me and thought maybe I'd done something stupid to myself, but I was just passed out and when I opened—"

The look on her face is changing with every word I speak. From concern to great concern to a coldness that comes across her face like a curtain.

"I know that sounds bad. But he's not abusive. He was only trying to help. And we're split up." I try to straighten up, and howl. "Please help my ribs," I say, voice breaking.

"We'll move you to an exam room," she says.

The police come twenty minutes later while I'm awaiting the results of my x-rays in exam room 4. An intern with ridiculously bad breath has told me he thinks my ribs aren't broken but are badly bruised, which he tells me hurts worse than broken ribs. I believe him.

I start the whole who's on first routine with the two police officers — one female, looking compassionate, and one male, looking tough. Nothing I say seems to make them understand that my injury isn't because of anything intentional on Jamie's part. They ask me how much I had to drink today and I know I'm being judged as much as Jamie is. Misjudged.

"We are pressing charges, Mrs. Flynn," the male officer says, despite the three times I have told him it's not Mrs. or Flynn. I just haven't gotten around to changing my MCP number or driver's license back to my maiden name. "Whether you cooperate or not."

"What time is it?" I ask.

"8:57," the male officer answers. "So will you cooperate or not?"

"Please give me a minute," I say. "I need to make a phone call." I'm lying flat on a stretcher, pushed back into a horizontal position by the intern who first examined me, and fully intending to stay there however long it takes to heal. "Could you pass me my jacket?"

I pull my cell phone out of my inside pocket and the female cop warns me not use it in the hospital.

"I have to," I say. "I can't move. Just give me five minutes for a private call, please."

The woman nods to the door and says, "You go check on him. I'll wait outside."

"Him" I assume is Jamie and I suddenly realize that his evening might be worse than mine. I feel a twinge of sympathy amidst my pleasure.

When I'm alone I hold down the number one on the cell phone until I see the call has been made. In seconds I hear her voice. As I have so many times in my life I ask her for help.

"Where are you?"

"Health Sciences Centre. Exam room 4."

"You okay?"

"I will be when you get here."

"Be there in ten minutes." I feel my shoulders relax a little.

ᕦ

The first time I used BJ was in downtown St. John's outside a coffee shop. I had been doing some early Christmas shopping and was to meet her at Auntie Crae's and was lucky enough to get a parking spot right in front of the store and coffee shop. By the time I made it back to the car to feed the meter before meeting BJ for lunch, time had run out. A Parking Enforcement Officer was writing a ticket.

"Wait, I'm here," I shouted to him from fifteen feet away. "I'm going to put money in."

He kept writing. "I already started the ticket. Too late now."

"Stay here," I said, pointing my finger at him. "I'll be right back."

I ran into Auntie Crae's, found BJ reading a newspaper,

every eye in the place either staring at her or trying not to look like they noticed her. I picked up her purse, grabbed her arm and dragged her out to the meter man.

"This is him. Now, tell him this is your car."

"You're BJ Brown," the man said.

"I am," BJ said with a broad smile and a nod.

"Wow, I'm sorry. I had no idea it was your car."

"Would you mind if we could forget about the ticket?" she asked. Broader smile and an arm touch.

"Already done."

"Thanks so much. I really appreciate it."

"I'm a big fan. I watch you every night."

"Thank you. Hearing that is what I live for." I stepped behind the guy and rolled my eyes at her.

"That last part was a little over the top," I said once the guy had left, three autographs in hand — one for him, one for his daughter and one for his mother. "That's what I live for?"

"Shut up. I got you out of the ticket. You know, you've never done anything like that before. Never took advantage of me like that. I thought you were different." She turned and walked away.

"I've gone to packed restaurants and sailed in with no reservation and no waiting," I called after her. "I've skipped line-ups."

She turned around. "But you've been with me. It just happened. You hauled me out here." Her eyes betrayed how hurt she was and I knew I should just say I'm sorry.

"Come off it, BJ. It was a parking ticket. Big deal. Fair play for all the downsides of being your friend."

"What downsides?"

148

a few kinds of wrong

"You're worth it. Don't get me wrong. But just like it's not always easy to be you, it's not always easy to hang out with you."

"How?"

"It's being treated like a pimple on your arse, like I'm not a person when I'm with you. It's having every lunch interrupted by 'Are you who I think you are?' And being the person who takes the picture of you and whoever owns the camera. It's being … invisible."

BJ stared at me a long time and I watched her deciding what to say. "Must have been cold there in my shadow. To never have sunlight on your face," she sang as I burst out laughing.

"You really are the wind beneath my wings," she said and squeezed my arm.

⚬

At the hospital BJ arrives in my room with two nurses and a resident in tow. The two cops aren't far behind.

"I can vouch that she has never been abused by her husband."

"Ex-husband," I correct.

"Not yet. Not officially. Whatever. I've seen Jamie Flynn pick up a spider and set him free outside. And I can guarantee that he loves this woman with all his heart, even though they're not together."

"A friend doesn't always know," the female cop said.

"This one does," BJ replied. "I know her and I know him."

"We have his admission that he kicked her, and Mrs. Flynn verified it."

"And we both say it was an accident," I join in.

"And I can vouch for both of them."

The officers leave with autographs and the promise that BJ will show up at the next RNC Association banquet.

The police are barely gone when Jamie comes in the exam room.

"Was it bad?" I ask.

"Awful. They thought I was a wife-beater. It was the worst thing ever."

"I have badly bruised ribs," I say. "That's pretty bad too."

They look at me in silence.

"What did they say in the end?" BJ asks Jamie.

"They said they were recording this and were keeping their eyes on me." Jamie looks close to tears.

"Best not try to kick in any doors again," I say, trying to lighten the mood.

Silence again.

"So, can you go home?" Jamie asks me.

"I have to wait for a painkiller prescription."

"Are they going to tape up your ribs or something?" Jamie asks.

"No, they don't tape ribs, especially if they're not broken," I say. "The doctor just said I have to rest for a few days and put ice on them."

"You're going to rest for a few days?" BJ says and laughs. "You'll be at work tomorrow, bruised ribs or no bruised ribs."

"You didn't tell her?" Jamie looks at me.

I shake my head and shrug.

"Tell me what?"

"Nothing," I say.

"What?" BJ turns to Jamie.

He starts to recount the morning at the garage and I feel like I'm sitting in the accused box at my own trial. Jamie is talking and BJ is shaking her head, saying things back to him, things I ignore because I can't hear any of them. Their noises fade into the background, becoming a carpet of sound that covers everything but doesn't resonate in any way. It's like they're the normal people and I'm on the outside. I'm the failure, the screw-up, the stick-in-the-mud. I'm bruised and broken, and all around me things and people seem intact.

The chatter in my room stops. I follow BJ's and Jamie's eyes to the doorway where Mom stands, her eyes full of something I can't identify. Maybe a mixture of fear or something else, maybe shame.

My ribs start to ache more and I notice the tension in my whole body. My jaw is clenched, my fists, even my legs are tense but I don't realize it until I will them to relax.

Without a word, BJ and Jamie walk out. Mom nods to them and mouths "thank you" to BJ.

"Are you okay?" Mom whispers to me, as if speaking loudly will hurt me. She touches my arm and I flinch. The act of pulling my hand away so quickly makes me cry out from the shot of pain in my side.

"Oh God," Mom says and a tear rears its ugly head.

"It's nothing," I say, trying to find a comfortable position. "It's a couple of bruised ribs."

"What happened?"

I just stare at her. Not speaking. I know Mom won't let it stay that way for long. Silences need to be filled, especially the uncomfortable ones.

"What happened?" she asks, her tone formal. She straightens up and pushes her shoulders back.

"Get out."

"What?"

"Get out of my room."

"Jennifer, I'm your mother," she says. Her hand reaches out for me then pulls back.

"You're a whore," I say and it feels ugly and wonderful. It feels like a surge of anger that washes some of my pain away. It is a hideous release and even the look on her face, her hand to her mouth, the tears in her eyes, makes me feel better. Her hurt lessens mine.

"So get out. And tell those other two not to come back in here either."

She turns and runs out the door. I hear voices outside and BJ shouting, "We'll see if she can look after herself," obviously leaning toward the door so I can hear, words directed right at me. And then there is silence in my room.

Fifteen minutes later the doctor gives me a prescription and asks me how I'm getting home. I cry for ten minutes before I call Michelle and ask her to pick me up.

"BJ told me not to," Michelle says. "She told me you upset your mom. That's a sin, Jennifer. I think it's good her and Bryce are together. And you should too."

I hang up the phone without saying goodbye and call a taxi. A nurse helps me get in the cab, and the driver helps me get in the house. The painkiller prescription in my jeans pocket remains unfilled and there's only a small bit of Bacardi left. I want to get in the car and drive but I can't. I pop six Extra-Strength Advil, lean against the arm of the couch, and turn on the TV.

An hour or so later, I hear a tiny knock at my door, like the rap of a child. As the door opens, I remember that I didn't lock the door. A bunch of flowers stand in my doorway wearing khakis, a white shirt and the leather jacket I gave Jamie for his birthday two years ago.

"Wow, walking flowers," I say.

Jamie moves the flowers aside and smiles. "Surprise," he says.

"Flowers. I must be really sick."

"I gave you flowers before. Lots of times."

"On Valentine's Day or if I was mad at you."

"Not true. I gave you flowers lots of other times. I picked a flower and gave it to you the morning after we first made love." He smiles and tilts his head in a way that makes me wish I could kiss him.

"Really? I don't think so."

"You honestly don't remember that?"

"No."

I remember everything about it. I can almost feel his lips all over me that first night in my bed. The way he smelled of sweat and Ivory soap, the way his tongue felt inside my mouth, the way his lips brushed my nipple, making me shudder before he took it into his mouth and sucked while I reached my hand down to the zipper in his jeans, unzipped them and released what had been straining against the denim.

My fingernails, short as they were, dug in his back in the moment we shuddered together.

The next morning I woke to a half-empty bed. With Jamie nowhere to be seen, I thought I'd lost the first thing I ever desperately wanted as a grown-up. Until he showed up at my bedroom door with a coffee and a red rose.

"For you, madam," he said and gently kissed me until the coffee went cold.

"That looks like one of my neighbour's roses."

"Hmm. Yes, well, it committed rose suicide when I went outside. Just leapt off the bush."

"Poor, sad rose," I said and laughed, stopping only when his lips covered mine again and we fell back down to the bed for another round of Jamie.

"Well, I did give you a flower," Jamie says, bringing me back to the present. "A rose, to be exact." He places the bouquet of wildflowers, complete with vase, down on my coffee table.

"I'm not supposed to be here. BJ thinks we're enabling your self-destructive behaviour."

"BJ is a bitch sometimes."

"So are you."

I nod. "Yet you're here."

"I am. But I feel bad because I kicked you." And when he moves to me, he touches my face and kisses my lips. I don't push him away.

11

THE NEXT DAY I wake up with a pain in my side and Jamie in my bed. There had been no sex but he had held me and kissed me and I welcomed him to share the bed with me. Our bed. The headboard and mattress we picked out two weeks after our wedding. The sheets we'd slept on so many nights. The bedspread on which he'd made love to me many times.

I stare at him as he sleeps. His eyelashes are long and golden. I've admired them since I met him. His nose is long and aquiline, the perfect Jamie nose, I often called it. His face has tiny pockmarks you'd have to be this close and staring in order to see. And his lips, his lips are full, full of so much I want but am afraid of. Yet I can't stop myself and I kiss them gently, just a brush.

He returns a long, soft kiss, his tongue playing around inside my mouth, making me curse the pain in my side. He keeps his eyes closed until he pulls himself away, opens them, revealing ocean-blue eyes, the colour always different depending on the lighting. The chameleon of eyes.

"I thought I was dreaming," he whispers.

"Not unless your dream involves me trying not to breathe with the pain in my side."

"In my dream, all your pain would be gone." He kisses my forehead.

The day goes well. Jamie tends to me, we rent a movie and drink wine in the evening, going to bed again with no pressure for anything but companionship and sleep. I don't ask him to leave. Not once.

I don't hear from Mom, BJ, or Michelle and I wonder what would have happened to me if Jamie hadn't shown up. I'd missed brunch and no one even bothered to call. I go to sleep grateful for Jamie and feeling a little less sore. The next three days are the same — relaxed, easy, boring. Jamie goes to work a couple of times to check in and tells me that Bryce knows where he is if he needs anything.

But on the fourth night he is there, things change. Lying in bed, Jamie's hand on my arm, I'm back on to him when I say, "I think my ribs are a lot better now."

"Good," he says.

I turn around and touch his face. "No, I mean I think I could move a lot now." I raise my eyebrows.

"Oh. Well …"

"You don't want to?"

"No. It's just that … the last time you said I was just to make you forget. I need to know that's not what this is about."

I stare at him. He closes his eyes. In a minute he is out of the bed.

"Jamie. I want you. I'm not saying I need you but I want

156

a few kinds of wrong

you. I don't know why. I haven't analyzed it. But I want you and that's all I can tell you." I say this even though I know there is an emptiness inside me I need him to fill.

I'm not sure who is hungrier. No words are spoken. Nothing. Only two people locked in something wild and passionate. It hurts my ribs — to the point that sometimes I can't breathe — but the explosion inside me once we get there makes it worth it. I roll over and Jamie holds me, telling me how much he missed me, how happy he is to be with me. He hardly pauses for me to say anything back and if he does, I feel no urge to fill the silence. I say nothing and try not to think about exactly what it is I am not doing.

❦

The phone wakes me up with a start and a quick jolt of pain to my ribs, having performed a less than careful move. In the darkness, I reach over to grab the phone, touch Jamie, and let out a yelp. This body I had lain next to for so many years startles me in the dark by its presence.

Jamie sits up and says, "What? What?" in the instant before the phone rings again.

"Who is it?" Jamie asks me as he reaches for the phone.

"Don't answer that," I scream and lie across him to grab it. No one needs to know he's here.

"Hello?"

"Jennifer," Mom's voice says. The clock tells me it's 2:53. I know this call will change things. Mom isn't the call-to-chat-about-things-at-2:53 type of person.

"It's your grandmother."

And like that the phone is back on the receiver.

"Wrong number?" Jamie asks.

"I'm not ready for this. Unplug the phone." My voice sounds frantic, even to me.

"What?" Jamie says as the phone rings again.

"Don't answer it."

"Why? What is it? Is something wrong?"

"Nan."

And Jamie says hello as I put the covers over my head and cry.

12

MOM RARELY CALLED the garage. She and Dad managed to stay out of contact most of the hours of the day. So when the call came that day a couple of years ago, when I saw Mom's number on the caller ID, I knew without picking up the phone that things weren't right. Dad was on the other side of the garage using an air gun so I couldn't call out to him and tell him to answer the phone like I wanted to.

I didn't say hello, just picked up the phone and listened.

"Hello?" a voice other than Mom's said from the other end.

"Hello. Who's this?"

"It's Maisie. Is that you, Jennifer?"

"What's wrong?"

"Is your father there?"

"He's in the garage. I'll get him." A sense of relief swept over me. She'd asked for Dad and skipped telling me.

"No, that's okay. Could you just ask him to come home? It's important."

Why? What's happened? Is Nan okay? Why isn't Mom calling? The list of questions in my brain didn't reach my mouth.

"Okay," I said.

I got Dad and, at his request, joined him on the ride to the house.

"Did she sound upset?" Dad asked on the way. He'd asked questions ever since I told him about the call and what Maisie said, my answers not giving him enlightenment.

"I don't know."

"Well, why didn't you ask?"

"I don't know. I was too surprised that she was calling."

I was half afraid when Dad made the turn onto Shea Street. I was relieved to see a quiet street, no signs of ambulances, fire trucks, or police cars. There was nothing outside to indicate why we were there. A tranquil street on a quiet Tuesday afternoon.

Walking into the house, while less tranquil, did not immediately answer our many questions. In fact, more questions sprang to mind: Why is there blood on the cabinets and floor? Why does Mom have gauze on her arm, shoulder, and neck? Where is Nan?

Dad kept his boots on as he walked to Mom, crouched down and asked her what happened. Mom tried to answer through the tears that came but nothing she said made sense.

Dad looked to Maisie.

"Your mom got a knife." A thousand words might be provided by a picture, but the picture in front of us was suddenly clarified by those five.

"Oh God, where is she?" Dad stood up.

"She's asleep. I gave her a tranquilizer. The important thing now is to get Grace to a hospital. She'll need stitches."

"Why would she do this?" Dad said to no one. He touched Mom's face twice, stood up, crouched down and touched her again.

"She was wild," Maisie said, looking straight at Dad. Grace called me. She'd grabbed the cordless phone and had herself barred in the bathroom. I could hear your mother screaming on the outside of the bathroom door, pounding on it while poor Grace told me what was going on."

"I was just doing the dishes," Mom finally said. "It was quiet. Your mother was watching TV. The next thing I knew she was screaming for me to get out, and before I could even think, she had the knife. She was so strong, Jack. You wouldn't believe it. I used both hands to try and get that knife from her, but she wouldn't let go. When she got my neck, the blood squirted out … I thought I was dead." Mom's voice broke into gulping sobs.

"She was lucky, Jack," Maisie said. "She got awful close to the jugular."

I swallowed. A loud swallow I thought everyone must hear, no saliva in my mouth. It felt like burning sand in my throat.

Dad got Mom's coat and gently put it on her. He slipped a pair of boots on her feet and tied them up. His hand rubbed her calf through her jeans, the way you'd rub a child's hair in passing. I looked away, jolted by the intimacy I wasn't used to seeing.

Dad stood up and turned to Maisie. "You said the

tina chaulk

contacts you got at Hoyles, you can get her in there quick."

"Dad, you said you'd never put her in there," I piped up.

Three words I never heard before or after from the headstrong man who, I was sure, believed until that moment that he could control the universe, or at least his small part of it.

"I was wrong."

Blood seeped through the bandages on Mom's arm and the gauze she had pressed to her neck. Above the deepening red of her gauze collar was such an expression of relief that my arguments not to put Nan in a home stopped before I could say them.

Maisie had told Dad before, several times, that Mom couldn't do it on her own but Dad always had a solution. When Nan started to wet the bed, Dad got Maisie to pick out the best diapers; when Nan would no longer stay in the bath, Dad relented to letting someone come in twice a week to do it, as long as Maisie would be that someone; when Nan left the house once in the middle of the night, Dad got a lock on the outside of her door; and when Nan's screams and banging on that door got too much, he got Nan tranquilizers and Mom gave them to her every night. Mom got her own tranquilizers too, the strain etching in her face and in the dark circles under her eyes and the once-manicured nails that became chewed-off nubs. But his wife bleeding in the kitchen, lucky to be alive, there was no fix for that.

"Stay with your grandmother," Dad said as they left.

"I'll help you clean this up," Maisie said, motioning to the blood and to the butcher knife in the sink. She bit her lip.

"I would have done it already, you know, but your dad had to see this. He had to see it all. That's what I figured when I saw this. The stress has been slowly killing your mother and he couldn't see it.

"Now, we'll just need a mop and bucket and a cloth. Where does your mom keep them?"

"I don't know."

Maisie blinked at me, her eyes going to the floor, then back to me. I realized that she expected I should know that information. And suddenly I wished I did.

"Well, let's look, hey?"

By the time Mom and Dad came home, everything was cleared away. The sink, cabinets, counter and floor were sparkling, the knife locked away in a cabinet downstairs. Nan was awake.

"Dear Saviour, what happened?" Nan asked when she saw Mom with twenty-one stitches, looking like a female version of Frankenstein.

"Accident. Don't worry about it. I'll be fine now." Mom looked to the window. "We'll all be fine."

Her words wiped the concerned look off Nan's face and replaced it with a smile. "Good," Nan said. "Long as we're all good."

I looked away from her happy face.

༄

The hospital at three in the morning is a surprisingly busy place. Again, there are smokers outside, although fewer than there were during my last evening visit here. The IVs and nightgowns of the evening smokers have been replaced by the black eyes and bandaged hands of the late-night ones. The smoking seems more furious, less about relieving a need than about relieving a tension, their draws deeper, the cigarette ends glowing red.

Jamie has driven me here in silence. He heard the news from Mom. He passed it on, had tried to soften it.

The emergency room nurse tells us Nan is in exam room 2 and that only family can go in.

Jamie rubs my shoulder. "I'll be here until you come out," he says. I turn and hug him. The surprised look of pleasure on his face after the simple action makes me follow it with a bigger, longer hug, the pressure of his arms around me hurting my side but making me feel that maybe everything could be okay.

I hear Nan before I open the door. The voice doesn't sound like Nan. It doesn't really even sound like a person at all. It's a loud moan, devoid of its humanity.

I stand outside exam room 2 for at least a minute, listening to this sound and wondering what is behind it, what altered form of Nan is inside and what will I do with it once I go in.

Nan has been so transformed in the past ten years. She was a plump woman who baked cookies and told me to "put out" to a guy so I could give up being a mechanic and get married. She believed chocolate could cure anything life could throw at you and that man never walked on the moon. She would tell me stories about growing up and what Dad was like as a boy, and she loved to sing, her music the only part of her that consistently clung on through her dementia. That happy, carefree, satisfied, complicated lady left when Pop Collins' heart stopped beating, late at night on the sofa where Nan found his cold body the next morning.

"I pressed my breast against him," Nan once told us, with tear-filled eyes. "Foolish, I suppose. I thought I could make his heart beat again with the help of mine. I tried to share my heart with him, just like I shared it all those years. And he took it with him. I've only half a heart left now without him.

Wasting away to the thin, frail Nan who started to forget small things like paying the light bill, then the names of loved ones, then onto sitting behind the steering wheel of her Chevy Impala when she was driving me to a family dinner at Swiss Chalet and asking me how she was supposed to start the car. Names, faces, recipes, knitting, gardening, history, laughs, games, all followed. All but music.

Then the Nan who lived with us, the one who kept us awake at night, who broke things, who knocked down the cans Mom set up outside her door to alert us that Nan had left her room, and who blocked up the toilet with Mom's new towels.

Then Nan in the Seniors' Home. The one who had resigned herself to die once Pop had, but who, in a rare moment of lucidity, told us the day she entered the home that this was the place she would die.

"I'll go to the garden here," she said that day.

Nan's view of death had always been a garden. "If there's no God, the garden will just be dirt, but if He's up there, it will be full of the most beautiful flowers, full of life everywhere, and I'll smile the biggest smile."

"And what if you go to hell, Nan?" I asked her every time she told me this.

"Weeds, my dear, all weeds and the devil will make me pull them forever."

Then the Nan who was the time machine. The blessed sanctuary where I could find relief from pain. The sound inside exam room number 2 makes me fear that sanctuary is gone forever.

Even when I turn the handle to the door I hold it there in my hand for seconds, knowing this line is about to be crossed and that I'll never be able to unsee what I'm about to see.

I push open the door and they stand next to Nan's bed: Henrietta, Chuck, Mom, and Bryce.

For a second I'm filled with anger that Bryce is here, in our space. He is not immediate family. Not any family in the strictest definition. I'm about to say exactly that when a renewed moan brings my eyes to Nan.

Her face is drawn and slack at once. Her lips don't move in the moan, one hand flails frantically, trying to communicate something and getting nowhere. I haven't seen a face so changed since the time I watched Dad's change from alive to dead, that grey, chalky look that replaced a ruddy healthy glow.

The mask Nan wears is horrifying because of the sounds, but mostly the desperation in her eyes. There is a wild, terrified person needing to understand what is happening.

I walk straight to her. "Nan, you've had a stroke and they're going to help you here." The moans become louder, her movements more pronounced, her left arm grabbing my hand in a fierce grip. "Nan, it's okay," I shout over her sounds. "We'll make sure you're okay."

"I don't think she knows who we are," Bryce says and the fearful look in her eyes and terrified sounds make sense.

"Mrs. Collins," I say, my experience telling me exactly what to do, "you're in a hospital and the doctors will be here soon. You'll be fine. You can't talk right now but we're here for you."

I watch her relax, eyes calm as the moaning stops.

"Aunt Henrietta, can I talk to you outside?"

Henrietta looks from me to Mom, to her husband. "Why?" she asks.

"Outside, please. I don't think Mrs. Collins needs to hear us."

"Oh for God's sake, why can't you talk to me?" Mom says. "Will everything have to go through Henrietta now? Are you eight years old?"

Her words sting and their impact is shocking. She said this in front of Aunt Henrietta. A woman Mom felt judged her through every second of her marriage to Dad.

Henrietta looks at Chuck with her bottom lip turned down and eyes wide in a gesture of "Well now, what have we here?"

I walk out. "Aunt Henrietta, please come out here," I say as I exit the room.

Mom rips open the door behind me and stands in front of me, legs apart and hand on hip.

"Why is Bryce in there?" I point at the room door.

"Why wouldn't he be? Your father isn't here so—"

"What? So, he replaces Dad everywhere? First in your

bed and now in there with Nan."

"Your grandmother has had a stroke. Like it or not, we're here as a family, and like it or not, that still includes Bryce. He was always family. You've said it yourself a million times."

"Before he fucked my mother."

For the first time in my life, I feel the sting of a slap on my cheek. I stand in stunned silence.

When I look at Mom I expect something akin to guilt or surprise on her face but see hurt and defiance instead.

"Don't you dare speak like that about me," she says, oblivious to the other people in the hallway who are staring at us. "You don't get to judge me. You have no idea."

"He's Dad's best friend." My voice breaks with hot raspy tears.

Mom grabs my arm and pushes me toward the all-too-familiar family room where a man is sitting but says, "Excuse me," then leaves when we enter. Mom, who would normally apologize for being lumpy if someone walked over her, does not respond, "Oh, that's okay, we'll leave," as I expect, but says, "Thank you."

"He was Dad's best friend," Mom says. "Was. Your father is dead, Jennifer, and I am not. I don't know why you can't accept that or why you seem so angry at me. Everyone tiptoes around you and tries to make you happy, despite your constant sadness. I cried for him too, you know. I grieved and I mourned. And so did Bryce. But while we were holding each other up, struggling through to get better and come out stronger and more supportive, you have just angrily clung to your grief, like proof of how much you loved him. Even Aunt Henrietta talks about it. We all try to work around you and deal with you with kid gloves. And you choose to judge us. All the time. No one has as much pain as you. Well, I slept with his shirt for weeks. I cooked his dinner for two months and put it in the oven until I'd throw it out the next morning and cry about it. I miss him too." Tears are streaming and it's difficult even to understand her words now. "You were never alone in this. You just chose not to see the rest of us."

I have no words. Maybe I could have gotten through this easier. Maybe I needed to share it. But I pushed everyone aside and they all know it. I just stare at her and blink.

"I."

She waits but no words come after "I."

"The word is 'we.' Everyone around you wants to help you and to hold you but it's this 'I' that gets in the way. It's 'we.' We. Not you against us. We against everything, whatever it is."

Mom paces around the room, clutching her fist to her chest. "Oh God, I've been waiting to say this. I should have said it sooner but I didn't know how to get through all of this." She points to me, to the space around me.

"You said you were never happy with him. So how the hell can you be so sad about him dying? He was just out of the way. You were just waiting for the joy, weren't you? You put it on his headstone, for God's sake."

"What?"

"Who puts anything about joy on a headstone? He was dead and you were looking for joy. Because you never loved him."

"Is that what you think?" She shakes her head. "I didn't say I didn't love him. He. And you. Were my life. Now I just want my life to include me."

"Well, why didn't you leave him? Or why didn't you stay away when you did leave? Why did you come back?" Finally the question I have waited so many years to ask is out there.

"Because." She pauses. "He told me about you."

"What about me?" I ask.

"He came to Nan Philpott's and told me how you couldn't stop crying. How you wouldn't eat or sleep. I came back for you. I'd do anything for you. Every night, when I'd call and pray that you would talk to me and you wouldn't, it killed me. I would have done anything just to talk to you again. So I came back."

I inhale, trying to catch all the air I feel is leaving me. My hand goes to my mouth. "Dad told you that?"

She nods, tears still falling, maybe for a different reason now, all the anger gone to some loving place.

"Then you were never happy because of me? You stayed there and ... for me?"

"Not just for you. For ... I don't know. It doesn't matter why. I came back. And I did love your father. Maybe not the way you think I should have, but I did."

"But I was ... Thank you."

"Oh, Jennifer. I've been wanting you to be happy, waiting for you to be happy." Her eyes don't move from my face. "I wanted that verse on your father's headstone for you, my love. You were so lost in sadness. I wanted you to see that the sadness would end one day."

She touches the side of my face and wipes my tears away. "I don't know how to make you whole again."

"Me either," I whisper.

13

DAD AND I were watching *The Cosby Show*. Claire Huxtable had her arms around a young Rudy, dispensing motherly love and advice. An ache started in my stomach and rose to my chest, making it uncomfortable to breathe. I had always taken my mother's hugs for granted, as much a part of her as not hugging or kissing was a part of Dad. Suddenly, Mom being gone and the absence of the potential for a hug overwhelmed me. I walked over to Dad and sat next to him on the couch.

"Yes?" He sat up straighter as he spoke. "Want a drink?"

"No." My arms went around his thick neck. I felt him straighten up even more, tensing beneath my touch.

"I love you, Daddy." As a child, I had said the words often but never while in an embrace. Usually reserved for bedtimes, the words were usually followed by a pat on the head and a smile. Occasionally, a "me too."

"You must be getting tired, little one," he said, first patting my back a little then pulling back so my hands came apart. I let my arm drop away. This was not the hug I needed.

"Mommy said she'd call when she got to Nanny Philpott's. Why didn't she call?"

He shrugged and looked away. "I don't know. Maybe she forgot."

Maybe she forgot. Three simple words said while Dad looked away. Said offhandedly. An offered suggestion. A possibility. But how could I forget them or forgive them?

My kind, loving mother could forget me so effortlessly while the man who showed me how to turn a wrench and how to wash my greasy hands sat next to me. Did not forget me. Stayed. Until he died, when suddenly he left me alone with someone who could forget me with ease, left me without that hug I'd craved that night and every moment since, no matter how many times my mother held me.

At least that was what I thought. Up until this moment when more words changed everything. She had called. She had dialled the numbers and asked for me, pleaded for me. Where had I been when he refused her? Refused me? Was I just watching TV or playing with my Hot Wheels cars or drawing the picture I remember drawing? The one where I tried out the look of our family without Mom in it. What simple task had I been doing while he changed our relationship forever? Did he pause to think better of hurting us both? I know him enough to know the answer. He was not a pausing man. Something was broken in his life and he sought to fix it with whatever tools he had: a wife, a small child, aching hearts.

And it worked. Mom returned, just like he wanted. Returned to a changed family, to a lesser one than before. As I sit here in this family room, staring at my mother, I want to be able to go back to the small child in that living room and speak the truth to her. "She loves you," I want to say. "She called and she would do anything for you, even make herself unhappy."

Mom does not know the truth and I can't find the words to tell it to her. I don't even know where to look for the words. Only three of them keep going around in my head, a continuous loop of "Maybe she forgot."

Uncle Chuck opens the door to the family room, bringing me back here to this new, awful chapter in my life. Mom and I both wipe our faces again, ensuring no remnants of tears.

Chuck says, "The doctor is in with Mrs. Collins. He wants to talk to all the family."

We walk towards Nan's room. Mom places her hand on my shoulder.

I let it stay there.

In Nan's room, the doctor holds a chart in his hand. Nan is moaning again but less so.

"Your mother has had a stroke," he says to Aunt Henrietta. "A very severe stroke on the left side of her brain. Her speech has been quite severely affected as has her right side, which is paralysed." Nan's moaning gets louder.

"My God." Henrietta puts her hand to her chest. "But I thought people with strokes don't have permanent damage anymore," Henrietta says. "There's medicine for that."

Nan's moaning gets louder again.

"Let's go to the family room," he says and nods to the nurse who is standing next to him.

a few kinds of wrong

We walk to the family room again. My stomach tightens as we walk through the door.

The doctor motions to the seats and puts on the practiced sad doctor look. I wonder if they teach it in medical school. He shakes his head and I know this is not good. I drop to the overstuffed vinyl seat, making the air push out of the chair. The chair sounds like it grunted.

"There are medications for your mother's kind of stroke." He looks to Mom now and then to Bryce. I can tell that he's not sure who in the room is this mother's child. "But there are a couple of reasons we won't use them. Because she was sleeping when she had the stroke, it took a while for staff at the nursing home to notice her symptoms. Too much time has elapsed for the treatments we have to work. Also, your mother has an advance healthcare directive, a living will, and it is very clear that we are to use no life-saving measures at all in the case of a catastrophic illness. No medications. No anything."

"But you have to," Henrietta shouts. "You can't just let her die. I never agreed with that living will thing. She wasn't of sound mind when she made that damned thing. That was you crowd came up with that." She points at Mom, wagging her finger.

"It was what your mother wanted, Henrietta. She was always clear about that. And she signed that long before she got sick. She signed that not long after your father died. She didn't want to live without him."

"Well, she wasn't in her right mind then. Jack agreed with me. It was you and Jennifer that got that signed."

I remember sitting around the kitchen table with Aunt

Henrietta while Nan answered questions from a checklist Nan's lawyer had given Mom.

I want to have life-sustaining treatment if I am terminally ill or injured. Yes or no; I want to have life-sustaining treatment if I am permanently unconscious. Yes or no. It all seemed so impotent there at the table, Nan in good health, the idea seeming sad but not plausible. Aunt Henrietta had argued against the whole living will idea, reminding us that God should and would decide when Nan should go.

"I think that's the point of the living will," I had pointed out. "It just says that no one except God will intervene."

"God made the machines and medicines that help keep people alive," she said, but Nan cut into the conversation.

"This is about me. And I'm telling you right now that I don't want one second on one of those breathing machines like Hope was hooked up to when she had her car accident," referring once again to her favourite soap opera. "I don't want none of them shockers to the chest or nothing. I wants the Lord to take me if He wants me, and God help the man that gets between me and my garden."

And that had been the end of that. Nan answered all her living will questions with a resounding no and signed everything, witnessed by the legal secretary in the office of Nan's lawyer.

"So what will happen to Nan?" I ask.

The doctor turns to me and says, "That's what we need to discuss. She appears to be unable to swallow."

No one speaks.

"That means she cannot eat or drink, but her wishes are not to have a feeding tube so—"

"What?" Henrietta says loudly.

"Without the feeding tube she will die."

His words hang there, loud despite how softly he spoke them.

"I don't think you can let her starve to death," Henrietta says, standing up then flailing her arms.

"She won't starve," Bryce says. "Thirst first."

The doctor nods and Aunt Henrietta starts to weep.

"Everything we know tells us that she will not suffer if we don't provide this for her. If we do provide IV fluids and then a feeding tube, she could survive indefinitely. But we have to remember her Alzheimer's. Her life would be," he pauses, "very difficult."

"Nothing she's not used to," Henrietta says too loudly for the size of the small room.

"She's had a stroke," the doctor says, looking directly at Henrietta now.

"Yes," Henrietta says. "I know."

"That doesn't take away her memory loss. She will regularly and routinely forget that she has had a stroke. She will not understand why she cannot talk or move or swallow or why the feeding tube and IV are attached to her. She will insist on trying to remove them from her body and will have to be constantly restrained to prevent this."

The horror of this strikes me hard, the idea of Nan being startled by her own imprisonment both inside and outside her body. I can't picture anything but the moaning person in room 2 who looks more terrified than I have ever seen.

"But if you give her the stroke medicine she won't be paralysed," Henrietta says.

177

tina chaulk

"I suspect there would still be damage, based on the severity of the stroke and the length of time now. But this is not an issue. The will is clear."

I want to have food and water provided through a tube or an IV if I am terminally ill or injured. Yes or no. She checked no. Her decision was made.

"How can you let this happen? How can you not fight for her to live?" Henrietta screeches at us.

"How can you not let this happen?" I ask. "You know what she wanted."

More than anything, I want what Henrietta fears.

The doctor puts his hand out in a calming gesture. "I can only go by this legal document. I can only do what it says."

"No, this is barbaric. Well, we'll take you to court," Henrietta says, standing up. "Come on, Chuck, let's go. We're going to get a lawyer." She stares at Chuck, waiting for him to go with her.

Uncle Chuck stays in his chair, his eyes focussed on the floor.

"Chuck, I said, come on."

He looks to her slowly, this man who has been run by her their whole married life.

"No," he says, his voice firm.

"No. What do you mean, no? Come on, I want to go."

"No. We should let the doctor do what your mother wanted."

"My mother didn't want to die of thirst surrounded by doctors and nurses who should help her."

I open my mouth but Mom lays her hand on my arm. I

look at her, see her warning to stay out of it.

Chuck looks up at Henrietta. "Your mother didn't want to be paralysed and not able to talk and not able to remember who she is or why she's like that."

I watch Henrietta struggle with herself. I know it will be hard to give into Chuck, but I also realize the power of the word "no" coming from someone after a lifetime of "yes."

"Doctor, is there anything else we need to know?" Henrietta pulls her cardigan tighter around her broad body.

"Do you have any questions?" he says softly.

"Will we know when it's close?" I speak up, my voice sounding foreign to me. "So we can make sure she's not alone when—" The lump in my throat stops my words.

"We'll see signs of dehydration but we won't know for sure. Perhaps it's best to have someone here for the next few days if you'd like someone to be with her when she passes."

When she passes. Such a nice, melodic line to refer to the end of a person's life, to the end of a person who created and raised two children, who baked wonderful bread, collected stamps, gardened with a passion, bluffed in Scrabble with a wry smile, and lived through seventy-nine trips around the sun.

Henrietta starts to sob on Chuck's shoulder and Mom rubs her sister-in-law's back. Sadness and resignation fill the room.

"We'll move her to a room as soon as we can. We can provide medication to calm her down and ease her ..." He pauses again. "Discomfort. Although we don't feel she has any discomfort. At least not physically."

"Please," Mom says. "As much as it takes. Don't let her suffer."

We sit in the family room for minutes, crying and sitting and talking. This reality starts to wash over us and we struggle in different ways. Henrietta clings to Chuck. Mom tends to me, seeming to want to make sure that I'm okay. Bryce tends to Mom but I can tell he wants to make sure that I'm okay. I'm not ready for it yet and don't acknowledge his presence. He leaves and in a moment returns. In the doorway, behind him, I see Jamie, and just like the last time I saw him in the doorway of a family room, I go to him, relieved he is there.

"Bryce told me," he whispers. "I'm so sorry."

"Me too," I say, not referring only to what has happened to Nan.

❦

Later that morning, with less than two hours of sleep, I turn into the almost empty parking lot of the garage. There is one familiar car there, besides all the cars that belong to customers.

I unlock the garage door and walk through, turning on lights as I go. In the office Bryce is sitting at the desk, but stands up when he sees me. He passes me before I can make it to the office door. He says nothing as he walks past.

"I need to speak to you."

"I have nothing to say to you," he says, standing still, his back to me.

"You don't have to say anything. I said I have something

to say to you." I start to walk. This is why I came here before I go home to sleep. I need to get this said.

He follows me into the office and I close the door even though there is no one else around. He picks a piece of lint off his pants.

"Were you and Mom together when Dad was alive?" I stare straight into his eyes, looking for his reaction as much as his words.

He closes his eyes and I clench my fist. In my mind the answer is as clear as if he said "Yes."

"You said I didn't have to talk." Eyes still closed.

"I lied."

"Is this what this is all about?" He opens his eyes and the blue pierces me. "Why didn't you just ask that in the first place?"

Because I was afraid to, I don't say. I shrug.

"No, of course not. Your mother and I were never together when your father was alive. Never."

I want to ask how but can't. I want to know, but my desire not to know is stronger. My need not to picture them together. A tender touch, a gentle kiss, him touching her, him taking off her clothes, caressing her breasts, him inside her. It makes me sick. And yet I want to know.

"The first time we kissed, we pulled away and didn't speak to each other for eight days. We both felt so guilty. I couldn't sleep or eat. I felt sick all the time. Like your father's ghost would come back and haunt me. Like I was betraying him. And finally I realized that I also couldn't eat or sleep because she was all I thought about. When she laughed, it made everything good. And I told her. And she felt the same. The not eating or sleeping, the guilt, the knowing that being around me made her happy. But mostly she was afraid of what you'd think. I told her that you'd want her to be happy. I guess I was wrong."

Happy. My mother sought it and I took it away. Even when I hadn't known about it, I had been used by Dad to rob it from her. At least the potential of it. Every moment of her life that was not happy had been, in some way, as a result of me.

The man I adored and trusted had taken it away from her too. Just as surely as I had with her second chance at happiness.

I sit down, my back to him, and look out the window to the garage. "There are some things that are hard to accept. Almost impossible. But I'm doing the best I can. I'm here, aren't I? And so are you." And I haven't beaten you over the head with anything yet, I don't say.

"Humph." I feel his hand on my shoulder just before I hear the door open. As I watch him walk across the floor to a car up on a ramp, I wish I could talk to him about how I'm feeling. He was always the person I'd tell if someone hurt me, and he would make me feel better. I mourn the loss of that person to turn to and wonder how much longer I can work here, with all these bad feelings all around me. For a second I feel a strong urge to visit Nan in the home, at least until I remember what it is I'm trying to forget.

14

THE AFTERNOON OF the day Mom left, I went to the garage after school to find that Dad was not there. Bryce told me Dad had to attend to some business, which I found odd as Dad rarely left the garage for any business. Others came to him, and Bryce did any external business that needed to be done. But Bryce had a couple of windshield wipers for me to replace so I got down to work.

This was one of the only times I was at the garage without Dad. I wasn't there very long before I realized I didn't like it so much without him there, without seeing him somewhere, without a smile from him or just the attention he gave me by answering a question or even signing my work order. Without Dad, it seemed, the garage ceased to be a magical place.

Dad still hadn't shown up by seven that evening. I'd been doodling in the office for a couple of hours when Bryce took me across the street to the A&W for supper. We drank thick chocolate milkshakes and ate juicy onion rings and whistle dogs. I could barely suck the milkshake through the straw.

"This is the best milkshake I've ever had in my whole life," I told Bryce.

He smiled and said, "Me too."

We sat in silence, neither of us seeming to know what to say. After I finished my onion rings and whistle dog, Bryce bought me a small apple pie.

"My mom left." I suddenly felt like I had to say it.

"Oh?"

"Yes, but she didn't leave me."

"No?"

"No. She's leaving Daddy. Not me."

He sucked on the now milky milkshake. "Does that make you feel better?"

My eyes started to fill with tears and I swallowed hard. I looked down at the table, then to the floor and nodded.

"It will be okay," Bryce said, his hand on mine for just a second, long enough for me to feel the calluses there. And, for just a second, I saw his eyes and something I would not understand until years later. I saw there the question: How could someone possibly leave their husband and home without leaving the child who lived there?

Silence again, until I asked the question I'd carried with me all afternoon, "Is that where Daddy is? Is he gone to look for Mommy?"

"He's dealing with it," Bryce said.

After the pie, we returned to the garage. Dad was waiting there. I ran to him and hugged his legs and told him, "It's okay, Daddy, I'll never leave you."

He stood straight and patted my back. "Let's go home."

When we pulled up to our driveway, I squealed, "Mommy's home," because there, sitting in our driveway, was Mom's station wagon. But as we neared it, I could see that the small stuffed elephant I left on the dash was not there and there was rust over the back tire well.

I looked at Dad.

"It looks like Mom's. We don't want people to talk."

"Talk about what?"

"It's best we not tell anyone that Mom is gone. No one will really notice. At least not if the car is in the driveway."

"Mrs. Murphy will. They have coffee every day."

"Mrs. Murphy knows your mother is gone. But she knows not to say anything about it."

I knew Mrs. Murphy and Mom would talk about everyone in the neighbourhood over their coffee, and I knew Mrs. Murphy would normally talk about it to someone else. How Dad could prevent that was a mystery to me. But I didn't ask. I didn't think I wanted to know the answer anyway.

Inside the house that first night, the phone rang four or five times. Each time, my heart would race with excitement, sure this call was Mom. Dad walked out into the kitchen for each call. I heard him speaking, the conversation shorter each time until I heard him pick up the receiver then hang it up. He left the phone off the hook until I could hear the loud, fast beeping sound, and when I told him about it he said that if I waited, it would stop.

"But Mom's going to call. She said she would."

"She's not going to call tonight. It's too late. That's a customer bugging me about a bill and I can't take it anymore."

Dad let me stay up late and I fell asleep during *Kate and Allie*. On the couch, not in my bed, where my mother made me go every night at nine, no matter what.

When Dad shook me awake the next morning, I mumbled that I was too tired to get up. And I was. At least until I realized that Dad had woken me. His hands on my bare arm were rough compared to Mom's gentle waking with her soft, lotioned hands. The realization that Mom was gone jolted me to wide awake.

I got dressed and went downstairs to the table where Dad was drinking instant coffee and swearing about how awful it tasted.

"What you want for breakfast? Cereal?"

I thought about it for a few seconds. "I'd like some chocolate chip cookies."

"Okay," Dad said.

"And some hot chocolate."

"Okay."

"With marshmallows."

"Sounds good. Better than this bloody coffee."

At school everyone, including my teacher, noticed the bag of roast chicken potato chips and Snickers bar I had in my lunch box, along with a bottle of Pepsi.

"I've been a good girl," I told them. "And I'm allowed a treat day."

"Apples are a good treat," my teacher, Mrs. Crane, whose husband was a dentist, told me. "Sugar will rot your teeth."

"Apples are high in sugar," BJ said, without looking up from her own peanut butter and jam sandwich.

"But they're nutritious and the sugar is worth it."

BJ shrugged. "Sugar is sugar."

That night, after working until almost 7:30, Dad and I stopped at Kentucky Fried Chicken on the way home and picked up a bucket with fries and creamy coleslaw. We brought the chicken back to the house and ate it in the living room in front of the TV. We munched on Chips Ahoy chocolate chip cookies for dessert.

The phone rang twice in the evening. Wrong numbers, Dad said. Still no call from Mom. After watching *Growing Pains*, Dad asked me if I wanted to go to bed and I said "yes" because my eyes kept going together. My bed seemed like a great refuge from the tiredness I felt, and I asked Dad if he could carry me. He did and lifted me up in the moment before I drifted off.

I woke up in the middle of the night to use the bathroom and saw light from the living room. Dad was sound asleep on the sofa and test pattern filled the screen. He was sitting up with his feet on the coffee table, his head bent over and slumped a little to the side. I wished I could pick him up and put him in bed the way he'd done for me. I turned off the TV and the lamp on the end table. He didn't budge. I thought about waking him up but knew Dad couldn't get back to sleep once he was woken up. That's the reason I knew I had to go to Mom's side of the bed and whisper when I needed something, rather than wake Dad up. So I let him sleep.

Before I left the room I stared at him a long time then tentatively kissed him on the cheek. It was the first time I had kissed him, the only time I recall kissing him, and I remember the feeling of the scruff on his face against my lips.

The next morning I watched him rub his neck while I ate my McCain Deep and Delicious chocolate cake and cream soda for breakfast.

"Slept funny?" I asked.

"Yeah. Something like that."

I went to the bathroom and stopped at Dad's room to peek in. He had pulled the bedspread up over the bed, but it looked lumpy. I went in the room to try and fix it. As I straightened out the bedspread, I saw the receiver off the hook of the phone on Mom's bedside table.

"Dad," I called, running out of the room. "The phone is off the hook in your room."

"What are you doing in my room?" he shouted, startling me.

"I was just straightening—"

"Stay out of my room." His voice was still loud.

"But your phone was off the hook."

"I must have knocked it off this morning when I was making the bed. I'll go put it back on."

He walked to his room then came back. "There. Phone's on the hook."

We sat in silence for a few minutes, as we did again and again every morning for the next two weeks. Two more weeks of late TV shows, exhausted mornings, eating junk food for breakfast, dinner, and supper, and going to Nan's to get my clothes washed. Two weeks of falling asleep on the couch every night. Of the sound of the phone not ringing.

Every night I'd go to sleep and wonder where Mom was and when she would talk to me again. I imagined her having an exciting life, dancing and going out and having fun, forgetting I was at home and how I might miss the cadence of her voice, how it lifted at the end of my name and went down when she laughed. I pictured her putting on her White Linen perfume and going out somewhere with a group of people. I saw her doing everything I had never seen her do before and was sure the only reason she could do that now was because she was no longer with me. And I told myself that her absence did not bother me, even though she was the last thing I thought about before I went to sleep at night and the first thing I thought about when I woke up in the morning.

One morning, as I ate my strawberry pop-tarts, Dad came out of his room dressed in the good black pants he wore to important meetings and funerals, and a wrinkled, white dress shirt. As he walked out, I saw him fiddling with his cuffs. He kept trying to put in cufflinks by himself, the pair Mom had given him on their wedding day. I finally grabbed the cufflinks and managed to put them in myself.

Dad smiled. He touched his shirt. "Too bad you can't iron."

"I can try," I said.

"Nah, I'll cover it up with my jacket."

"Where are you going?"

"Just a meeting," he said. "More of a negotiation. But I'm pretty sure I'll win." He smiled.

"I know you will," I said. And I believed him.

After school Dad was waiting for me in the car outside. I could see someone on the passenger side, but it wasn't until I got close that I saw it was Mom. She waved and smiled. I walked slowly toward the car, torn between being happy to see her, confused about why she had suddenly come back into our lives, and wondering where she had been.

"I love you, baby," Mom said when she hugged me, and I said the words back, even though I wasn't sure I believed what she said.

෨

The first full night of vigil with Nan, I insist on staying and tell Mom and Aunt Henrietta to go home. I know I won't sleep, so what's the point in going home?

It is so hard to watch this broken woman in her bed and not be able to make things right. She is a shell of herself — drugged, moaning, the piercing blue eyes only peeking through half-opened lids from time to time, sparkling with fear at times, resignation at others. I brush her hair three times, rub lotion on her elbows, the way she did every night she remembered to do it. I read to her from a magazine I found down the hall, pausing over and over to wipe the blur away from my eyes. I pace the floors, sit down, stand up, and even lie next to her in her bed, holding her, breathing in tandem with her breath.

I catch small naps until Aunt Henrietta bursts into the room at around 8:30, barrelling past me and straight to Nan's bed, wailing with great loud shouts of "Oh God" and "Oh Lord Jesus, help her" between sobs as she rests her head on Nan's bed. Thankfully, Nan is asleep.

I smile. Right here in this room with my dying Nan in the bed, my aunt weeping all over her, I smile and fight the urge to laugh. The scene brings back a memory of Nan at our house, one evening after Henrietta had visited.

"The scientists should study her brain," Nan said, nodding after Henrietta.

"What?" I asked, a chuckle in my voice.

"She could take the best of anything and make it something bad. There must be a part of her brain for that and if the scientists could see it they'd figure out a way people could not be like it."

I nodded then and as I watch Henrietta sobbing on the bed I wonder what Nan would think of the show.

"I'm going," I say.

Henrietta doesn't stop her wailing. I'm not even sure she realizes I'm in the room so I just leave.

Outside the hospital, the day is cooler than yesterday, fog hovering over the city like a symbol of how I'm feeling. I'm beyond tired and know I still won't be able to sleep. I need something real to cling onto. I want to fix something, so I decide to go to the garage again. The pain in my side is tolerable, especially when I take a couple of Atasol 30s.

When I get there, the garage is bustling. It fills me to walk in the building. The guys all ask me about Nan. I can still feel leftover tension in the air and I wish things could be like they used to be. I wish I could feel like the guys would do anything for me. But they've already chosen Bryce over me so the feeling is gone. Jamie is under a car up on Ray's ramp. He's holding a wrench. He looks comfortable. Jamie is becoming. I'm not sure what he's becoming but I think I like it.

Bryce sees me and follows me to the office.

"Got an engine job in here?" I ask him.

"You need some sleep."

I look at his baggy eyes, the dark circles, the shoulders hunched just a little. "So do you."

"Go home."

I stare at him, fighting back the urge to tell him to get out. But I want something else.

"I need something hard to do. I need to get in there and figure something out, maybe take a whole car apart. A nice, big, engine job. Understand?"

And I know he does. He stayed at the garage for fourteen hours the day after Dad died. He worked for two weeks straight, weekends and all, after his wife died.

"No engine job," he said, shuffling through the work orders, "but there's a mystery electrical problem here. Everything shuts down when this car goes up a steep hill. Something's loose somewhere. Might be a long time to figure out where."

Wires and fuses make minutes then hours pass. Tilt the car, she stalls. Put her level again and she's fine. Tracing connections from spark plugs to engine to dash to sensors, to the Electronic Control Unit. Nothing. Most times this would frustrate me, but three hours pass and I'm in blissful oblivion.

"Hey," I hear outside the car door. I look up to see Jamie standing there with an egg sandwich off the snack truck and a Pepsi. He passes them to me and I shake my head. "Not hungry."

"Tough. You have to eat."

"Nan can't."

"You're not her. Listen, I promise if you were seventy-nine years old with Alzheimer's and after having a stroke, I wouldn't give you this sandwich and drink, but you're not, so please eat."

"Put them in the office. I'll get to them when I finish this." I point to the car.

"What's the trouble?"

"Electrical. Stalls. A little beyond spark plug replacement," I say and bend to get back to work.

"Really? Well, I might not know everything about cars but I know that TPS connector looks loose. Might cause a stall on a hill." Jamie winks at me, smiles, and walks toward the office.

I stare after him, mouth open.

"I fixed one a few days ago with Alan," Jamie says to me over his shoulder. He goes in the office and places the sandwich and Pepsi on the desk then leaves again.

After putting the Throttle Position Sensor connector back on, I go back inside the office and drink the Pepsi. I have been thirsty but didn't know it until I start to drink. I can't stop thinking about Nan and how dry she must be. I promised I'd be back to the hospital by four so Henrietta could be home when Sarah gets home from Day Camp. It's only a little after two, but I can't stop thinking about Nan, and there are no work orders left. This is summer, a slow time of year when everyone is more focussed on vacations than oil changes and brake jobs. Bryce comes in and I get up.

"I'm going to see Nan."

"Your mom just left there."

I just look at him, my eyes searching his face for some reminder that I love him rather than feel the way I do. "I don't need you to fill me in on Mom. I'd rather you not speak to me about her at all."

"Okay. I thought we were past it."

"No, we're not. You might be fine with it and she might be fine with it, but it still makes me want to throw up. So we'll all get through this thing with Nan and deal with it, but I don't want to deal with that." I point to him as if he is the "that" instead of just one half of it, one third of it really as I'm in the mix too.

"You have to accept it. And then we can get back to some kind of normal."

"I don't know where normal is anymore."

"Doesn't mean you can't start to make your way there. Like I said, you have to accept it. It's the way it is."

I tilt my head. "Then how come Aunt Henrietta doesn't know. If it's so acceptable, why haven't you shared it with everyone?"

Jamie comes in and my question hangs there.

"What's going on?"

"Nothing," I say and leave the office. I walk away and Jamie follows me.

"Where are you going?"

"I'm going to see Nan. I don't think I'll be going home tonight. Henrietta has something with Sarah tomorrow and someone should stay with Nan all night."

"I'll come by later with some supper."

I nod. "Okay."

Jamie smiles and walks back to the Honda Civic he's working on. He crouches by the back door, turning a ratchet with the same passion he plays guitar or sings or makes love. Everything he does is Zen. He flicks his hair out of his eyes and squints at something in the car. I feel such an intense surge of something that is not hatred that I grab the workbench to counter the weakness in my knees.

ॐ

I shower at the house, change into shorts and a t-shirt that reads *Sarcasm is just one more service I provide*, then go to the hospital.

Aunt Henrietta and Uncle Chuck are both in the hall outside Nan's room.

"The nurses are changing her," Chuck says. "She soiled the bed."

I'm not sure what soiled means but it's a good term that doesn't commit to much detail. It's as much as I need to know.

"Oh."

"It was a bad smell," Henrietta says. "I asked the nurses about it and they seemed to know. Even before they lifted the sheet and looked. Didn't they?" She looks to Chuck for confirmation.

He nods.

"Smelled some bad," Henrietta says.

I'm glad I wasn't there. I've watched Nan fade into this remnant of who she was, her body just waiting to die, clinging onto life somehow. To have to add the bad smell to the bad sights I've seen, the awful sounds I've heard, the feel of her rubbery skin. I want to remember her for the good stuff, but I fear that these horrible things will sear themselves into my memory, blotting out the good.

"Remember when Nan rode Jimmy's motorcycle?" I say about the day my second cousin brought over his new Harley, and Nan, at age seventy-one, strapped on a helmet and insisted he take her for a ride. I need to remember a better Nan.

"Got nothing to lose," Nan had said.

"She could have been killed," Henrietta says and tsks.

"And miss all this," I answer back, trying to remember Nan's smiling face on the back of that bike instead of the snarl on Henrietta's face now.

"It was such a nice day," I say. "All the neighbours were out around and they all stood on the road and watched and smiled and cheered. I can hear Nan's yahoo now."

I close my eyes, trying to find the picture of her smile. And I do. For a minute I'm back there in the driveway, the warm wind on my face, Dad laughing, Mom saying "Oh my God," Henrietta squealing for Jimmy to get Nan back in the driveway now.

The nurse opens the door and I hear her say we can go in. She leaves the door open and in the time it takes to open my eyes Nan changes from fun-loving daredevil to paralysed invalid about to die. I close my eyes but she's still there, still dying in that bed.

"I'll be back before Sarah gets out of camp," I say to Henrietta and walk away.

"Where are you going? You haven't seen her," Henrietta shouts after me.

"Yes, I have," I answer.

15

MOM'S CAR IS in the driveway when I get to her house. I hesitate before going in. Bryce is at work so I know he won't be here. But will his clothes be in the laundry hamper? Will his fishing magazine be on the coffee table? I knock even though I'm sure the door is unlocked and even if it isn't, I have a key in my pocket.

Mom's face pales when she sees me. "What is it?" she asks. "Is she …"

"No. No."

Mom steps back and I walk into the porch.

"Why did you knock?" She pulls her hair behind her ear as she speaks.

I don't answer and she says, "Oh."

"I came to get our photo albums. I want to bring them to the hospital and look at them. All of them. Nan's too. Of Dad and you and Henrietta but mostly pictures of Nan."

She touches my face and smiles, even though her eyes are sad. "Yes," she whispers. "Let's go get them."

Mom walks into her room but I stay outside, just outside

the doorway, thinking back, seeing, without going inside, a new book on Dad's bedside table. But it's not Dad's anymore.

"They're in here," Mom says.

"That's okay. I'll wait in the living room."

"No. Come in. They're just in my bottom drawer."

"No," I say more firmly. "I'll wait in the living room." I walk away before she can argue again or realize why I don't want to go in, a look of guilt on her face, a realization of how things have changed.

I'm standing in the living room with my arms crossed when she comes in with a pile of photo albums.

"There's more," she says, laying that stack down and returning for more. There are big albums with smiley faces and pictures of trees on their fronts, the pictures inside kept safe on sticky pages under sheets of cellophane, and small ones made of black felt with old, ripple-edged black-and-whites stuck into tabs. Lifetimes of pictures, not looked at in how long, I wonder. Has Mom looked at them since Dad died? Do they make her happy or sad? I wonder how they'll make me feel.

Mom brings in the next load, a pile of seven books in her arms. I reach out to help her lay them down.

"Got any boxes or bags? I can carry them in."

"How about I help you with them? I was thinking of going to the hospital again anyway."

I open my mouth to tell her no. I want to be alone when I look at these. But then I realize why I want to see these pictures. I want to remember the good times. And the only way to really do that is to look at the pictures with someone else. To say out loud that you remember that pumpkin and how Nan cut her finger on the knife while she carved it and had to go to the hospital for three stitches. To ask what the name of that cat was again, the one Nan said Henrietta hugged away as a little girl.

"We'll still need the boxes," I say and Mom smiles.

⚘

Mom and I have the pictures in the trunk of the car. We wait until Uncle Chuck and Aunt Henrietta leave the hospital before we retrieve them. I make two trips, insisting Mom stay in the room with Nan. Someone has to be with her. Just in case.

It's not that Henrietta wouldn't want to see the pictures. It's just that the memories contained in these albums would be skewed by her perspective on them. Nan's green dress would make Nan look washed out instead of beautiful — the strong Nan who curled her hair and applied lipstick every morning. Dad's old car would be the one that Henrietta got transported to the hospital in the time she got kidney stones, rather than the vehicle Mom used to drive me to my first day of school. The black cloud of Henrietta would obscure the view in all the memories in all the pictures. In my mind, I can hear her now, as I open the first book, full of fairly recent shots when Pop was dead but Nan was still Nan: *Look at Mom smiling. Poor Mom. She didn't know there that she'd end up here like this.*

Mom and I travel back in time with the photos, our own portable time machine. All of us younger. Many of them taken before I was born. Pop Collins in his uniform before he went to Italy and Africa with the 166th Field Artillery Regiment of the Royal Newfoundland Regiment. Mom and Dad's wedding day, Bryce standing next to Dad.

It pops into my mind: *If Dad knew then, I bet he wouldn't have asked Bryce to be the best man.* The thought makes me gasp.

"What's wrong?" Mom says and looks at Nan, unconscious in the bed.

"I'm a lot like Aunt Henrietta. Aren't I?"

Mom laughs. "Well, you're about half her size."

"No. I don't mean in looks. In the way I …" I can't find the words. I can find lots for Henrietta: wet blanket, damper, negative Nellie, black cloud, whiner, moper, complainer, glass half empty. The list could go on but I don't want to make them refer to me. Even though the more I think about it, the more it's true.

"You didn't used to be like her," Mom says and turns the page of the photo album.

"No?" I say it like a question because I just can't remember ever feeling any way but shrouded in this darkness.

Mom shakes her head and starts to sing. "My little ray of sunshine, you're my little ray of sunshine, shine through the day and all through the night, you're my little ray of sunshine."

I hadn't heard the song in years.

"The last time I heard that was my wedding day. You sang it at the reception and then Jamie sang it."

The moment, the memory, is like a blow to my body and I suck in air then blow it out, but it still doesn't feel like any breath is getting in my lungs.

Mom singing in front of everyone, the song she sang to me as a child and even through some of my adulthood. Jamie coming up to sing with her then Mom sitting down, Jamie finishing the song. I was his ray of sunshine then too. Not a dry eye anywhere at the wedding. Such a feeling of joy in me and a certainty everything would always be wonderful.

"I have to go." I'm almost to the door before I finish the sentence.

"What? Why?" Mom stands and the photo album in her lap falls to the floor. Pictures that had been carelessly inserted in the back of the album scatter all over the floor.

"I forgot I have to do something." I bend to pick up the pictures but stop and turn around instead.

"But I don't have my car."

"I'll come back for you," I say. I nearly crash into a nurse as I run down the corridor. Unlike so many times before, when I've run away from something, I know exactly where I'm going and exactly what I'm going to do when I get there.

☙

When Jamie arrives at the house, seven hours have passed since I left the hospital. Six phone calls have come in, although I only heard the phone ring once. After I heard Mom's voice on the machine, asking when I was coming back for her, I unplugged the phone and turned down the answering machine. Five other messages have gone unheard but they are there. I heard the clicking of the tape as it

201

tina chaulk

engaged for each message, the whirring as it rewound the outgoing message every time. No voice mail or digital answering machine for me. Only the mechanical whirring of the cassette can ensure that a message gets taken.

One bottle sits empty on the coffee table and the second is three-quarters full in my hand. I've passed out once and woke up again. I've eaten a slice of bread with nothing on it, just to help the burning in my stomach. I've taken four Atasol 30s for the pain, in my side and other places. I've watched soap operas, a game show, and the evening news. The top story was that the price of gas is going up again tomorrow.

Jamie doesn't look happy when he enters the house with his key. The one I gave him. The one I just loaned to him so I wouldn't have to keep letting him in. Jamie stands there.

"Where have you been? Your mom's been trying to call you."

"I've been right here." I stand up and fall back into the chair, unable to balance on my feet.

"You left your mother stranded at the hospital." He places his lunchbox down and takes off his workboots, flashing me back to Dad doing the same thing every day. Something in the way he unlaces his boots reminds me of Dad, the way he flicks the laces away once they've been unwrapped from the top hooks, the way he pulls the laces out a bit, leaving them slack for when he puts them on again.

"Bryce is really pissed off," Jamie continues.

"With me?" I try to make it sound like that but it comes out a slurred mess, even to me.

"Yes, with you. I can hardly understand you, you're so

drunk. Why don't you just go to bed?"

"Bryce is pissed off with me?" I bang my chest on the word "me," harder than I want to. "Well, fuck him and fuck my mother too. Oh, right." I slap my forehead. "He's doing that already, isn't he?"

"Come on, let's get you to bed." Jamie puts his hand under my arm as if to help me up but I push him away.

"You are my little ray of sunshine, my little ray of sunshine," I sing.

"What?"

"That's me, Jamie." I burp and continue talking. "Don't you remember? You sang it to me." I point to him, hit his shoulder by mistake on the word "you" and hit myself on the word "me."

"I remember." He stands up and looks down at me.

"I think that's funny. Don't you? I mean I must be the world's littlest fucking ray of sunshine. You must need a magnifying glass to see me."

"Stop swearing. You never swear."

"No, the little ray of fucking sunshine doesn't swear."

"Jesus."

"Ooh, now you're swearing too. Only you're taking the Lord's name in vain. That is some serious shit, man."

Jamie just stares at me, looking down.

"Don't do that. Don't look at me like that," I scream, and try to push him away. He moves in the second before I reach him, and I fall out of my chair onto the floor, rum tumbling after me, pouring onto the hardwood floor. I grab the bottle and hold onto it like a drowning man holds a life preserver.

"Like what?"

"Like you're mad and like you're pitying me. Don't fucking pity me."

"I don't pity you. I pity the rest of us that have to put up with you."

I'm lying on the floor hugging the bottle. My shirt is getting wet from the puddle of rum that's spread its way over to me.

"You're sucking us all down into your darkness. Your grandmother is dying and all you care about is yourself and your bottle."

"Aww, Jamie's mad. You hardly ever get mad, Jamie. Why are you so mad?" I know how much he hates to be pushed, to be made fun of, and I push the button.

He walks out of the room and I hear the bathroom door close.

"Jamie fucking perfect Flynn is mad. Call the newspapers," I shout to no one. "Jamie's sooky. I'd say Jamie came home tonight figuring he'd get some. Figuring good old Jennifer would go down on him. A good screw maybe. Ha. Oops. I shouldn't use 'Jamie' and 'good screw' in the same sentence."

I start to laugh. I'm laughing for a couple of minutes and still no Jamie appears. No rise out of him.

I lay my head back on the floor and start to sing, "You're my little ray of sunshine, my little ray of—"

I'm being lifted off the floor. The bottle falls out of my hand and I hear it crash on the floor, an explosion of glass. I start to kick, but in what seems like three strides, Jamie has me in the bathroom.

"What are you doing?" I scream and start hitting him with my fists. He's carrying me in a fireman hold, at least until he plops me in the bathtub.

"My ribs," I call out as Jamie turns on the cold water in the shower. I kick out at him but he moves away and I miss. I try to stand up but he easily pushes me back.

"Jamie." I start to cry, shivering, my clothes soaking through. He is wet too, his hair down in his eyes until he slicks it back with his hand. He starts shivering with me and with his hair out of the way I can see again his eyes, the pity still there, mixed with rage and determination. He holds me and I sob into his chest, hitting him at the same time.

"I used to be a ray of sunshine, Jamie. How did I get here? How did I get here from there?"

"Something broke," he says over the water pounding us. "Something inside of you broke. And you haven't tried to fix it yet."

"How do I fix it?"

"I don't know. You just have to let it go. Let it go, babe."

It feels like we're back in the parking lot and all I want is him not to say the words that will change everything. Only this time I want him to say something that will make it all right, will heal this part of me.

Jamie turns off the water and slowly takes off my clothes. I'm quiet, letting him hold me and dry me all over. He winces at the now purple shoeprint on my side.

"Sorry," he mouths.

"I know."

tina chaulk

He wraps the cotton robe that hangs on the bathroom door around me and starts to gently dry my hair. After a couple of moments, he lifts me up again and walks me to the bedroom where he lays me on the bed. I reach up to him, to his lips, but he pulls away.

"Good night." He doesn't wait for me to say anything. He closes the door before I can think of what I want to say.

In the silence and the darkness of my room I find myself feeling sleepy. It surprises me after a cold shower.

As I nod off, I hear Jamie in the bathroom and I know he is cleaning up the mess in there. My last conscious thought is that of all the wrongs in my life right now, without even trying, somehow, he's the only right I have.

16

ONE NIGHT, ALMOST seven months after Dad died, I worked extra late, picked up a bottle on the way home, dropped by the cemetery, and was ready to collapse when I walked through the front door of my house. Jamie greeted me with a scowl. He was waiting on the couch, sitting in his pyjama bottoms.

"What is it?" I asked as I put my keys down on the little table next to the door.

"What is what?"

I pointed at him. "The face. Did something happen? You look … pissed off."

"I'm surprised you noticed."

"So, I'm the one you're pissed off with?"

He wriggled on the couch, moved over a little, pulled his hand through his hair. It was only then that I looked behind him and saw the table, set with silverware and candles burned down to nubs. I searched my mind and found the date I had been writing on work orders all day.

"Shit." I tapped my forehead with a closed fist. "I'm so

sorry. I don't know how I forgot." I walked toward him, stopped by his stare.

"I emailed you to make sure you came home at a decent time. I know better than to expect you for supper without a special invitation."

I started to walk toward him again. "I said I was sorry." I could smell candle wax and food I couldn't quite place.

"It's not like it was forty-seven years or anything. It was five years, for God's sake. Five years."

I walked to the kitchen, opened the oven and looked in. Steak and baked potatoes in a casserole dish, looking like they'd been there for hours. It was 10:12 at night. I'd had two bags of potato chips and four coffee all day but still didn't feel hungry. Something told me to take the food out anyway.

"I didn't forget. I knew all day that there was something about the date. It bugged me all day."

I tried unsuccessfully to pick up the dried-out steak by attempting to stab it with a fork. I gave up and dumped the contents of the casserole dish onto a plate. There was silence and when I turned around Jamie had one arm crossed and his jaw clenched.

"That makes it worse, Jen. You knew and tried to think of it and couldn't."

I sighed and shook my head. "Jamie, I'm tired. I don't have—"

"You're tired? You're tired. Well, maybe it's because you worked sixteen hours today. And yesterday and the day before that and the day before that."

I pulled the bottle of Bacardi out of the paper bag I'd laid on the counter and poured a large glass.

"Maybe you're tired because every night you come home and lower down that shit before you pass out. Well, I'm tired too."

I sipped on the drink and turned away from him.

His hand grabbed my arm and made me spill some of my rum.

"Don't you dare touch me like that," I shouted as I wrenched my arm away.

"What other way can I touch you? Like this?" He pulled me close, his face an inch or two away from mine. "Like this?" His left hand groped my right breast.

I brushed his hand away, tried to push him away from me. "Don't."

He pulled me close again, his breath in my ear, his hand gentle on my shoulder. "I want you, Jen. I want to be with you."

I pushed him away again, harder this time, with the force of the sudden anger that rose up in me. "That's what it's always about with you, isn't it? Is that what this poor, angry man act is about? Not getting it enough? You're horny, is that it?"

"No." He raised his voice enough to make me jump. Jamie never raised his voice. "That isn't what *this* is about. I want to hold you, to be your … your husband, your partner. I want to be there for you. I haven't held you in months." He touched my hand.

I stared at him, seeing how much he meant it. I watched his sad eyes look into mine and I tried to find any part of me that wanted to be held by him.

"Let me go," I whispered.

"I don't know why I thought you'd remember today. Or why I thought you'd want to spend it with me. I mean I'm alive so I'm not worth your time."

"What the hell is that supposed to mean? Are you mad at me because my father is dead?"

"No. I'm not mad. I'm so frustrated." He shook his fist at nothing. "It's like you've cut me out of your life. All you do is work all the time and then you go to the cemetery and then you get drunk." He looked away then back to me. "My therapist says that you—"

"Your what?"

"My therapist. I'm seeing a therapist. About you, about us."

"Oh my God, you're not serious." I put my hand up in the air. "You make everything into such a big deal."

"It is a big deal. You are stuck in this grief. And your work. Dr. Morgan says that you—"

"I don't care what he says," I screamed. I pointed at his face. "Do not talk to him about me. I'm none of his business. If you think you need to talk to some shrink then you can but it has nothing to do with me."

"It's everything to do with you. You're a workaholic, and that and your grief are destroying us."

"I am not a *workaholic*. I just work a lot."

He stabbed the air with a caustic laugh, a sharp "ha" that made me jump. "That's a good one. Like you're not an alcoholic, you just drink a lot. Like your nan doesn't have Alzheimer's, she just forgets a lot."

"Get out."

"What?"

"Get out of my house. Now." The words were out before I had a chance to think.

"Your house? Our house."

"Oh no. *My* name is on the mortgage and always was. This is *my* house."

He stared at me a long time, and I watched him. He went from livid to composed to sad, his face morphing into something that made me feel bad about myself, that made me wish I could ask him to stay. But I wouldn't.

After he went to our room, I heard the slamming of drawers and the squeak of coat hangers moving along the rod in our closet. I poured myself another drink, gulped it down and poured another before I sat in front of the TV and turned it on. I knew he wouldn't leave. He was in our bedroom, making those noises, the sounds of leaving, so I would go in and tell him I was sorry and ask him to stay. Like we hadn't argued before, like he hadn't threatened to leave half a dozen times in the past couple of months.

The glass was up to my mouth, the television on a repeat episode of *House MD* when he walked out of the room, accompanied by another sound. The glass stayed against my lip but I didn't drink from it. I didn't move. I didn't even turn my head toward him, just heard that squeaky wheel on the bottom of his suitcase as he rolled it across the floor, heard the front door open, felt the cold wind blow inside. I knew he was standing there with the door open, waiting for me to turn my head and, as surprised as I was that he was leaving, I wouldn't give him that satisfaction.

"I'll wait for you. I'll wait forever, if that's what it takes. Just get yourself straightened out and I'll be waiting. You just need to call." He spoke those words and then finally closed the door, leaving a sad, aching silence behind him.

For two months I did not speak to him. Even after he sent me Dr. Morgan's card and the key to his new apartment with the note:

> *I mean it. I will wait forever.*
> *Love*
> *Jamie*

I did not even try to speak to him until that day I heard a song on the radio. And something cruel that Saturday morning told me I should go to him, that I should use the key to his apartment and surprise him; told me it was okay to feel again and to want to be held again. Something softened in me that day, and before I could remain that way, Jamie hardened it again.

☞

Henrietta's snoring when I enter Nan's room makes me grateful poor Nan is drugged enough not to hear it. If Nan woke up, she wouldn't be confused about why she couldn't speak or move but why a train was roaring through her room.

It's four in the morning and after waking up at home to find Jamie not there, I couldn't get back to sleep. I wanted to make up for the previous day so I decided to go to the hospital. Henrietta would be able to get Sarah off to camp. I drank a couple of big glasses of water when I woke up. Between that and the previous night's cold shower, I'm not feeling too bad.

Henrietta is in the extra bed in Nan's room. I try to wake her with a gentle shake as I whisper her name. She snorts but does not wake. I shake her a little harder and say her name louder.

"Oh Jesus, what?" Henrietta shrieks as she sits straight up in the bed, hand to her chest. "Mom?"

"No. It's me, Jennifer. You can go on home now. I'll stay here."

"Chuck got the car. I'll have to call him."

I dig around in my knapsack and pull out a twenty. "Get a taxi."

"I got my own money."

"I know but I should have been here last night and I wasn't, so take the taxi on me."

She nods and takes the money. "Where were you?"

"I was sick."

"Your mother seemed mad at you." Henrietta stands up and pulls on her raincoat. "You know she'd never say nothing, but she seemed mad."

"Yeah." I look over at Nan. "How is she?"

"Moaning sometimes. Nurses got to give her some meds around seven. Make sure they don't forget. Sometimes they gets busy at the end of a shift when they have reports. I knows that from when Chuck's mom was in here. We don't want Mom to wake up too much." She turns to Nan. "She gets scared."

"Okay." I wonder if she's changed her mind about letting Nan go.

"Make sure, now."

"Yes, I will. Seven. Meds. I got it."

213

tina chaulk

Henrietta picks up her purse and walks over to Nan. She kisses her forehead and whispers, "I love you." There is such genuine love in that kiss, I feel drawn into it and when Henrietta stands up, I find myself hugging her. I don't remember ever hugging Henrietta. She stiffens, pats my back, and pulls away.

"What's that for?" Henrietta says and pats my arm. "I'm not the one dying, you know?"

"No, but you're the one here. And you always are. Whenever we need you for anything, you're there. Much as ..." I stop myself.

"What?"

"Nothing. Just thank you. Now, go home and see Sarah. And I'll see you later."

Once Henrietta leaves I sit in the chair next to Nan's bed. We're lucky to have an empty bed in the room but I won't lie there. If I get too comfortable, I might miss something. Might not be there when Nan needs me. So I sit in a chair instead and stare at Nan.

Her lips are dry and cracked. Even when she is asleep, she licks them, searching for a moistness not there. It's been hours since she's swallowed anything. She is dying of thirst and hunger and we are watching, sitting on our hands and clenching our jaws. I wipe lemon glycerine cotton swabs on her lips, hoping the small amount of moisture will relieve the aridness of her body.

Nan's breathing is rhythmic and the darkness in the room, broken only by the crack of light coming from outside the almost closed door, lulls me. I pull a thermal blanket up over me and rest my feet against the metal side of Nan's bed.

In what seems like two seconds, I wake to loud groaning. Nan is awake and staring at me with the eyes of a wild, caged animal. Every time she opens her mouth, her dry, cracked lips split a little more and she cries louder. I run out into the hall screaming for a nurse. One comes out of the nursing station and runs to me.

"Did she get her meds?" the nurse asks me in the room. She is tall and thin, wearing thick glasses and a concerned look.

I look at my watch: 8:15. "I don't think so. She was supposed to get them at seven. I was asleep."

"I'll check," she says, leaving the room.

Nan is moaning and scared, her head moving around like she's trying to escape something. I touch her white hair, smoothing it. To my surprise, it seems to settle her. Here she is. Nan. Starving, thirsting, dry, brittle, scared, immobile, but all I see is her white hair and those bright blue eyes I thought I'd never see again. She could have been medicated asleep until she dies but now I have them here, these brilliant eyes somehow shining with moisture, staring at me, barely blinking. There is no longer fear in them. There is a serenity about her as I continue to stroke her hair and I hum. It's not a song really, at least nothing I recognize. Just a peaceful, humming melody, a kind of lullaby.

The nurse appears after a few minutes and does not speak as she sets about placing the needle in the little shunt in Nan's hand, where an IV would be attached if her will had expressed her choice to live.

"She won't be awake very long once I put this in," the nurse whispers.

215

tina chaulk

I nod. I don't take my eyes off Nan.

"That's okay, Nan," I say softly. "I love you. I love you so much, you know?" I get a blink in return. But I have said it and as the nurse leaves, as Nan drifts away from me again, as those blue eyes close, the sky leaving me again, I'm grateful that I got these few peaceful moments with her. That I got to say those three important words to her. I know with all my heart how much I'd regret it if I never got to say them.

Even though Nan is sound asleep, I continue to smooth her hair and hum, hoping that even in her sleep, she can feel how much she means to me.

❦

It's just after ten when a man wearing a clerical white collar knocks on the half-open door of Nan's room, smiles and says hello.

"Mrs. Collins?" He points to Nan.

"Yes."

"And you are?"

"Her granddaughter. Jennifer." My hand goes out and he shakes it.

"I'm Father Carl March. You can call me Carl, though, if you like."

"Okay."

I notice a yellow stain on his blue, wrinkled shirt — sleeves rolled up, exposing the gorilla-hair on his arms. I wonder if he has to comb that hair. His muted brown eyes are under heavy lids. His hair, a little curly, is receding and is kept short. A tiny nose centres his face.

"I'm the Anglican chaplain here and I just came by for a visit. Your grandmother is listed as Anglican."

"That's what we wrote on her forms."

Nan stopped going to church the day after Pop's funeral. She still believed in God and some form of heaven, but she said that she stopped talking with Him.

"I knows He's there and all, I just got nothing to say to Him anymore," Nan said once to Henrietta, who insisted someone as old as Nan should hedge her bets and go to church, just to make sure God knew where she was.

"Oh, my dear, don't you worry, He knows where I'm at. Don't need no church or no priest for that," Nan argued.

Carl smiles. "I'm just here to see if anyone needs anything. Perhaps offer a prayer."

"I think it may be a little late for that. She's going to die."

"And you?"

A glib answer like *I don't think I'm dying* comes to mind but I don't say it.

"I'm okay." I look at my feet. "Well, at least as good as can be expected."

"It can be hard to watch a loved one die." His voice is soft and soothing.

Is that voice something that makes you choose to sit with dying people and their families or is it something you learn?

"I don't know. This seems necessary." I sigh. "Makes it easier than … something quick, with no time for goodbye." My stupid voice breaks.

217

tina chaulk

He bends his head down to meet my eyes. "You know, my ears are for anyone. You can see they're made to listen."

I look at his ears and notice how large they are. They almost stand straight off, as if he'd bent them forward enough times that they stayed that way. And I laugh out loud, cover my mouth in embarrassment and laugh again, joined by him, until my laughter suddenly becomes tears.

He sits there. Not speaking. Not touching. As I cry for long minutes.

Finally I get to the point where I can talk and I say, "This isn't just about Nan, you know?" I don't know why I need him to understand that.

"No?"

"No. She's sick and she didn't want to be kept alive if she was sick. It's right. It's ugly and horrible but it's right. And I got to say goodbye. And even 'I love you.'"

"We don't always get to say goodbye, do we?"

I shake my head, the new lump in my throat blocking my words.

"Who missed your goodbye?" Not, Who did you not get to say goodbye to? Different question somehow. "And your 'I love you.'"

"My dad," I whisper. "Her son." I point to Nan. "I thought I'd get to say I love you to him eventually. Even though we never said it, I always felt it. But now, I'm not even sure how I feel about him."

"Sometimes we feel mad when someone we love leaves us, especially if we don't get to say goodbye."

"I feel mad at him but not because of that. Because he lied to me."

218

a few kinds of wrong

The man is just sitting there nodding, not dragging stuff out with "and how does that make you feel?" Yet I want to keep talking to him.

"Sounds like you're going through a lot."

"Really? Just because my dad died and my nan is dying and I'm getting a divorce and my mother is sleeping with my father's best friend and I just found out the person I've felt betrayed by all these years didn't betray me but my father did?" Saying it all seems overwhelming yet makes me feel lighter.

"Oh, well, if that's all there is." He shrugs. "No big deal."

"You're going to break into some psychological mumbo jumbo now, aren't you?"

"No. But I could, if you want, give you the name of a grief counsellor here."

"No." I look around the room, everywhere but at him. "I don't like the mumbo jumbo."

"Mumbo jumbo is not really my thing. I'm more about listening. And praying."

"I prayed when my dad had a heart attack. I prayed for him to live but it didn't work."

"Maybe you prayed for the wrong thing."

I shoot him a glare.

"If God answered all the prayers for people to live, no one would die. Sometimes we need to ask for His help in getting through a very difficult and painful time. Did you ask for that?"

"No."

"Would you like to do that now?"

219

tina chaulk

"No."

"Okay. Would you like me to pray for your grand-mother?"

I shrug. "I guess so."

He stands up and I follow. We stand over her bed. Carl bends his head down and closes his eyes. I keep my eyes open, looking from him to Nan and back.

"Dear Lord, please help your servant, Laura Collins, and welcome her to your kingdom when she gets there. Ease her suffering and allow her to see the light. And please do the same for her family as they grieve her loss and continue to deal with other losses. Grant them the peace that only you can give and allow them to feel your love through their pain. Amen."

"Amen," I say.

But he's not finished. He takes a small vial with a ring on it from his pocket. He uses the oil from the vial and makes a cross on Nan's head. This anointing and the words he is saying, the whole scene, makes me turn my head away. Suddenly his soft voice blessing her and asking the Lord in his love and mercy to uphold her by the grace and power of the Holy Spirit makes this more real than anything the doctor has said to us, even more real than my words when I told Carl that Nan was dying. Nan is dying. Not in the abstract, not in just words. I am here in a hospital and a priest is anointing her. As Carl says the Lord's Prayer, I join in, barely whispering the words my voice is not strong enough to say out loud.

I sit down and whisper, "Amen."

"You okay?" Carl asks.

I shake my head. "Not okay. Not sure what word I'd use."

"I hoped that might help give you some peace as well."

"No. The only thing that gives me peace about this, that I try to keep in my mind, is the garden."

I look at him and the question on his face.

"Nan says that when she dies, she's going to see the most beautiful garden ever in heaven. She even calls dying going to the garden."

Carl sits down in a high-backed, blue chair and smiles a broad, beaming smile. "That's a wonderful image."

"Do you think it's true?"

He shrugs. "I think there's light and love in the afterlife, so why not flowers?"

"Dad probably got a 73 Challenger that needed a lot of work when he got to heaven."

"Well, I'll let you in on a little secret," Carl says, leaning forward. "I'd rather the car than the flowers. I have an 84 Camaro and she's my baby."

I laugh. And it's real and free. It is a laugh. I picture Dad at his car and Nan in a garden and I laugh some more.

"I haven't laughed in a long time. Seems wrong to do it now."

"Why?"

I point to Nan.

"She doesn't like laughing?" Carl asks.

"Loves it," I whisper. "If she's here now, with us, if she understands anything, she's enjoying the laughter."

"Then that must be a good thing." Carl is grinning.

"She loved a game of poker too. And cigars. Well, those

221

tina chaulk

Old Port, wine-tipped ones. I remember she'd save the tips for me when I was little and I'd hold them in my mouth, acting like I smoked, tasting the wine flavour and the tobacco. Back then that seemed cute. Back when you could still get candy cigarettes and they weren't called candy sticks."

I look at Nan, sleeping peacefully, looking so unlike the woman I'm remembering. I want Carl to see her too, to know her as something other than this sick, dying person in the bed.

"She rode a motorcycle once and she loved soap operas, especially the guys, especially if they had their shirts off." I giggle. "She called their muscled abs a sex pack no matter how many times Aunt Henrietta corrected her."

"She must have been very proud of you." Carl smiles but his eyes are full of a sad empathy.

"In some ways. She hated that I worked as a mechanic. She thought I should have kids, especially when I got married."

"And did you consider them?"

"I guess you consider anything before you dismiss it."

He nods.

"Guess I was always afraid I wouldn't be good at it. I can fix machines but a kid is something else. And now I think maybe I might be like Mom, and if I had a kid I would feel…"

He waits a while before he speaks. "Feel what?"

"I don't know." I look him straight in the eyes. "I really don't know how I made her feel." My eyes searched the floor. "You're easy to talk with. You're not like a priest."

Carl laughs and the guffaws echo around the room. "I don't know if that's a compliment or not. If it's any consolation, you don't seem much like a mechanic."

"No, I guess not."

"Do you want to talk about what your mom felt?"

"No."

"Okay." Carl rubs the back of his ear, making it bend forward even more.

We stay in silence for a moment.

He stands up. "Well, I think I've taken up enough of your time. I better go see some other people around here." He hands me his card and writes another number on the back. "This is my office number and my pager number too. Feel free to call me. You know, if you want to talk or need anything, anything at all."

"Sure." Even as I say it, I know I wouldn't mind talking to him again, if he drifted back into my life somehow, but that I'll never reach out to him. "Thank you."

"I'll keep you in my prayers. And the garden and the Challenger too." He smiles and walks out the door, leaving the room much emptier than when he walked in.

17

WITH CARL LONG gone, I sit back in the chair and drift off to sleep again, my mind full of cars and flowers. I try to think about the garden — Nan's, with Dad's car in the corner of it, far enough away that Nan won't get mad about the fumes or the sound of the engine, but close enough that Dad can see Nan and the flowers.

I don't intend to go to sleep. I just find myself losing consciousness and drifting into a peaceful state, carried off by exhaustion. Carl left at 10:30 and I see 11:15 on my watch. But in what feels like the instant between closing my eyes and opening them again, Nan's room transforms.

I wake to a sound, a gasp that is loud enough to echo around the room although I'm not sure that the sound was ever made. With half-open eyes, I see an image of someone sitting up in bed. The cobwebs in my head dissipate as I realize this figure is Nan. She is sitting, ramrod straight, her arms outstretched in front of her, her face reflecting something I can't see. I look at the wall where she stares, just to make sure there is nothing remarkable there. Her face remains slack but her eyes are as full of life and wonder as the day she got on the motorcycle.

"Nan, what is it?" I whisper, looking from her to the wall, where I hope I will see what she sees.

As if my words have broken a spell, Nan falls back down in her bed with the small thump of a ninety-pound woman on a mattress.

I stand and watch her. Two deep breaths. Two more shallower. Then nothing. The silence of her not breathing fills the room and I hold my own breath as long as I can, until I gasp and touch her, knowing she should have breathed again now. I know what is happening despite resisting it. A certainty made of absence.

I touch her wrist, searching for a pulse. The lack of one tells me this is not a dream. I run out to the hall and scream for help.

It's not like the movies. No drama or paddles or crash cart or CPR. A life has passed and it is accepted. Quietly. Respectfully even, but I remember more of a drama when we put our dog Twinkle to sleep. It is me, a nurse, and a shell that once carried a woman I loved. There is no doctor. No one looks at the clock and pronounces the time. I glance at it and see it's 11:48. I was asleep for maybe thirty minutes and now Nan is gone.

I'm quietly crying, the tears spilling in silence down my cheeks. The nurse asks if I need to call anyone and when I answer yes, she guides me to a family room.

Halfway down the hall I stop. "Will she still be there when I go back? Can I go back?"

"Yes. She'll be there for a while. You can go back."

The family room is empty and when the nurse shuts the door, it's the loneliest feeling I have ever had. In every way, I am alone.

I dial Mom's number. When her voice answers, I don't speak. I cry, sobs overtaking me.

"Is she gone?" Mom's voice is a whisper.

I nod then realize I'm on the phone. "Yes." My voice is low and thick.

"Is there anyone else there with you?"

I shake my head, unable to speak.

"I'll be there as soon as I can get there. And I'll call Henrietta."

"Okay." I want her there now. I want her shoulder to cry on and her presence to make me feel less lonely.

I call Jamie and repeat the non-conversation. He will be here soon too.

I sit in the room, afraid to go back and afraid to stay. Which is lonelier? I wonder. To stay here in a place her life never was or to go back to a place where it existed but does no more.

A man comes in the family room with a small, crying boy of maybe five or six. I put my head down, wiping my face with my palms, get up, and walk out without meeting either of their eyes. I don't need to know what pain lies there.

On the way back to Nan's room, I stop crying. I feel like I'm returning to an empty room, a place where there is no Nan. And I can't find a tear now because I know what happened when she died. When she passed. Once that phrase seemed too easy to me, not enough to say about a death, but I felt her pass and the word seems perfect now.

Walking into Nan's room, I see Carl standing next to the bed. He looks at me with a peaceful sadness.

"I'm sorry." His words are soft.

"She's gone," I whisper.

"I was still on the floor. Another loss. I wondered if I could be of some help. Would you like me to say a prayer?"

Another loss. I think about the man and child in the family room.

"Yes."

"Would you like to join me?" He places his hand out, inviting me to take it. I don't hesitate. I want to touch someone alive and feel connected. I hold his hand as he prays.

"Depart, O Christian soul, out of this world in the name of God the Father Almighty who created you, in the name of Jesus Christ who redeemed you in the name of the Holy Spirit who sanctified you. May your rest this day be in peace and your dwelling place the paradise of God.

"The Lord is my shepherd, I shall not want. He makes me lie down in green pastures ..."

Carl continues to say the Twenty-third Psalm, Nan's favourite, and all I can think of is her in a green pasture, in the garden she had imagined. Peaceful, still waters nearby.

"Even though I walk through the valley of the shadow of death, I fear no evil; for thou art with me; thy rod and thy staff, they comfort me ..."

Something comforted her, something she saw made her face light up in wonder in the moment before she left what surely was her valley of the shadow of death.

Carl finishes his prayer, opens his eyes, looks to me. Closes them again.

"Dear Lord, please grant a peace that only you can give to the family of Laura, who are left here mourning her loss. Let them be comforted by memories of her. Comfort them with your love. We pray this in your name. Amen."

I keep my hand in Carl's and keep looking down at what was Nan.

"I think she saw the garden."

"I hope so."

"No, I think she saw it right here. I think I watched her see it. She sat up in bed. Sat up straight and reached her arms out to something. Her eyes were focussed on something that seemed to fill her with amazement. Like it was the most wondrous thing she'd ever seen. There was no fear there at all." I shake my head. "Whatever she saw must have been beautiful. I could almost see it myself in her eyes and I kept looking where she was looking to try to see it for real. And then she was gone. Just gone. And I knew. It was like I felt her …" I take a deep, gasping breath, gulping in air to fill the empty lungs I feel I have. "… leave," I whisper. "There was Nan and then there was nothing." I point to her with my free hand. "Like this is a container, drained of her. This is not Nan."

I look at him, searching for something. "I felt the instant she left, the moment this body became empty. Her breath stopped only a second after she did."

"I know."

"Have you felt that before?"

He nods.

"With Dad it was so sudden and so much going on. It felt violent somehow, chaotic. But this was so peaceful. Like she just quietly slipped away." I raise my voice. "And she sat up, Carl. She was paralysed and she sat up and saw something. I so wanted to see what she saw."

He squeezes my hand.

"Jen?" Jamie is standing in the doorway and I'm holding hands with this man wearing a wrinkled blue shirt, standing over Nan's body. I let Carl's hand go. I walk toward Jamie and him toward me, meeting halfway.

He holds me and whispers, "I'm sorry."

I tuck my head under his chin, against his chest. His hands smooth my hair. I feel his tension, know he's waiting for my sobbing tears but I don't have them.

"I'm okay," I say.

I don't move. Something wet falls on me, dampening my hair. I realize I'm the lucky one to have gotten to be in the presence of Nan's change from life to death. I hear Jamie sniff.

Lifting my head up, I pull close to Jamie's ear and whisper. "Nan is okay now too."

18

"SHE'S BEEN LIKE a rock," I hear Mom say to someone at the funeral home.

"She was there when she died?" asks the woman Mom is talking to. I walk away, not hearing her answer.

I have spent over forty-eight hours coming to grips with it all. I've told the story of Nan sitting up so many times that I tell people I won't tell it anymore.

"Another stroke," the doctor explained to Henrietta about Nan's sitting up. She most likely had another stroke when I saw her sitting up, her electrified brain seeing who knows what psychedelic trip. A nice, scientific answer to a question I never felt I had to ask.

This room is filled with family and friends and neighbours. Voices meld into one large blanket of sound. I've been here for four hours now so far today and six hours yesterday. I've smiled at everyone who said they were sorry. I've listened to stories about Nan, about Dad, about me as a precocious child. My hand has been shaken by dozens of people, my shoulder patted a hundred times.

Two people I've never seen before are in front of the condolences book for Nan. Henrietta is in a corner, dabbing her eyes as she talks to Mrs. Wells, who lived next door to Nan and Pop. Mom and Bryce are standing near the casket, she talking to someone, he close by. But not too close.

The casket is open. Nan is wearing the powder-blue dress she has kept in a garment bag, ready for her funeral, since before Pop died. The pearls around her neck are fake. Henrietta has had the real ones for years. Nan never planned on getting buried in the good stuff. Sarah has Nan's engagement ring and I have her wedding ring, although I know I'll rarely wear it.

Rings and mechanics don't go well together. I learned that when I was eight years old and saw Harold Winter get his wedding ring caught on the edge of the garage door as it was being raised. He couldn't get the ring untangled from the door. The garage door kept going up, taking the ring with it, finger and all.

But I'm wearing Nan's ring today and I twist it around my left middle finger as I wonder what the point of this whole thing is. Is all this smiling, shaking hands, small talk, and reminiscing about comforting us or about comforting the people who walk in to sign the book or is it just obligation for them? Are people happy to have this duty done when they leave here? Do they go for fish and chips and talk about how thin Nan looked? At how she looked so good in the dress? Do they notice how the dress is pulled back, the extra material gathered underneath her, having been bought and zippered into a garment bag when she was forty-odd pounds heavier? Do they talk about how Henrietta's hair looks like a poodle's, her stylist going overboard on the tight curls? Do they see the looks between Mom and Bryce? The way they look at each other but try to pretend they don't?

The last time I slept was before Nan died. My eyelids are like lead weights and I'm exhausted, but whenever I've had the opportunity to lie down, sleep has eluded me. Nothing helps, not even the wine I've had the past couple of nights. I don't like wine but I wanted something that might help me sleep but wouldn't make me lose myself. Also, I've noticed that Jamie doesn't bug me about wine. He and I have shared a glass before bed, before the time when he sleeps and I stare at the ceiling, thinking of things I wish I could get out of my mind.

I lean against a wall. I feel myself wavering. Desperate to rest. Needing to escape this place. Wanting so much not to be a rock.

"I'm going to go home and get showered. Maybe change my clothes," I tell Mom. "I'm really tired."

"I know." She touches my shoulder gently. "You don't have to come back this evening if you don't want to."

"No. I'll be back. I just need to get freshened up."

On the way home I pause to turn into a parking lot. I get out, walk in the store and make my purchase. No need for perusing or hesitation. Take it off the shelf. Bring it to the counter. Pay my money. A cheap price for sleep.

I crack the bottle in the car, taking several gulps, enjoying the warmth. I turn the air conditioner up on bust. The air outside is sweltering. I continue to drink, sitting in the car in the parking lot, the urge to move, the desire to sleep suddenly replaced by the joy of numbing.

A woman walks by, stops, and looks at me, letting me know that she sees I'm drinking in my car. I raise the bottle to her in the sign of a toast and nod. Then I drink some more.

I move the car, not because I've already thought of where I want to be. I haven't gone now in over a week, after months of going every day. I continue to take long swigs from the bottle as I drive there, unconcerned by the presence of people in other cars who might see me. By the time I reach the cemetery, the bottle is half gone.

I drive through the cemetery, down the small lanes that permit me to get close to Dad's grave and stop next to Dad's row. From where I am I can see the place where Nan will rest tomorrow, or what was Nan, next to Pop's grave.

I feel no connection to the place anymore. The only thing in here, I now know, are the empty cases of the people who once existed. Dad and Nan and Pop are no more here than they are in my car. They are more likely in my car. Is Dad here with me now? Nan? Pop?

"Dad, are you here?" I shout. "I love you." I take another drink. "But I don't understand. How could you stop me from talking to Mom, how could you lie to me about her not calling? How does a father do that to a little girl? I might not have cried myself to sleep every night, but I thought she didn't love me. And you could have made that easier on me."

Thoughts I have been trying to push out of my head keep pushing back. I rub my forehead then hit it against the steering wheel.

"Goddamn it! It was a lie. And it's your fault. I've spent my life thinking she didn't care enough to call, and she has spent her life thinking I was too angry to speak to her, that if she didn't return to her miserable life with you, that she'd lose her kid. Well, we know now." I scream every word until my voice drops to a whisper to say, "But is it too late?"

I look at the verse on his headstone. *Weeping may endure for a night, but joy cometh in the morning.* How much joy did she miss? How much weeping had she done? Because of him. Because of me. I gasp for a breath, suddenly feeling like I'm drowning.

I'd looked at that headstone hundreds of times and felt anger every time, at how she could have considered any kind of joy when our world had ended. Now it sears questions into my brain. When will I find joy? How can I help Mom find hers?

"Oh, Mom," I say out loud.

And my eyes close slowly as I place the bottle firmly between my legs so it won't fall when I go to sleep.

ℰ

It takes at least a minute for me to realize where I am when I wake. A cold has settled over me. I left the car running and the air conditioner has done its job too well. The cold only reminds me of the bottle between my legs and the warmth inside it. It's 7:20. I slept for almost three hours and yet I still feel as tired as I did at the funeral home.

The funeral home. I told Mom I'd come back in the evening. I consider calling a cab, but sitting here, I don't feel drunk. And it's been three hours. In the cold. I put the cap back on the bottle and lay it down in the passenger seat.

The parking lot at Carnell's Funeral Home is full and I

circle around a few minutes before a space comes open. After a couple more drinks, I search the glove compartment for gum I know I have there and find it. I put three sticks in my mouth and chew all the way to the funeral home; my feet falter from time to time. Shouldn't sleep in the car, I tell myself. Now my balance is off as I try to walk again after sleeping in one position too long.

A small group of people are outside the funeral home smoking, and as I approach them I realize I'm not walking straight at all. My best attempts to alter my course and keep steady fail. I overcompensate as I try to correct my path, and sway more the harder I try not to.

I slow down. One foot in front of the other. Take your time. Go slow and no one will notice, I tell myself. A man glances at me, nudges a woman next to him and nods. She turns and looks at me too.

"What?" I say louder than intended. They both look away and shake their heads in unison like some choreographed judgement of me.

I slow down even more inside the funeral home. Methodically, I take each step to ensure my feet go the way they're supposed to go. I don't recognize the people gathered in the doorway of Nan's room. I get inside and lean against a wall, knowing I'll be fine as long as I stay there.

Mom isn't in the room, neither is Bryce or Jamie. Henrietta, Chuck and Sarah are encircled by people. A woman is crying over Nan's casket. I don't know her. How could someone care so much about Nan that she would weep over her and I wouldn't even know her?

A firm hand on my shoulder jolts me. I lose my balance for a second and place my hand on the wall for support.

"How are you?" BJ asks. "Sorry I wasn't here earlier but I got here as soon as the newscast was over."

"I nod. "S'okay."

"Where's your mom? Is she coming this evening?"

I answer with a shrug.

"I suppose you got Michelle's email?"

Shaking my head sets me off balance again as I have stepped away from the wall. I start to fall.

BJ grabs my arm to catch me. "Are you drunk?" she whispers, leaning into my ear.

"No," I say loud enough to make several heads turn.

"Come on, let's get you home before your mom gets here." She places her hand firmly on my arm, pulling me away.

"No, I'm fine. I told Mom I'd be here." More people turn to look at me.

A man I don't recognize at first walks toward us. As he gets closer, I see that inside the navy-striped suit with the white shirt and navy tie is Carl.

He smiles briefly. "Can I help?"

"No, we're good," I say. "BJ this is Father Carl March and this is BJ Brown." I'm thankful for the diversion.

"Yes, I recognize you," Carl says to BJ. He extends his hand and BJ shakes it,

"Jennifer is not feeling well and I'm going to take her home."

"No. I'm fine and I'm staying. Carl, are you going to the funeral?" The words come out garbled and, realizing that, I repeat them again, more slowly now. "Are … you … going … to … the … funeral?"

"You asked that already," BJ says.

"I know that. Excuse me, but we're having a conversation here." I try to push BJ a little, but it's too hard and she moves a couple of feet.

"Jesus. I can't help you anymore. Go sleep it off," she says and walks away.

"Would you like me to go the funeral?" Carl says. His hand finds its way to my arm, lifting me slightly, guiding me to the wall again.

"I wouldn't mind. Up to you, I guess."

He nods and stares at me. His eyes withhold judgement. His half-smile seems reserved.

"Jennifer, you seem very tired. Would you like me to drive you home so you can rest?"

"I have my car. I can drive myself."

"Perhaps you're too tired to drive. I'm afraid you'd fall asleep on the way home."

My heavy eyelids, half-closed, make arguing with him seem stupid.

Yes, okay," I say, changing my mind in the time it takes for his eyes to lock onto mine.

He again takes my arm. I can feel a muscle in his arm flexing as it keeps me on course, out the door, down the hallway, out the front door and toward the far right of the parking lot where he guides me to a black Toyota Corolla.

"This is such a minister's car," I say. His hand is on my head, ensuring that I don't conk myself on the door jamb. He leans over to buckle my seatbelt. His hair smells of vanilla.

"Hmm, you smell good."

"Thank you." He closes my door and walks around to his side of the car. My eyes are closed before we leave the parking lot.

19

WHEN I WAKE up I'm on my sofa and Carl is across from me in a chair. I bolt upright.

"What's going on?" I ask.

"How much do you remember?"

"Not enough, I don't think."

"You were at the funeral home and were a little, um, under the weather. I drove you home."

"How long ago was that?"

Carl looks at his watch. "About two hours. I didn't think it would be right to put you to bed so I laid you down here. I was afraid to leave you alone, you know, like that."

Once again I'm surprised how little judgement appears in his face.

I'm quiet for a couple of minutes and Carl lets the silence stay.

"Thank you though. For the ride. And the staying with me."

"No problem." He stands like he is about to leave.

"Would you like coffee or something? You really could

stay. I don't mind." I hear something in my voice and hope it doesn't sound desperate, although I fear it does.

"I really should be going." He is looking down.

"Oh." I look away and want to ask him again if he'd stay. Just for a bit.

"Well, okay, if you have decaf." He sits back down. "Anything else will mean I'll be up for the night."

"I only have instant decaf." I wonder if it's still fit to drink. The bottle of instant must have been in my cupboard for a year or more. I don't usually do decaf but sometimes Jamie would.

"Instant would be fine."

I feel like he's taking pity on me but that doesn't stop me from not wanting him to leave. The thought of being alone is worse than any pity he might feel.

I move into the kitchen and take down two mugs from the cupboard. In the open-concept house the kitchen adjoins the living room so we can continue to talk. But Carl sits in silence as I fill the kettle. I chip some coffee crystals out of the hardened mass in the jar and put them in the mugs.

I lean against the counter until the water boils and the electric kettle shuts off. I pour water into the two mugs and stir. Some of the coffee doesn't dissolve and I fish the floating crystals out with a spoon.

"Was my mom at the funeral home?" I ask, as I come out of the kitchen.

"No, she wasn't. But your friend BJ wasn't too happy with you when you left."

"She rarely is lately."

"Is she a good friend?"

I nod. "Better than me, that's for sure." I return to the kitchen for milk and sugar. Thank God, Jamie has stocked the kitchen.

"Why'd you say that?"

"Let's just say I've been a bit of a burden lately. And I was never a very good friend to begin with. Always wondered why she was my friend, to be honest with you."

"People usually keep friends because they enjoy their company. Obviously BJ is not as hard on you as you are on yourself."

I shrug. "Mom says I got that from her."

"You seem close to your mother." He sips his black coffee. I can see him hide a cringe at the taste.

I don't answer, not knowing what to say.

"Is that a yes or a no?"

"Dad was always the one I was close to. We spent a lot of time together."

Carl nods. "It just seemed that when your mother came to the hospital, you relaxed and let her be there for you."

Again, I don't know what to say. "I've been kind of mad at Mom."

He nods. "Yes, the best friend." He straightens up. He stares at me and starts to pick at his upper lip, like he's thinking hard about something.

"Pretty bad, hey?" I almost smile, feeling finally vindicated that someone understands how bad that would be.

"And it makes you mad? Not happy that two people you care for—"

"Of course it makes me mad. You don't do that. There's appropriate times of mourning and even then …"

He picks up the mug, brings it partway to his lips then sets it down on the cocktail table again. "What's an appropriate time for mourning, do you think?"

I shrug. "A couple of years."

"Most experts say that things should at least start to get a little better after about six months. And it's been?"

"A little over a year."

We sit in silence.

"So you think something is wrong with me." I almost make it a question.

"From what you say, things have not started to get better for you. And I wonder why."

"Because I loved my dad a lot, I guess."

He nods but I don't see affirmation in his face.

"I worked with him. At his garage. Our garage. Well, my garage now. Spent most of my time with him. He was a great guy. We …" I shake my head.

"What?"

"I always thought he was a great guy. But lately I've found out things. That he did things. I don't know."

"And? Where does that put you?"

"I don't know. I feel like I've thought things about my mom for years that were wrong. And that's because of my dad. All the things I thought were wrong."

"All of them? Every single thing?"

"Well, no. But some of the important things." I stare at the ceiling, thinking, looking for what I'm trying to say. "My mom always said she loved me and I never believed she did, not really. And Dad never said it, but I always thought he did. Now I'm not sure what's true."

"Did you tell them you loved them?"

I shake my head. "Not since I was a little girl. I guess I always thought I'd have the time to tell them. That sometime in the future, when Dad was one hundred and ten, there'd be some deathbed scene where I'd say it. But, well, you know."

"Did that matter to you? When you lost your dad? That you hadn't said it?"

From somewhere tears rise up inside me, up into my throat. I swallow them but they continue to come and the more I fight, the more they flow.

"I wish I'd said it. Out loud. To him." I whisper the words, knowing that the louder I speak, the thicker my voice will sound. "And I'm afraid if I don't say it to her, she'll never know it."

"So, what's stopping you?"

My tears don't deter him and I relax with them, feeling them washing something away. He doesn't look away or seem uncomfortable with my feelings.

"I'm mad at her."

"Okay."

"Okay?"

He shrugs. "Well, I could say that you can love her and be mad at her the same time. I could say that your father is gone and your mother is the one left here, in your life. I could say that the way you reacted when she came to the hospital after your grandmother died showed me that you love her and that you depend on her in some way." He smiles. "But you probably don't want to hear that."

243

tina chaulk

I stare at him. It feels like hours before I shake my head. I look away and find myself somewhere between wanting to cry and wanting to scream.

"I'm tired," I say. "It's going to be a hard day tomorrow and I'm already so tired.

"I've upset you."

"No. I'm just tired."

"Okay." He stands up, runs his hands down his pant legs to straighten out the wrinkles. "You still want me there tomorrow?"

"Up to you, I guess. I'm not going to stop you." His hurt look makes me flinch. "But it would be nice to have you there."

"Then I'll do everything I can to be there."

I stand up too and walk him to the door.

"See you tomorrow," he says, and I can't get goodbye out and close the door fast enough.

As soon as he's gone, I call a cab. I pat my dress pants pocket to make sure my keys are there and realize they're not. Carl must have taken them out when we got here. I look around and get a sick feeling that maybe he took them with him. That I won't be able to get in my car. I need to get my car and the thing I want most, which is lying on my passenger seat.

I find the keys exactly where I always put them, on the little table next to the door. Before I can open the door to leave, I hear a key in the lock. I unlock the door, knowing who's on the other side.

Jamie opens the door, and even though I knew it was him, seeing his face startles me.

"What are you doing here?"

"Coming to see you." He stands up straight. "Waiting for him to leave."

"And what if he didn't?"

Jamie doesn't respond, just looks away as he lays his keys on the table by the door. "Where are you going?"

"To pick up my car. Please, Jamie. I'm exhausted and I just want to get my car and get back here."

"You okay to drive?" He taps his foot then purses his lips.

"Yeah, why?"

"I heard you weren't when you got to the funeral home."

"What? Who said that? BJ said it, didn't she?"

"Lots of people said it. Did you drive in that state?"

"No."

"Then why was your car in the parking lot? Why did people see you fall out of it when you got there?"

"I didn't fall out. My God, did you come here just to interrogate me?"

"Well at least four people told me differently. Now who should I believe? The four sober ones or you? And I'm not interrogating. I'm looking out for you."

"I don't remember inviting you here," I say to his feet.

"Oh, that's the way it is, is it? I don't remember you inviting me any other night for the past few nights either."

He is standing between me and my friend on the passenger seat, and I fight the urge to push him away.

"I just let you stay those other nights."

"Let me? Let me? How nice of you to let me. You let me do everything, don't you? You let me stay here, you let me look after you, you let me cook for you, let me clean up your messes for you. You let me screw you. You're all about letting."

I turn away from him.

"And did you let the bottle open and go down your throat? And did you let yourself stagger into the funeral home where your grandmother is being waked? Did you let yourself make a show of yourself in front of everyone?"

I hear a horn blowing outside.

"I'm getting a cab. I don't want you here when I get back." I open the door and walk out.

Jamie comes behind me. "I don't think you should drive, Jen. It hasn't been long enough."

"I'm fine." I don't turn around to face him. "Just go, Jamie. You don't have to deal with my shit now. We're not together anymore, you know."

"I deal with your shit every day. Not a day has gone by since you left me that I haven't dealt with your shit, either me missing you or wishing for you or lately, lying in bed with you, so close I can touch you, so close you let me inside you but so far away it could be a stranger there next to me. Knowing that the only reason I'm there is because you let me. Because you need something else, someone else, to help take away your pain. So whether I'm here or a million miles away, I deal. With. Your. Shit."

His words are followed by the sound of footsteps walking away. I turn to tell him that I'm sorry, that I feel something every time I see him, and how grateful I am for him.

But something else, something sweeter and less demanding, beckons me and I walk toward the cab.

20

THE PHONE WAKES me out of a dreamless sleep. I answer the phone without thinking and Mom's voice says hello. "How are you?" she says. Her tone is tinged with something, a coldness.

I shake my head to try and make my voice sound like I haven't just woken up. The clock says 10:30.

"Okay," I croak then clear my throat.

"I wanted to know if you're going to the funeral with us."

"Us?"

"Yes. Us. The family. We're leaving from Henrietta's house, sometime around one."

"Um, yes, sure."

"You can come over here this morning if you like."

"No, that's okay. I'll be at Henrietta's by one."

Silence.

"Is Jamie there now?"

"No."

"Could you not? Could you?" Mom pauses then stops.

"What?"

"I hope you'll be feeling well when you get there."

"What do you mean?" And then it hits me. But I wait. Let her say it.

"Nothing. Just that I know you weren't feeling well enough to be at the funeral home last night and I hope you don't feel like that today." She pauses between words and I can almost see her searching for the way to say what she wants to say.

"I'll be fine."

"Good."

"See you at Henrietta's." I hang up without a goodbye and without hearing hers.

After a long shower, two glasses of water and two cups of coffee, I look in the back of my closet. Still hanging in a fancy garment bag is the dress Mom bought me to wear to Dad's funeral, never taken out of the bag.

Black, three-quarter sleeves, sensible neck, hangs just below the knees. I'd picked it out when Mom insisted, when I was still in a daze and would have agreed to anything. I tried on three others before we got that one. I hadn't worn a dress since my wedding day but I didn't tell Mom I wanted a pantsuit. I just followed her, got in the car as she drove, stood there as she picked out dresses, put them on in the change room. She opened the changing room door, then she guided me out and turned me around in the better light. Until she found this one.

The night before, the night Dad died, I had slept at Mom's house, not wanting to be alone in my house. People came and went, bringing soups and cakes and casseroles like they contained some healing salve, like their cooking would make things all right instead of just giving us the trouble of figuring out where to put things and who owned what casserole dish that had to be returned.

Maisie was there. The sensible one who organized the food but didn't bring any to add to our burden. She turned off the light over the door sometime around 9:00 p.m.

"They won't leave you alone if you don't turn off the lights," she said, turning off other lights around the house until there was only one small lamp left on in the living room. "And you'll need your rest now."

After Maisie left, Mom turned off the one remaining lamp and we sat in the dark, surrounded by blackness, encompassed in silence. Our breathing sounded like loud waves crashing over the shore, and all I could think about was that Dad was no longer doing it. Every breath in and out was one Dad didn't get.

It seemed like a long time before Mom spoke. "I can't go to bed. Not without him there."

"I'll go with you," I said, although I found her words odd considering how she and Dad so rarely went to bed at the same time.

Mom sat on the edge of her bed until I'd finished putting on an old nightshirt of hers and come into the room. Only when I walked over to Dad's side of the bed and turned back the sheets, did Mom get in.

The pillow I laid my head on felt like a cruel hug — warm, smelling of Dad, yet empty of him. One of his hairs lay on the white pillow case and I put my cheek against it. Mom moved and her feet touched mine. They felt like ice

a few kinds of wrong

and I jumped. When she moved her feet away, I searched the bed for them and placed my feet against them, the cold somehow reassuring. Until I thought how cold Dad's feet must feel now and pulled away. I turned over and pulled my knees up, trying to stop the shivering that had started.

Mom cuddled my back, and as sleep found me, I wondered if Mom and Dad always slept like that. I'd never seen them snuggled together in the nights I'd come in their room seeking refuge from colds or dark nightmares. But Mom's arm draped over my side felt practiced, like it was a natural place for it to be.

The night had been punctuated with the first moments of waking, when I could still believe it was a dream, before I realized it was Mom lying next to me and not Jamie. In those moments, I felt an empty, painful longing, not just for Dad but for Jamie, and when the tears lulled me back to sleep they were for both of the men I loved.

ᕬ

I don't put on the dress until 12:28, just before I'm going to leave for Henrietta's. I don't feel comfortable in formal clothes, especially a dress, and want to wait until the very last minute to get dressed. I unzip the bag and look at the dress. I hadn't remembered the small, braided pattern in the rayon. I run my fingers along the pattern and feel, rather than see, that it's a series of leaves and flowers.

For Dad's funeral, I didn't get the bag unzipped. I took it down from the closet and laid it on the bed. I found black shoes I intended to wear with it, with just the hint of a heel. I put on concealer to hide the dark circles under my eyes, made of restless sleep. I added foundation, eye shadow, opened my drawer, took out the new pair of pantyhose Mom bought me. Laid them next to the bagged dress on the bed.

Then I walked to my closet, put on an old AC/DC t-shirt I bought at the Value Village, my jeans, a pair of socks from my drawer, strolled down the hall, slipped on my workboots and walked out the door.

Outside, the air had smelled fresh, like I had breathed for the first time. My lungs filled. There was never a conscious decision not to attend the funeral. That thought, as far as I can remember, did not form. Just as the thought not to go to the funeral home any of the days Dad was waked there did not come. No thoughts not to look at Dad in the casket. My idea was just to go to work. The garage was closed that day, out of respect for Dad, but there were cars waiting to be fixed and paperwork to be done. And I did it. Non-stop, not even a cup of coffee, for eight hours, until Mom came in, while I was face and eyes into a transmission job on a 92 Mustang.

"Your father was late for our wedding," she said, standing over me as I bent under the hood. She was still dressed in the black skirt and blazer she'd bought two days before.

"Really?" I didn't think I'd ever heard her talk about their wedding before and found it on odd time to do it then.

"I told him I wanted his hands clean for the wedding pictures. Clean fingers, clean nails, everything."

I looked down at my hands, covered with grease, dirt so deep it filled my pores so that no amount of scrubbing could get it out.

"But he went to the garage that morning," Mom continued. "And worked until a little over an hour before the wedding. Until Bryce went and got him. His hands were filthy so he and Bryce got a bottle of bleach and soaked your father's hands until they were white enough. Too white, really. Only Bryce was already dressed in his tux, and you know you can't use bleach without splashing some here or there, and Bryce's tux got a big, white spot right on front." Mom started to laugh until tears came to her eyes.

"I was in the back of the church for ten minutes, waiting for him," Mom said, still chuckling and wiping away tears of laughter. "Your Nan Philpott thought he'd run away. But in came him and Bryce, your father stinking of bleach, his hand blood red with the stuff, and Bryce with a big sunflower pinned over the white spot on the front of his tux. Your father's hands were so raw, I could only get the ring down to the first knuckle, he cringed so much." Mom laughed again.

"He wouldn't have minded you not being there today, you know," she said, the laughter stopping as I finally understood the reason for her story. "But *I* wish you'd been there."

I wiped my hand on an old rag, leaving plenty of dirt on both the rag and my hands. "Sorry."

Mom nodded. "I still can't believe it. I saw him lowered into the ground, saw them sprinkle dirt on him and I still can't believe it."

If Dad had walked into the garage at that moment, I

don't think I'd have been surprised. I hadn't seen anything. I watched him on the floor in the garage, saw the paramedics try to revive him, but nothing else. As I slip the dress I'm wearing to Nan's funeral over my head, I hold no memories of the finality of Dad. Paramedics, the doctor's shaking head in the family room, Jamie's words. The headstone with Dad's name on it. Nothing I touched or felt or saw myself. Not like with Nan. Dad's presence, unlike Nan's, still feels around me, in part, I know, because I let it. Because I let the whiskey stay in the file cabinet, the message on the answering machine, and leave the toolbox open.

Jamie's words come back to me. Dad remains because I let him. I let everything. Except let Dad go.

๑

I expect just family when I get to Henrietta's, at least until I try to park the car. Their driveway is full and the street is lined with parked cars. I recognize the Millers' Pontiac Grand Am, the Wilsons' Mazda 5, and the Heffernans' Windstar. This isn't going to be the quiet family preparation for the funeral I expected.

I hear wailing before I get inside the front door. Aunt Henrietta is at maximum decibels, hands flapping around as she cries loudly. Uncle Chuck is beside her, rubbing her back.

"Jennifer," Mom whispers and slips her hand on my back. "You look lovely." She smiles a little. "The dress still looks good."

I could have put that dress in a line-up of two dresses

and not recognized it, but Mom sees it and knows it in a second.

"It fits you well." Her hand traces a line down my arm.

Bryce is on the other side of the room, his black suit immaculate, the crease in his pants even more profound than usual. His nod to me is slight. Maybe someone else wouldn't even think it a nod but I've gotten that nod before.

He walks toward me and as he gets close Mom steps away, a magnet pulling away from a like magnet.

"You okay?" His eyes are red.

I shrug my answer. "You?"

"I'm going to miss her."

"Me too."

Bryce stares at me a long time and then turns to walk away. The sight of his back, the thin rim of hair around the perimeter of his head, they make unexpected things come out of my mouth. "I miss you too."

He stops. Doesn't turn around. "I've always been around." He continues to walk away, goes back to the corner he'd been standing in a minute before.

A flurry of whispers starts around the room and I look to see that BJ has just entered, Michelle two steps behind. Michelle wears a black, short dress, while BJ has a perfect skirt suit — navy, sleek. She is turning heads even at a funeral. My Uncle Chuck's eyes start at BJ's heel and stop somewhere around her chin. Henrietta doesn't seem to notice Chuck's assessment. She is too busy getting over to BJ, to show everyone there that she knows a local celeb.

Henrietta hugs BJ. BJ returns it, folds her arms around my aunt in a warm embrace. Except for Nan and Mom, I usually step back from huggers or stand stiffly with my arms halfway up, unsure how to react to their uninvited displays of affection. Still, it doesn't stop some people, the huggers who hold you even if you show no interest in it. I see one such hugger has sighted me and is on her way over.

"Oh my God, Jennifer, I still can't believe it," Michelle says, enveloping me. My one hand finds its way to Michelle's back for a pat — maybe a bit too hard — before I pull away.

"Remember when she'd make us sugar cookies?" Michelle asks.

"No."

"Really? That time we went to her house after school and she made them? Maybe grade four?"

"Oh, yeah," I say, nodding even though I'm no closer to remembering some, one-off sugar cookies from so many years ago.

"She made great sugar cookies," Michelle repeats.

"Really?" BJ catches up with us. "I didn't get any sugar cookies."

"Jennifer took me to her Nan's when we were little for sugar cookies. All the time. Didn't you, Jennifer?"

I nod, wondering if there was another time other than the one Michelle just mentioned. She had said "that time."

"I knew you'd come to the funeral but I'm surprised to see you here." I look to both of them. "I honestly thought this was just going to be family."

"We're pallbearers," they answer in stereo.

"Henrietta asked us yesterday afternoon," BJ says. "I was going to tell you last night but—"

"Yeah, okay. I got it."

Looking around the room I wonder who else is a pallbearer. All these things have been planned and decided with no input from me. Things, just as they always have, have chugged along without me.

"Who else?" I ask.

"You don't know? I figured you picked us out," Michelle says.

"No, I've been—"

"Drunk," BJ finishes my sentence with a word I wasn't looking for.

"Preoccupied," I say. "What's your problem anyway?" I turn to BJ.

"There's another pallbearer now," Michelle interrupts and places a hand on my shoulder.

He stands in the doorway to Henrietta's living room, framed by the oak door trim and the green with yellow bees wallpaper on the surrounding wall. His eyes are searching for only a few seconds before they land on me, stop and stay focussed, first on my face, then on my dress. He places a hand on his chest, takes in a deep breath and smiles. I wonder how he can still even want to look at me after all I've said and done to him.

His dark navy suit highlights everything about him — his blue-grey eyes, his perfect body, the natural blond highlights in his hair. Unlike him, I can't find my breath.

Henrietta intercepts him, stands in front of him, and pulls him into a hug. He moves his head, his eyes still on me.

"And Maisie," Michelle says.

"What?" I pull my eyes away.

"Maisie is a pallbearer too. And Mrs. Connors and—"

"I think the important ones have been covered," BJ says. "Let's get a meatball. I see some on the table over there." BJ pulls on Michelle's sleeve as she walks, physically moving her along, however lightly.

For a moment, I'm standing alone in the room, although I can see that several sets of eyes are on me. Mom, Bryce, BJ, but it's Jamie that my eyes hunt for. As he disentangles himself from Henrietta, he starts to walk towards me. Halfway across the room he stops, his eyes losing their lock on me, moving to my side. I turn to see what he sees.

Another set of eyes meets mine. How long have they been there? How long has he been an arm's length from me?

"How are you?" he asks.

I turn back and Jamie is walking towards the meatballs too.

"Did you get any sleep last night?"

He is wearing a pressed black jacket and pants, making his collar seem whiter. His hair is blown dry and styled. The whole package makes him look more and less attractive.

I nod then turn away, but my mind wants to say something, to erase everything I said the previous night from his memory. I exposed myself and it still feels raw. He stands there looking at me, and without turning my head I know that Jamie is watching us. Probably from the corner of his eye, but he is watching us. I have no doubt.

"About last night," I start and then stop, not knowing what to say next. "I'm sorry. I think I spoke too much."

"No, you didn't." He rubs the back of his ear and I wonder if the habit is the reason his ears stand out so much. "We just chatted."

"I felt like I opened up a bit too much."

"Maybe you need to open up even more."

I glance at Jamie, who is staring at us now, not at all trying to be subtle. I see the jealousy he's always had for me. Can't he see that Carl is only an instrument of something scary?

"I think I've opened up enough." I speak the words and look away. "I'm not sure I can take much more."

"This is a difficult time. Just know that everything you said to me will be kept in confidence. And you have my number if you need it."

I nod. "Thank you."

Carl smiles and touches my hand. "I'm going to say hi to your aunt again. She had some questions for me and I don't think we got through them all."

He walks away. Jamie's eyes haven't moved from me even though I can see that Michelle hasn't stopped talking to him long enough to take a breath.

I back away until I'm against the wall. I look around and see Jamie, BJ, Bryce, Mom, Michelle, Carl, and Henrietta. All around me is everything I want to avoid. They are milling around and talking and eating meatballs. My time machine is gone and her loss has gathered all my wrongs in one room.

21

AFTER MOM'S RETURN to our house when I was a child, my life changed for a time. I came home from work with Dad before five every day and we all sat at the table together to eat. Dad picked up his dishes from the table and insisted I do the same. He didn't sit in his recliner chair in the corner and read the paper. He sat next to Mom on the couch and watched TV with her, his arm looking strange around her shoulders as he fidgeted.

When I went to bed I'd hear them talking, listen to them as they both went to bed at the same time, Mom's voice coming from the bedroom or sounds I didn't understand then coming from them. Roses, delivered to our door by Howse of Flowers, sat in the centre of our table, their vibrant red colour brightening the house and Mom's face every time she passed by them, then bent and smelled them. She changed the water in the vase every day and put some kind of tablet in the water, and a little bleach, and they seemed to last longer than I ever imagined cut flowers could.

But, after a time, the flowers faded and no new ones came to the house. At around the same time, things slowly returned to the way they used to be. A day here and there of Dad and me working a little later, suppers kept warm in the oven until we arrived, Dad stopping to pick up the paper on the way home. Silence filled the house after I'd gone to bed, nothing but the sound of television or the rustling of Dad's paper. The spare bed, Dad's bed sometimes, left unmade in the morning.

I woke up early one morning to a muffled sound. Tracing it to the kitchen, I saw Mom crying over the crinkled crimson flowers in the garbage. No matter how hard she tried, those roses could only last so long. I just watched, didn't let her see me as she wiped her eyes and blew her nose. I couldn't understand how someone could love flowers so much.

Still in my pyjamas, I crept to the front porch, to where my sneakers were. I slipped them on and went outside, barely closing the front door. An early morning fog shrouded the street but I could see sunshine over the horizon, the promise that the fog would lift.

We had no flower garden, but Dad had fallen behind in his mowing and our lawn was covered with dandelions. I knew they were weeds, knew that Dad cursed on them every year when they would arrive and hold fast, with a stubbornness only nature could provide. But I always thought they were pretty flowers. I'd said it once to Mom and Dad.

"Foolishness," Dad said. "They're weeds and they're ugly."

"I like them too," Mom had whispered, her hand touching my face with the gentleness of new snow on the ground, her smile both happy and sad, as her smile so often was.

When I got back in the house, Mom was eating cereal at the kitchen table, the cover of the garbage bucket closed, her red eyes free of tears. At least until she saw the armful of dandelions I held, pulled out of the ground as close as I could get to the root so they would be long enough to fit in the vase that had held the roses.

As she took the dandelions from my arms and put them in the vase that had been washed and laid upside-down in the draining tray in the sink, she tried to speak. But she only mouthed the words "thank you" with lips wet with new tears that flowed down her face and dripped off her chin before she wiped them with her sleeve.

I was eating my cereal, staring at the yellow plants crammed into a vase too small for their number, before she spoke out loud. "They are the most beautiful flowers I've ever seen. They mean more to me than you will ever know." Tears glistened at the edges of her eyes again.

Something told me not to ask how that could be when she'd wept over the remains of beautiful red roses this morning. I just smiled and said, "I'm glad."

This memory comes to me at Nan's graveside where flowers and tears are everywhere. We have just left the church where the family had entered together just before the service started: a dramatic scene where double doors were opened and everyone in the church turned to face us, to see the pained.

It had felt reminiscent of another, smaller scene: me in a

a few kinds of wrong

dress in church, all eyes turning to look at me. Only my dress had been white instead of black. And Dad had been by my side, Nan in the front row of the church.

Just as on that day, my eyes looked for, found and locked onto Jamie. He was sitting one row behind the pews reserved for family and I suddenly wished I had asked him to stay with me, to sit with me. He is as much family, more so, than some of the people seated in the reserved area — distant cousins who never visited Nan once, who didn't even bother to look at us when we came in the church, whose phones vibrated throughout the service and who typed messages on those phones. Text messaging, the new way to get through a boring family funeral.

When I walked up the aisle to the front of the church, I saw other faces I knew. All the guys from the garage were there. Bryce was there, his eyes not on me but on the woman next to me, holding my arm.

Bryce's hands, just like Jamie's, BJ's, Michelle's, Maisie's and others, were covered by crisp, white gloves, hands folded together in front of them. I had watched Jamie squeeze one hand with the other several times, and it struck me that this was the first time I had seen Jamie unaware of what to do with his soft, skilled hands.

Now Jamie's white-gloved hand holds a red rose, just as my hand does, as we await our turn to toss the flower onto Nan's coffin that has just been lowered in the ground. Henrietta insisted this flower tossing be included in the burial service, the red roses looking dramatic against the white coffin Henrietta picked out. If nothing else, Henrietta has a flair for drama.

Jamie's rose goes on there, the last of the pallbearers'. Now it's Henrietta's turn. She wails as she throws it down, just as she had when the casket was lowered into the ground. Mom had gripped me at that moment and I stepped back, unsure my legs would hold me up if I didn't move them. Seeing her lowered into the ground brought a gasp to my lips then a sob. Mom wrapped her arm around me, took much of my weight as I slumped against her. Bryce and Jamie both stepped forward to catch me but I recovered, Mom's strength bracing me so that I stood up on sturdier legs. Henrietta, her face buried in an old lace handkerchief of Nan's, had missed that drama.

It's my turn to throw the rose on top of the mishmashed pile that already sits on the coffin. Sweat is dripping down my face from the hot sun and I wipe my forehead with the back of my hand. As the flower leaves my hand I hope it pales in comparison to the garden Nan is in now, that somewhere she is laughing at our silly attempt to bring beauty to this moment, that she is shaking her head at Henrietta's orchestration of this event, of her loud sobbing as the rose hits the coffin. I let out a little laugh and smile a smile that resonates through my body. People turn to me, most with questioning looks, some with concern or sadness, but Mom squeezes my hand and when I look at her she is smiling too, tiny creases at the corners of her eyes accentuating their twinkling.

Henrietta wails again then speaks. "That was a beautiful service." Her voice is loud and it rings around the group. "Just the way I planned it."

"Hope she doesn't hurt her arm trying to pat herself on

the back," BJ whispers in my ear from behind me, and I stifle another laugh. I turn to her but BJ is gone.

"Going back to Henrietta's?" Mom asks.

"In a while." I turn to her. "I have something to do first."

"You don't want to go with us?"

"No, I'll be along in a bit."

Jamie lingers, back a bit from the grave. He seems to be waiting for me but I walk toward someone else. I planned this while still at Henrietta's. After standing against the wall for a long time, watching the people there, sad but not broken, damaged but not destroyed, I made up my mind.

Carl is talking to someone and, as I step next to him, he immediately turns, ignoring the other person, who seems miffed and walks away.

"That was a nice service." Carl smiles and squints in the sunlight. "Quite the turnout."

"I felt like the priest didn't get it right. Henrietta didn't either." I look to the place where Nan's body rests now.

"Left out the cigars and motorcycles, hey?"

"Yeah, yes, exactly that." I look at his face. "You get me, don't you?"

He smiles again and tugs on his ear. "Like I said before, it's all in the ears."

"I was wondering if maybe I could talk to you again." Suddenly, the idea of not seeing him again, of not speaking to him, fills me with a dread.

"About what?" he asks.

I give him a look that has "you're an idiot" all over it. "What do you think?"

tina chaulk

"Well, there's different issues. Do you want to speak to me about religion?"

"No. Other stuff, really."

"You do have some other stuff. There's grief, the breakup of your marriage, unresolved issues with your mom—"

"Well, they're not really unresolved. I just have to get used to the two of them being together."

"I don't mean that."

I stand up straight, push my head back. "Well, what do you mean?"

He shrugs. "I don't know. You said you didn't want to have kids because you were afraid it would make you feel like your mom felt with you. You never did say what that was."

"It was nothing. Really."

"Sometimes it's the nothings that are the biggest things to deal with."

I don't even open my mouth to argue. "So, will you talk with me some more?" Even as I say it, I'm nervous at how much he sees in me, things I don't even think I understand.

"I would be happy to be your spiritual counsellor. But, if I'm honest, I think you need more than that."

"Fine. I tried." I turn to walk away but he stands in front of me.

"Do you really want to do that?"

I stare at him. "I just asked for some ears, but hey, you can't do that, right?"

"I didn't say that. I said I think you need more than I can provide. You're dealing with terrible grief."

I search for a non-existent pocket I can put my hand in. I

place my hand on my hip but it doesn't feel right. I let my arms hang by my side and suddenly that feels stupid, like everyone must see how I don't know what to do with my hands.

"You asked me for help. I just think you need the right help."

"I didn't ask for help. I just wanted to talk with you, that's all."

He stares at me and it's like I can read his mind, his thinking that that's exactly what it means to ask for help.

"Do you know someone like that? Someone who can give me more? Can you maybe give me a name?"

He nods. "You're reaching out. That's a big step, you know."

"I'm just asking for a name. When I meet the name, that will be a major step." I look down and kick the dirt, the pointy, black shoe looking strange on my foot. "It's going to be hard, isn't it? It's going to feel bad and hurt to talk about stuff."

"How's doing nothing been making you feel?"

"So, do you have a name?" I ask after I feel my silent pause answers his question.

He takes out his card and a pen and starts writing on the back of his card, resting the card on his left hand. "Why now?" he asks, looking up from the card.

"I don't know. Back at Henrietta's I felt kind of, I don't know, left out. Feels like I'm standing outside a bus and everyone is getting on and off, moving around, eating meatballs, making plans and I'm just standing here watching the bus."

Carl hands me the card. "You have an awful lot of support

and love around you. That's more than many people have."

The card feels heavy in my hand. I turn it around. A woman's name, Joan Craig, is written there, and a phone number.

"You sure about her?" I ask Carl.

"Who knows if two people will click or not, but I think you'll like her. She's kind but no nonsense. She won't be one to reach out and touch your hand or anything."

"She won't?" I like her already.

"No. But she'll help you with what you need."

"I don't even know what that is."

"To let go of some things you've been holding onto for too long. To accept things you've been pushing away."

"And she won't hold my hand?"

"You have lots of hands to hold. I don't think you'll have much trouble finding one."

"Well, you two look cozy," I hear Jamie's voice say. I wrap my hand around the card.

"We were just saying goodbye." I stare at Carl, my eyes trying to relay the message that I don't want Jamie to know what we've been talking about.

"Yes, we were. You call if you need anything." He puts his hand on my shoulder. "You take care now and you too, Jamie." Carl puts his hand out then cringes when Jamie shakes it. I see the veins in Jamie's hand as he squeezes.

"Thank you, Carl."

He gives a little wave and walks away, pausing to talk to Henrietta and shake her hand as well before he gets in his Corolla.

"Going to Henrietta's?" Jamie asks.

"Why aren't you mad at me?"

"What?"

"Why aren't you mad at me? After last night and yesterday, you should be mad at me."

"Who says I'm not?"

"Well, you sure hide it well."

"Look who's talking." Jamie chuckles.

"I'm going back to Henrietta's for a bit," I say.

"And then?"

"Then what?"

"Then, I don't know. I'd like to see you later. Maybe we could talk." He looks down on the word "talk."

"Maybe. We'll see. I'm pretty tired already, but we'll see. No promises."

"I don't expect them from you."

His words catch me, like a cold splash of water on my face. "Maybe everything's just been moving a bit too fast, Jamie. Maybe I need time to think about us."

"I'll take that. At least you think there's an us."

"No promises," I say. The wind is blowing my hair in my face and I pull it back, away from my face.

"No promises." Jamie nods. "Right."

He walks away and I'm left standing by the big pile of dirt that will cover Nan in a couple of hours. I glance at her casket in the hole, remember what's in there and what's not, then walk away.

22

THE NEXT MORNING I wake up groggy but determined that this day will be different.

"Back to normal," I say out loud, wondering as I say it what normal really means.

The garage is open again today and I have to start being responsible again. I've missed so many days with my ribs and then Nan. Who knows what Jamie is after screwing up there? And the guys are probably still pissed about me firing Bryce and then leaving. I've left everything at odds and ends and it's time to get back to business.

On the way to the shower I see the half drunk bottle of wine on the coffee table, the only thing I could find in the house at two this morning when I couldn't sleep. I'd promised myself that I wouldn't drink, that I could spend the night alone and without any kind of sleeping aid. I watched TV until midnight then stared at the ceiling, a continuous feeling of unease and wakefulness, until one when I got up and hunted for something. A couple of glasses of the homemade wine Uncle Chuck had given me several years ago sickened me, the taste almost not worth the warmth it sent through me. That and two Gravol let me sleep after three and made it nearly impossible to wake up at seven.

The shower doesn't make the sick feeling in my stomach go away. I try to think about the day at hand. First, I have to check on payroll, then see what's outstanding in the bills, what parts are on order, and what customers have been waiting the longest.

I'd placed an ad in *The Telegram* for a mechanic the day before things changed between me and Bryce — when Jamie had bugged me about moving on and I'd wanted to show him that I could. I could fill the extra bay we'd had since Dad died. Or at least I could put the ad in the paper. I wonder what has happened to the applications and applicants. Would Bryce have handled it? He's not the best people person. Jamie? He's too much a people person. He's probably hired everyone who applied.

A flash of Jamie makes me stick my face in the rush of water from the shower, hoping to wash it away. Only then do I realize how hot the shower is as I feel it burning my face. No use. Jamie's face is still there in my mind, looking kind, looking loving. I told him yesterday that I need time to think about us, that it feels like everything is going too fast. Why then does it feel like it's not going fast enough?

☞

When I get to work, the office has changed. Hanging baskets on the wall hold completed work orders, two metal file organizers sit on the desk, full of files bearing neat labels like "payroll," "parts," and "invoices." To one side of the desk is a stack of what I can see are résumés and cover letters. Nothing else sits on the desk except two pens and a desk blotter that is a current calendar, replacing the one from 2004 no one ever bothered to change.

I have mixed feelings about this order when I'm used to chaos. I know this is Bryce's work and my first instinct is to be angry about how he took over, how he organized my well-unorganized system.

But mostly I feel that this is the perfect start to my new beginning, to the one I vowed to myself as I lay awake last night. This place has changed. This familiar, safe, routined place has once again changed, but this time it's more than just one missing man or an empty bay and open toolbox. This is a change in the routine that had surrounded those things, had kept them safely enshrouded in the past. A clean desk: the proverbial clean slate.

"I didn't expect you here today." A voice behind me jolts me out of my thoughts. I'm afraid to turn around and face him, afraid he will see the truth inside me, the changes I have promised myself. If no one knows my plan to change, no one will know if I fail.

"I didn't expect to see this." I don't turn around but continue to look at the desk.

"Me and Bryce did that." I know he's lying. Jamie is clean but his idea of organizing involves making neat stacks of coupons, bills and papers. No need to sort through them, just as long as they're neat looking.

"It was just Bryce. I know you better than that."

"But don't get mad at him. You can get mad at me. I let

him do it. It's only been a couple of days now but it's working out."

I turn and I know he sees it. He steps back. He is so in tune with me, so aware of me, I feel naked in front of him.

"None of us let anyone do anything. We just don't stop the things we want to happen. That's not exactly the same."

"No?" His left eyebrow punctuates the question.

I shake my head and turn back to the desk. "I think it looks great here." I touch the stack of papers in the corner. "Are these the applications for the new mechanic?"

"Yeah. We left them there. Not sure what you wanted to do. The best ones are on the top. There's four or five pretty decent ones there. Bryce and me went through them."

"Thanks."

"You okay?"

"Yeah, I'm good. Now, I have to get moving on this paperwork and there seem to be plenty of work orders there for you. Let's see, something easy." I start to shuffle through the work orders.

"I'm already on an engine job."

"What?" I turn around and face him.

"Bryce is helping me. So is Ray. I'm replacing the valve seals."

"That's an eight-hour job. We can't charge the customer if you take longer.

"I came in yesterday evening and worked on it a bit. And early this morning."

"Early?"

He shrugs. "Couldn't sleep."

I fight a smile and think of Jamie's white shirt that

second day he came to work.

"What did you do last night?" he asks.

"Not much. Watched TV. The usual."

He opens his mouth, looks like he's going to say something but doesn't.

"Better get back to it," he says.

I don't see Bryce until about noon. I don't know if he's busy or just avoiding me, but the lack of interruptions means I get caught up on paperwork. I call six mechanics for interviews, double-check all the paperwork Bryce has done and find nothing lacking. I send out numerous invoices, ones Bryce hadn't gotten to yet. I should never doubt Bryce. He was practically Dad's partner and knows every part of this business as well as, probably better than, I do.

I decide to teach Jamie more about it too. If he can learn how to do an engine job, he should be able to create an invoice. It's time he shared some of the burden. Time I let him. I don't doubt he'll be eager to do it. I just have to be willing to take the burden off me and share it.

Bryce grins when he sees me. "You look almost happy there in the middle of all those papers."

"Well, you sure made my job easy with this new office we have here."

Bryce blinks his eyes and wobbles his head on his neck, pulling back in a sign of surprise.

"I have interviews scheduled for tomorrow," I say.

"For the new mechanic?"

"Technician. They want to be called technicians now."

Bryce snorts. "I'll take a mechanic over a technician any day."

"So, will you join in the interviews? Help me pick out the mechanics from the technicians?"

"You sure?"

"Positive. You can pick up on some of the vibes I can't. Dad always said you could smell an asshole a mile away."

Bryce smiles. "I didn't know he said that."

"Yup."

"But I can smell an asshole a mile away. And we've got to deal with one now. An unhappy customer is asking for the owner."

I look out the window onto the garage. There's a man pacing back and forth by the front counter. In Ray's bay, Jamie and Ray are under the hood of a van.

"Let Jamie look after it."

"But—"

"Jamie is owner too. He's part owner of dealing with assholes. Maybe we'll give him the title of asshole handler."

"I'm not sure he can do it."

"Let's let him try."

"Yeah, okay."

Bryce walks to Jamie, talks to him, points to me in the office. I wave. Jamie shrugs at me, scrubs his hands then goes to the customer. He shakes the man's hand. The customer, a new one I don't recognize, seems to shout, his arms waving around, his finger pointing at Jamie, then around the garage.

Dad had two ways to deal with upset customers. Which he used depended on the customer and the complaint that customer brought forward. He always listened, at least in the beginning, to any complaint. If it got heated right away, he tried to calm the customer down. If the customer seemed unreasonable or wouldn't listen, he'd offer a discount, a full refund, or if the customer was rude enough, tell that person to take his business elsewhere.

"Some customers aren't worth the money," Dad said more than once. "And you need to figure out which ones right away."

Or, if the customer seemed reasonable, if they spoke in a respectful manner, Dad would do anything to keep that person coming back. He'd double-check something himself, investigate and provide a full refund if necessary.

Jamie looks like a cat just placed in a bath. He's bouncing back and forth from foot to foot and looking in at me. Finally, he walks into the office.

"He's crazy." Jamie pushes his hair back with his hand then puts his palm on the top of his head. "What am I supposed to do with him?"

Not my problem pops into my head, but he looks so frustrated, and my mixed feelings about him pull me toward helping. "What's his beef?"

"He says his car smells like mechanic. Says someone really dirty must have worked on his car."

"Who worked on it?"

"Bryce."

The name, the sheer ridiculousness of the idea sets both me and Jamie off in peals of laughter. Tears soon run down my cheeks, feeling familiar yet foreign, the pain usually accompanying them replaced by amusement.

Bryce arrives in the office. "Jesus, are you trying to piss him off more? He thinks you're laughing at him."

"We are," I say through another laugh and start again.

Tears are running down Jamie's face too and he wipes them away, straightens up and tries to act serious, only to lose it again and start guffawing. He sits on the floor, half under the desk so the customer won't see him. Thinking it a good idea, I join him.

Bryce surprises me by sitting down too and asking us to let him in on the joke. Between giggles, Jamie and I tell him, but Bryce just stares at us like we're crazy. "Why is that funny?"

"You?" Jamie and I start again and Bryce stands up.

"Guess I had to be there," Bryce says. "I'll offer him a full cleaning?"

I nod, laughing too much to answer with a word. I wave my hand for him to go ahead. He leaves and it's another minute or two before Jamie and I start to have longer pauses between the laughter.

"It's so good to see you laugh," Jamie says. "To laugh with you." His face is mostly smile.

The comment makes my laughter stop. We're still sitting on the floor, leaning against opposite walls, the floor we made love on between us.

"What's different?" He looks right in my eyes before I can look away, before I can make them say something other than the truth. Denying that anything is different is futile.

"It's hard to explain." I look down at my clean hands. Even the pores are free of grease. "Impossible really."

"Will you ever be able to explain it?"

"I don't know. I'm processing stuff."

"Can I help?"

tina chaulk

"You always do. Somehow. Even when you don't do anything, you're the voice inside my head."

He stares at me a long time. Outside this room air guns roar; someone is smacking a brake drum that sounds like gunshots. Fumes — carbon monoxide, Varasol, grease, oil, brake fluid, antifreeze — permeate the air. Nothing, though, distracts me from his eyes. We have a wordless conversation and he finally closes his eyes, turns his head away, perhaps having seen what he had to see.

"I better go see how Bryce got on with Mr. Clean." He chuckles.

"Okay." And even though he is no longer there, I stay on the floor and smile.

☞

Later that afternoon, I'm a little disappointed that her car is in the driveway. My determination is too great to avoid the task at hand but I wouldn't mind a little forced procrastination. The Toyota Echo sitting in the paved drive takes away that hope.

I know she is watching *Days of Our Lives*, think that maybe I should have decided to come here later, after her show, when maybe she would be gone out somewhere shopping for groceries or walking along Rennie's Mill River. But she is here and part of me knew she would be, the part that wants this more than I don't want it.

I knock. She peeks out the corner of the living room window before coming to the door.

"What's wrong? Why didn't you use your key?" Mom asks.

"Nothing's wrong." I hand her the coffee I have brought

for her. "Thought you might want a coffee."

She takes the coffee, stares at me a moment then tells me to come in.

In the foyer she stops and turns around. "You've never brought me coffee in the middle of the day before. What's really going on? Did you and … Bryce have a fight?"

I shake my head and wonder why she paused before his name. "No. I just want to talk to you." I walk past her and sit on the couch, motioning for her to sit too.

"Sunday," I say, after she sits down.

"Yes?"

"Any plans?"

Her mouth drops a little and her eyes blink faster than usual.

"Bagel Cafe sound good?" I ask.

A smile spreads across her face and into her hungry eyes. "That sounds wonderful."

"Good. That's what I wanted to say." I stand up. "I'll see you then."

"Jennifer," Mom says as she lays her hand on mine. "What did you really come here for?"

I weigh the options. No matter what, she knows I didn't come here to confirm our Sunday date. But I can still walk out of here without saying anything else. So easy to say nothing. To do nothing. To let things happen. I reach into my pocket and feel cardboard. Carl's card with Joan Craig's number on it. Carl's words come back to me: *How's doing nothing been making you feel?*

"It's just. Well, you know. You must know. I mean, I've been awful to you." I look down and search the burgundy

279

tina chaulk

shag carpet for something to help me find the right words or even to tell me a way to say them.

Mom hesitates, lets go of my hand, her other hand on the coffee cup. She shifts around on the couch. Her mouth opens and closes twice with no sound until she decides on the simple word "oh."

"I'm not good at this, Mom. I don't think I ever will be but I want to say I'm sorry. I said awful things and thought awful things. And the truth is—" My voice breaks. I clear my throat and try again, open my mouth but my words wobble in my throat.

"It's okay." She reaches out again and I know she wants to make everything okay. But it's not.

"No, it's not okay. The truth is … that you don't know the truth. That when you left Dad, when you left us, I didn't know you called for me. Dad didn't tell me. He didn't ask if I wanted to speak to you and I didn't say no. He told me that you probably forgot to call, probably forgot about me." A sob grabs my voice and it comes out as a gasp.

Mom's hand goes to her chest. "Oh my God."

I watch her as the truth settles in.

"Oh my God. Jennifer. You must have—" It's her turn for her voice to break.

"When you came home, I didn't understand. Not until that night at the hospital when you told me."

"Why didn't you say something then?"

"Because I wasn't sure I believed you at the time. I couldn't believe he'd do that. Not to me or to you."

Mom closes her eyes. "I can."

Her words stab me, confirming that I really don't know

280

a few kinds of wrong

the man I've mourned, that I haven't really been mourning him at all. I've been grieving the loss of someone I don't even understand.

"He liked to control," Mom whispers. "He always did."

"Not me. At least not when I was growing up."

The pity on her face as she looks at me makes me want to run out of this house and to something warm in a bottle. But before me is something warm and kind and loving. I sit down.

I breathe deep, sucking in what feels like every bit of air in the house. Mom stares at me and our coffee is long gone before either of us speaks.

"I don't know what to say." Mom's voice seems small. She looks away, looks down at her fingers, and I see now that she isn't wearing her wedding ring. She definitely had it on at Nan's funeral. I remember feeling it as she held my hand.

I stare at her hand, can't take my eyes off the white line around her finger where her ring once was. It reminds me that mine still sits on my dresser, in the little dish I always put it in while I worked. Thinking of the ring still there makes me think about Dad's message on my answering machine and the whiskey in the office filing cabinet — the multitude of things holding me firmly in place, keeping me from budging, let alone moving.

There are words inside me waiting to be released. "Mom, I love you, you know?"

She pulls her head back and blinks, like I've just smacked her in the face. But the smile on her face shows me something different.

"I adore you," she says. "I always have."

"I know. But I don't know if you realize that I always loved you." I don't say the awful truth that is in my mind. That I'm not sure I always knew it myself.

෮

That night, I find myself outside BJ's TV studio, a shaking inside me becoming more intense, a want becoming a need. I'm in my car and I wait until she comes out in the parking lot and beep my car horn.

She stops still, stares at the car a moment then walks over. "What's up?"

"Want to go for a drink?"

"What's wrong?"

"Nothing. Want to go for a drink?"

Her mouth stretches out to a disapproving line. "Coffee?"

Without a word, I reach out my hand. She and I watch it tremble.

"Let's take my car," she says and closes the door.

"I thought a restaurant, maybe," I say, when I see that she's driving to her house.

"I don't want the hassle and I don't want to be noticed." She glances at me. "Don't think you do either."

"No."

We drive to BJ's house in silence. Inside, she takes a bottle of rum from her cupboard and pours me a drink before we sit down. I gulp it down and pass the glass back for a refill. She complies.

"This is really not good," BJ says.

I pull out Carl's card and turn it over to show her the name written on the back.

"Who's Joan Craig?"

"A counsellor. I got her number from Carl. Father March."

"What do you want from me?" BJ says, an anger in her voice I didn't expect. I had imagined a pat on the back.

"What?"

"What do you want from me? Why are you here? You could have bought a drink for yourself. You didn't need me."

"I do need you." I shake my head. "Not for a drink."

I watch the beautiful face that looked hard and cold a second ago morph into someone soft and kind.

She shakes her head. "I'm not going to watch you go down. I will watch you get help and I will hold your hand but I will not watch you go down." She points at me and flashes a wry smile. "You are worth keeping and I won't let you go."

"You won't have to."

After I finish the drink and BJ fills my glass again, we move to the living room where I sit on a recliner chair and BJ sits, as she often does, on the floor.

"When are you seeing this Joan Craig?"

"I haven't made an appointment yet. But I'm going to call."

She nods but the way she looks away tells me that she doesn't believe me. I want to make her trust that I'll call the counsellor but can't find a way to start to do this. I can't even find a way to make me know for sure that I will. I just know that in this moment I intend to.

"You don't open up to people. I find it hard to believe that you'll open up to a stranger."

I nod and take a deep drink. "I want to tell you something about my dad. Something I'm trying to get my head around."

As I start to tell her, I'm not sure if it's because I want to prove to her, and myself, that I can open up, or if I really want to share this burden.

⊙

On Sunday morning, I leave Jamie in my bed and go to the garage. There are no windows in the main area, so it's dark as I enter from the front customer area. I turn on a light but it wouldn't matter if I didn't. I could find my way around here blindfolded.

I need to see clearly to do this. A strange sensation of dread and exhilaration comes over me as I stand in the centre of the garage, eyes focused. Mind focused. Body refusing to move.

I know I've been here a while before my body kicks in. I've been talking to myself, out loud, the whole time.

"Just like a band-aid. Do it quick. Tear it off and then you can't go back."

I know I can't do it all fast. It will take time. But the first step can be done with three movements. Three, easy, swift movements I've done so many times I know that if I had Nan's memory loss, in the last stages, I could still do it. As automatic and easy as breathing. Yet all three seem so difficult now.

The breathing. I'm trying not to be aware of it, but I can't stop speeding it up, slowing it down, trying to make it normal but not knowing what normal is.

"Just do it. You'll do it and then you'll sit on the floor and cry and it will be easier. It's not that big a deal. Stop making such a big deal about it. Just step ahead and do it."

This is like the pivotal part in a movie, I think. The heroine stands and is about to make the big move and then everything will be fine. All the wrongs will go away. But this is not a movie. This is my life and, even if I can do this, it will change one thing, it won't change them all. It won't make me look at Bryce and Mom together and not feel a little sick to my stomach. It won't stop this trembling inside of me that makes me want to go back home, stopping to get a bottle along the way. Ripping this band-aid won't see Joan Craig for me and bear my soul at my first appointment with her next week.

It will close one door and allow me to stand in front of another, waiting to step into something new. If I thought it would make everything better, make everything bad go away, just like in a Hollywood movie, I wonder if I'd even want to do it.

In my mind, the camera pulls back on the scene. It watches me step forward and walk the few steps to the toolbox. I close the top drawer, close the middle drawer, then pull down the door cover and snap it into place.

Band-aid off. But I don't slump to the floor and cry. I don't lean against the toolbox. I just stand there and nothing feels different.

tina chaulk

"Big whoop. You closed a box," I whisper.

I unfasten the cover again then slowly open the small drawer on the bottom right corner. A Kit-Kat bar sits there, looking deflated. I pick it up and feel that it has been melted and hardened so many times that, without the wrapper, it would be unrecognizable as a Kit-Kat bar.

I open another drawer. Dad's chain stares at me. I lay the bar down and pick up the chain. It feels so light in my hand yet so heavy.

"Your father would want to be buried with it," I remember Mom saying in the days after Dad died. "You should go get it."

"Then he should have died with it on," I snapped. "He left it in the box, so it stays in the box." My angry words were not meant for her. They were, I know now, directed at him, at his leaving me.

I slip the chain around my neck and try to close the clasp but can't. I pull it off and try to turn it around so I can see the clasp and close it.

"Need some help with that?"

I freeze. I'm torn between wanting to tell him to get out, to get angry at him for interrupting the moment, and running to him.

"Yes."

I don't turn around. I put the chain around my neck again and feel the slight weight taken away from me. I lift my hair up and out of his way. I don't feel his hands, only the sensation of the chain and pendant as they hang on my chest, settling there in their rightful place. Connected.

He turns me around. "It looks right there."

"Feels right too." I intend to speak in a regular voice but it comes out as a whisper.

"The drawers are closed," he says.

"The whole box was closed for a minute. But I knew I had to take some things out first."

He just stares at me, looking down at the pendant from time to time.

"We have a new tech ... mechanic starting soon," I say. "I figured it's about time to make room."

"Making room sounds like a good idea."

Jamie smiles. His warm hand finds mine, folds around it. As I grasp his hand back, I notice something for the first time. Something that almost makes me pull my hand away. But I don't. I let it stay. How could I not have noticed? It makes me feel a new certainty that this hand is supposed to be in mine.

Through days and nights of lovemaking, of him holding me, touching me gently at times, fiercely at others, of his gripping me in the shower that night. Of all the times he has touched me in the past days and weeks, it's the first time I feel the roughness of his now calloused hand.

Many thanks to the Newfoundland and Labrador Arts Council for their support of this book in the form of two Professional Project Grants; the Newfoundland Writers' Guild for critique and encouragement, especially to Helen Fogwill Porter — every writer should have a mentor like Helen; the 2007 Winterset In Summer Literary Festival Committee for their generous New Writer's Grant which helped with the writing of this book; to everyone at Breakwater Books for encouraging me and believing in this book, especially Rebecca Rose and Kim O'Keefe-Pelley, as well as Annamarie Beckel who is a kind, supportive, and thorough editor, and Rhonda Molloy who always makes things look so good; to Father John for advice and a sharp eye; to all my friends but especially Kim Wiseman — no one could have a more thoughtful friend — Kathy Skinner, Pam Hollett, and the Strident Women — this book would not be this book without you; and to all my family, especially the ones who have to put up with me every day: Sam, Ben, and my first and most important reader, Vince.

Tina Chaulk lives in Conception Bay South, Newfoundland and Labrador, with her husband and two sons, while writing and working in a variety of freelance technical roles. *a few kinds of wrong* is her second novel.

ALSO BY TINA CHAULK

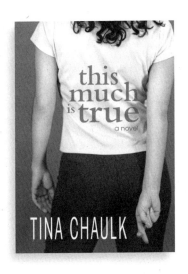

THIS MUCH IS TRUE

Is it okay to tell a lie? Lisa Simms thinks so. *this much is true* is a romp through the 1980s, about a fish out of water struggling to find her place in the world, all while sheltering her parents from the truth.

FICTION
ISBN-13: 978-1-894377-18-8
FORMAT: Softcover, 296 PP, 5.25 x 7.25, $19.95